CITY OF BRICK AND SHADOW

Tim Wirkus

TYRUS
BOOKS

Published by
TYRUS BOOKS
an imprint of F+W Media, Inc.
10151 Carver Road, Suite 200
Blue Ash, OH 45242. U.S.A.
www.tyrusbooks.com

ISBN 10: 1-4405-8276-9
ISBN 13: 978-1-4405-8276-9
eISBN 10: 1-4405-8277-7
eISBN 13: 978-1-4405-8277-6

Printed in the United States of America.

10 9 8 7 6 5 4 3 2 1

Library of Congress Cataloging-in-Publication Data
Wirkus, Tim,
    City of brick and shadow / Tim Wirkus.
        pages cm
    ISBN 978-1-4405-8276-9 (hc) -- ISBN 1-4405-8276-9 (hc) -- ISBN 978-1-
4405-8277-6 (ebook) -- ISBN 1-4405-8277-7 (ebook)
    1. Mormon missionaries--Fiction. 2. Missing persons--Fiction. 3. Latin
America--Fiction. I. Title.
    PS3623.I754C58 2014
    813'.6--dc23
                                2014026402

Cover images © iStockphoto.com/CSA-Printstock.

This book is available at quantity discounts for bulk purchases.
For information, please call 1-800-289-0963.

Acknowledgments

Novels aren't written in a vacuum and I'd like to thank some of the people who most contributed to this one:

Thanks to Yishai Seidman, who is a generous and insightful reader and a heroically dedicated agent. Thanks also to Ben LeRoy, Ashley Myers, and everyone at Tyrus and F+W Media who worked on the novel.

Thanks to rigorous and engaging creative writing teachers, especially Patricia Russell and Steve Tuttle.

Belated thanks to Paulo Rogério Silvestre for the kind detour through the Praça da Sé.

Thanks to John Steinbeck for *Cannery Row*, Herman Melville for *Moby-Dick*, Kate Atkinson for *Case Histories*, and Jorge Luis Borges for "The Garden of Forking Paths" and "Ibn-Hakam al-Bokhari, Murdered in His Labyrinth." Also thanks to *The Killers* (1964), directed by Don Siegel and starring Lee Marvin, Angie Dickinson, John Cassavetes, and Ronald Reagan.

Thanks to everyone who read all or part of the book-in-progress, particularly the members of T.C. Boyle's fall 2011 fiction workshop.

I'd also like to acknowledge the generous support of the University of Southern California's Provost's PhD Fellowship which afforded me much-needed time to finish this novel.

A big thanks to Paul and Janice Wirkus for, among many other things, being adventurous readers.

And finally, thanks to Jessie, the best sounding board of them all.

I like a look of Agony,
Because I know it's true—
Men do not sham Convulsion,
Nor simulate, a Throe—

The Eyes glaze once—and that is Death—
Impossible to feign
The Beads opon the Forehead
By homely Anguish strung.

—EMILY DICKINSON

PART ONE

CHAPTER 1

Years later, when he was no longer a missionary, no longer living in Vila Barbosa or anywhere near the sprawling behemoth of a city that contained it, Mike Schwartz often wondered if there was anything that he and Elder Toronto could have done to prevent the disappearance of Marco Aurélio. Surely there must have been signs suggesting that the man they had baptized was on the brink of vanishing, or, by all indications, simply ceasing to exist. On the not-infrequent nights that he had trouble sleeping, Mike sat at his dining room table nursing a glass of warm milk and composing mental laundry lists of, not excuses, but factors that had stood in their way. Topping each night's list was Vila Barbosa, the dreaded neighborhood itself.

Even before he was transferred there, Vila Barbosa terrified the young Elder Schwartz. A mere mention of the neighborhood's name caused his young missionary heart to speed up, his palms to sweat, his bowels to tighten and groan. As the city's most notorious slum, the neighborhood enjoyed an almost mythic status. Everyone—both Elder Schwartz's fellow missionaries and the residents of the city's other neighborhoods—had a favorite story about Vila Barbosa.

For instance: An evangelical preacher denounced a handful of local criminals over the pulpit one morning around Christmastime; the next day, the dead, mutilated bodies of the pastor, his wife, two older children, and baby were found in front of the church, arranged in a gory Nativity scene.

Or this one: Over the course of a decade, a popular churrasqueiro kidnapped the neighborhood's poorest children, cooked them up, and served them as pork from his grilled meat cart.

Or this: One hot, sweaty summer, the neighborhood's stray dogs banded together into one massive, snarling pack that roamed the dusty streets with impunity, driving the human residents into their cramped homes for three days until, just as suddenly as they had joined together, the dogs disbanded and returned to their usual vagabond ways.

Even if these stories were exaggerations, Elder Schwartz knew they must contain some grim truth of the terrible neighborhood. In his nightly prayers, he asked earnestly and often not to be sent to Vila Barbosa. He had only been working in his second area—a downtrodden but friendly neighborhood—for three months when he got a phone call from headquarters telling him he was being transferred. As requested, he showed up the next morning at the mission office, luggage in tow.

"Any guesses where you're headed?" asked Elder Pelourinho, his then-companion, as they stepped into the tiled upstairs chapel of the building.

"I don't know," said Elder Schwartz.

He knew where he didn't want to go, but the possibility had nagged at him since the phone call the night before.

"I bet you're heading to the interior," said Elder Pelourinho. "You've been in the city for a while."

"Maybe," said Elder Schwartz.

He hoped so. The two of them sat down in one of the hard, wooden pews and waited for the transfer meeting to begin. The chapel was about half full of missionaries engaged in similar conversations—*Where will I go? Who will I work with?*—in the usual blend of Portuguese and English. The missionaries were all young, at the end of their teens or the start of their twenties. With their scuffed dress shoes, their frayed slacks, their stained ties, and their graying white shirts, they looked like a mangy, nervous convention of junior accountants. On a morning like this, they all tried with varying degrees of success not to fixate on the amount of time they had left before their two years were up and they could return home to civilian life and the relative freedoms it offered. For his part, Elder Schwartz grew more and more nervous the longer he sat, increasingly convinced that Vila Barbosa and all its attendant horrors awaited him.

At nine-thirty, President Madvig, the leader of the mission, entered the chapel and the room went silent. A blond, fleshy former football player, he towered over the podium as he welcomed the elders to the transfer meeting. As President Madvig spoke, Elder Schwartz fought back the urge to vomit with fear, concentrating so intently on controlling his stomach that he didn't listen to the president's words of welcome, or to the opening prayer, or the opening hymn. He didn't listen to where the other elders were being sent, and he barely listened when President Madvig said that in Vila Barbosa, Elder Toronto would remain as senior companion, and would be joined by Elder Schwartz.

The other missionaries in the room applauded heartily, likely offering up silent prayers of gratitude that they had avoided this dreaded assignment. Elder Schwartz stared straight ahead, marshaling control of his terrified guts. He stood up, his fingers white as they clutched the bench in front of him. The other missionaries continued to applaud. As if Vila Barbosa itself wasn't bad enough, he would be working with Elder Toronto.

Everybody knew Elder Toronto but nobody knew what to do with him. He was one of the mission's most seasoned elders— almost twenty-one years old and nearing the tail end of his twenty-four months of service. A vocal presence at mission conferences, he compulsively disagreed not only with the comments of his fellow missionaries, but also with those of President Madvig himself. Elder Toronto would raise his hand, his face scrunched into a this-hurts-me-as-much-as-it-hurts-you expression of faux apology, and then systematically explain the flaws in the articulation, reasoning, or underlying motives of whomever had spoken before him.

While President Madvig clearly had an exasperated respect for Elder Toronto—he made him the senior companion in all of his pairings, listened carefully to his frequent objections, even solicited his opinion from time to time—the same could not be said for the various church authorities who occasionally visited the mission. At a conference a few months earlier, a visiting Seventy had presented a new method for soliciting teaching referrals from church members. His plan involved a pocket-sized picture of Joseph Smith, a few carefully selected scriptures, and the same techniques of salesmanship that had made this man his millions in the private sector. Following his presentation, the Seventy cold-called on a few missionaries in the audience and, utilizing the commitment pattern, asked them to implement his method.

"Elder," said the Seventy to the first elder, "will you use this plan to ask the members in your area for referrals?"

"Yes," said the first elder.

The Seventy called on a second elder and asked the same question.

"Yes," said the second elder.

The Seventy called on a third elder—Elder Toronto—and asked the same question.

"No," said Elder Toronto.

The other missionaries in the audience watched the Seventy's face adjust unpleasantly to this unexpected, unacceptable response.

"Elder," he said, "you won't use this plan to ask the members in your area for referrals?"

"No," said Elder Toronto, scrunch-faced. "It's manipulative and it's doctrinally unsound."

After Elder Toronto elaborated further, the Seventy, clearly gobsmacked by this insubordination, spent forty minutes lecturing the roomful of elders on the importance of humility and obedience.

Under different circumstances, a missionary like that might become a folk hero among his comrades. But Elder Toronto treated not only authority figures, but also his fellow missionaries, with condescension bordering on disdain. Regardless of the company, he couldn't resist correcting even the slightest error in the reasoning, behavior, or attitudes of those around him. His junior companions quickly learned to either take these corrections in stride, or expend considerable time and energy mounting doomed resistance to Elder Toronto's formidable powers of reason. And although Elder Toronto claimed an impersonal love of truth as his driving motivation, whenever the recipient of his arguments inevitably conceded the point, Elder Toronto's eyes gleamed with unmistakable self-satisfaction.

Elder Schwartz's trainer, Elder Amorim, had worked with Elder Toronto for a trying three months near the beginning of his mission. The experience had made an impression. Elder Amorim and Elder Schwartz might be walking down the street in companionable silence, when, out of the blue, Elder Amorim would emerge from a quiet train of thought with an angry recollection from his time with Elder Toronto.

"He corrected my grammar," Elder Amorim might say to Elder Schwartz, still indignant months after the fact. "*My* grammar. I'm a native speaker, it's his second language, and he's correcting *my* grammar. Can you believe that?"

Or maybe Elder Amorim would bring up the way Elder Toronto spent his p-day. On their one day off in the week, while Elder Amorim washed his clothes or wrote letters to his family or just lounged around the apartment, Elder Toronto sat at his desk in his tattered basketball shorts and faded green T-shirt reading books, magazines, and newspapers, none of whose titles appeared on the approved missionary reading list: *A Field Guide to the Birds of South America, Analyzing Firearm Ballistics, Essential Writings of*

Friedrich Nietzsche, Understanding Game Theory, The New Journal of World Dance History, The Calcutta Gazette, Cooking for a Crowd, Introduction to Logic, Bandeirantes: A Legacy of Discovery, The Joys of Organic Chemistry, An Advanced Training Manual for Interrogators, The Lusiads. He did this all day long, reading and reading, never uttering a word to his companion.

One p-day, Elder Amorim, on spotting Elder Toronto's current book of choice—*The Psychology of Human Sexuality*—called him on it.

"Do you really think this is the best use of your time, Elder?" said Elder Amorim.

Elder Toronto turned around in his chair, his eyes still on the book.

"Trust me," he said, "it's not as interesting as it looks."

"I'm still not sure you should be reading it," said Elder Amorim.

Elder Toronto lowered the book, assuming as worldly wise a countenance as someone just out of his teens can muster.

"Well," he said, scratching at the stubble on his unshaven face, "maybe you're right. Maybe I shouldn't be reading this. Maybe we should go out and knock some doors instead."

This was not a bluff—Elder Toronto had scheduled teaching appointments before on their day off, much to the chagrin of his beleaguered junior companion.

"No," said Elder Amorim, "this is fine," and he never brought it up again.

At least twice a day during their time together, Elder Amorim would tell Elder Schwartz a story like this from his apparently boundless repertoire, the moral of each one being that Elder Toronto should be avoided if at all possible.

Now, as the other missionaries continued to applaud President Madvig's announcement, Elder Schwartz turned around to see

Elder Toronto—a tall, skinny American whose boyish face, if it had resembled a cartoon turtle's a little less, might have been pleasant—standing a few rows behind him. Elder Schwartz walked back to join him. They shook hands and sat down on the pew.

"I don't think I know anything about you," said Elder Toronto.

Elder Schwartz only nodded, scared that if he opened his mouth, he would lose all control of his stomach. He sweated out the rest of the meeting in silence.

• • •

Two months later, the trouble began in earnest.

It was morning, the sun still low on the horizon, the air still cool at the already crowded Thursday street market. The two missionaries—Elder Toronto and Elder Schwartz—were looking for new people to teach, stopping anyone who could spare a minute, anyone who accidentally made eye contact with them.

Elder Toronto had become embroiled in a conversation with a tenacious elderly woman, debating the theological implications of the miracle of the loaves and the fishes. Despite having nothing to contribute to the conversation, Elder Schwartz stood next to him, as per the unbending mission rule requiring each elder to stay at his companion's side at all times. This tableau had become a familiar one—Elder Toronto deep in conversation with a new contact, Elder Schwartz standing next to him, arms folded, silent. With his slipshod spoken Portuguese skills, Elder Schwartz generally stayed quiet, preferring invisibility to the sometimes concerned, sometimes angry, sometimes pitying, but always uncomprehending reactions of the native speakers he attempted to address. As Elder Toronto's dialogue with the elderly woman wandered down increasingly obscure and heated paths, Elder Schwartz looked around at the booths lining the crowded street.

His eyes were sweeping over the various wares of the market—mangoes, homemade cleaning supplies, bananas, pirated CDs, nuts, spices, hand-sewn dresses, tangerines, apples—when he saw Marco Aurélio pushing his way through the crowd. He wore a new suit, the armpits of the gray jacket dark with sweat. His forehead was bruised and bleeding.

"Marco Aurélio," called Elder Schwartz, yelling to be heard above the noise of the crowd.

Elder Schwartz yelled again and Marco Aurélio turned from several yards away. When he saw Elder Schwartz, he didn't smile or wave or come over to say hello. Instead, he turned and pushed his way in the opposite direction, bumping into a man carrying a crate of oranges, squeezing past two conversing nuns, ducking behind a booth that sold knockoff soccer jerseys, and then disappearing.

Elder Toronto, deep in conversation with the elderly woman, had been oblivious to the whole thing.

"Hey," said Elder Schwartz, pulling at Elder Toronto's elbow.

"What are you doing?" said Elder Toronto, brushing him away. He apologized to the elderly woman, who had already leaned her half-full grocery basket back onto its wheels and was pulling it toward one of the fruit stands.

"Wait," said Elder Toronto, but the woman just shook her head at him and kept walking, obviously appalled by the poor manners of the two young foreigners.

"Come on," said Elder Schwartz, already jogging in the direction that Marco Aurélio had taken.

Elder Toronto followed after him.

"What's going on?" he said.

They ran behind the booth selling soccer jerseys and found a narrow alleyway leading to the next street over. A kid with a battered cavaquinho in his lap sat against one wall of the alley, listlessly smoking a joint.

"Did a man just run through here?" asked Elder Schwartz in his best attempt at Portuguese.

Unsurprisingly, the kid looked at him blankly. Elder Toronto repeated Elder Schwartz's question in his smooth, nearly native diction and the kid's eyes lit up with comprehension.

"No," he said, sounding genuinely sad that he hadn't. "No."

He picked absently at the strings of his cavaquinho, shaking his head as the two elders walked to the end of the alleyway.

"What's going on?" said Elder Toronto, wrinkling his round forehead.

Elder Schwartz told him what he had seen—Marco Aurélio, beaten and sweaty, fleeing at the sight of the two elders.

"I don't think so," said Elder Toronto, a patronizing smirk on his face. "That doesn't sound like Marco Aurélio."

"It was him," said Elder Schwartz.

"If it was him, why didn't he come over and talk to us? And why would he run away?" He asked the questions patiently, as if he were addressing a small child.

"I don't know," said Elder Schwartz. "All I know is that when he saw us, he ran. And he looked like someone had beat him up."

Elder Toronto shook his head.

"No, Elder Schwartz," he said. "It wasn't Marco Aurélio you saw." And then he started walking back toward the market, signaling the end of the discussion.

Elder Schwartz wouldn't leave it alone, though.

"It was definitely him," he said. "Something's wrong."

"Fine," said Elder Toronto. "We'll go to his house and talk to him. But you'll feel silly when he tells us he's been home all morning."

If he had been home all morning, however, he wasn't there by the time the elders arrived, a concerning fact, Elder Schwartz pointed out, considering Marco Aurélio's near-hermitic tendencies.

"Maybe," said Elder Toronto.

"I saw what I saw," said Elder Schwartz.

"We'll see."

But when they checked back at his house later that afternoon, he still wasn't there.

And the next morning, nothing.

"He never leaves his house," said Elder Schwartz. "Something is up."

Elder Toronto creased his face at this, but didn't respond.

After another day of not finding Marco Aurélio at home, Elder Toronto finally acknowledged that something might be wrong, that Marco Aurélio might actually be missing. For Elder Schwartz, this rare concession from Elder Toronto inspired not satisfaction but a sour sense of dread.

THE ARGENTINE

They say that within a week of the Argentine's arrival in Vila Barbosa, three people were dead and the Argentine was the most powerful man in the neighborhood. This was back when Vila Barbosa was still in its infancy, still just a few dozen squatters living in flimsy wooden shacks scattered over the area's then green and rolling hills. They say it happened like this—that one day an enigmatic foreigner with square, white teeth and a three-piece suit showed up at the neighborhood's little general store offering to buy the establishment from its owner at the time, a struggling pig farmer named Fernando. The amount of money the foreigner offered in exchange for the store was absurdly low, even by the neighborhood's cash-poor standards, and Fernando told him so, asked the man if he was crazy or just stupid. The foreigner replied that he was neither, that this was the most attractive offer Fernando would get for the place, and that he would be foolish not to take him up on it. The man smiled, flashing his square, white teeth at Fernando. He said he would give Fernando some time to think the proposition over. He tipped his hat, wished Fernando a good morning, and walked out of the store.

The other people who witnessed that first interaction—two men playing dominoes on a barrel of rice, a woman buying a box of salt—later remembered that the whole exchange had played like an odd joke, an encounter staged solely for the foreigner's perverse, personal delight.

They couldn't place the man's accent, foreign certainly, but from where? The incident would likely have been forgotten if, a few days later, Fernando the pig farmer and store owner hadn't been found lying face-down in a muddy pond at the edge of the neighborhood.

They pulled the body from the water, cleaned it up as best they could, and found a long, deep slit running across Fernando's neck, the sliced edges of skin puckered and white from soaking in the pond. While the neighborhood had been prepared to write this death off as the accidental result of an uncharacteristic night of drunkenness on the erstwhile store owner's part, the slit in Fernando's throat cast the situation in an altogether different light. They remembered the odd scene with the foreigner a few days earlier, remembered the foreigner's cryptic, possibly threatening statement.

On noting that a light was on at the general store, the neighborhood's self-appointed sheriff, a wiry, tenacious man with a bushy moustache and a bulldog glare, deputized the two strongest men in the area and the three of them marched up Vila Barbosa's highest hill to the little general store that sat atop it. Inside, they found the foreigner standing behind the counter wearing Fernando's canvas shopkeeper's apron over his crisp, three-piece suit.

"What can I do for you gentlemen today?" said the foreigner.

The self-appointed sheriff told the man he was under arrest for killing Fernando to gain possession of the general store. The foreigner reached under the counter. The sheriff told him not to try anything funny. The foreigner pulled out a piece of paper. He said that it was the deed to the store, that Fernando had signed it over to him, that he had paid Fernando a fair price for it, and the whole thing was all very above board. The three men from the neighborhood looked the paper over, but as none of them could read, they could neither confirm nor deny the foreigner's claims. They handed the paper back to him.

"You're under arrest," repeated the sheriff. "You and I both know that you killed Fernando."

The foreigner shrugged.

"How do you intend to arrest me?" he said. "Where is your badge? Where are your handcuffs and gun?"

The sheriff shook his finger at the foreigner. He said they'd be back and then the foreigner would have to pay for what he had done. On leaving the store, the three men spread word among the scattered shacks that there would be a meeting that evening to decide what to do with the murderous foreigner.

At sundown, the residents of Vila Barbosa gathered behind the sheriff's house. They agreed that the foreigner was clearly to blame for Fernando's murder, and that he must be brought to justice. Some of the more hotheaded residents proposed storming up the hill right then, tearing the foreigner from his ill-gotten home, and hanging him from the nearest standing structure. There were shouts of agreement. The self-appointed sheriff waved his arms in the air and yelled at the crowd to quiet down. When they had stopped shouting, the sheriff said that it would be wrong to answer lawlessness with lawlessness. He said the proper course of action would be to detain the foreigner and transport him to the city where he could be tried and sentenced by an actual judge. After some debate, the people agreed that this was the right thing to do and the sheriff and his two deputies set off with a shotgun and a length of rope to restrain the lawless foreigner.

The next morning, the residents of Vila Barbosa found the sheriff and one of his deputies dead at the base of the hill. Both men had been clubbed to death, their bodies a mushy, purpled mess. A few brave souls hiked up the hill where they discovered the foreigner and the other deputy playing dominoes inside the store. The foreigner didn't look up at them.

He said, "Tell the rest of the neighborhood we'll be holding another meeting tonight. Tell them to be up here in front of my store by sundown."

He laid down a domino and smiled at them.

At sundown, as ordered, the residents of the neighborhood congregated on top of the hill. Men, women, and children murmured nervously, their eyes fixed on the entrance to the little general store. They wondered aloud if this wasn't a mistake, if they shouldn't have taken some time to organize themselves, to make the foreigner meet them on their own terms. For all their hotheadedness the evening before, when confronted with the intimidating reality of their opponent, the residents of Vila Barbosa had to admit that they just wanted to avoid trouble. They were afraid of this stranger, certainly, but if he didn't plan to kill any more of them, it made sense to leave well enough alone.

As the sun touched the horizon, the foreigner emerged from the entrance of the store, the brawny deputy lurking a few steps behind him. The foreigner had abandoned his three-piece suit in favor of the simple clothes of the region. He still wore the shopkeeper's apron, his hands thrust into its large front pockets. He crossed in front of the gathered crowd until he stood just to the side of the little store, the sun directly behind him, silhouetting his person. The residents of Vila Barbosa squinted and shielded their eyes as they watched him, waiting for him to speak. Finally, he addressed them. He said he was so pleased to see them gathered by his store. He said that he looked forward to doing business with them, that he imagined they could have a long, profitable relationship together. He said that he hoped the string of terrible accidents—Fernando, the sheriff, and his deputy—would end soon and the people of Vila Barbosa would learn to be a little more careful. And then he smiled, revealing his thick, white teeth, thanked them again for coming, and wished them all a pleasant evening.

Since none of Vila Barbosa's residents felt a pressing desire to stick their necks out, they all decided to let the foreigner go about his business, as long as he allowed them to go about theirs. Yes, he had doubled, and then tripled the prices of the items he sold in the little grocery store, necessary items that the people couldn't do without, but ultimately they decided that this was a small price to pay for their personal safety.

When addressing the foreigner, they called him simply, "Sir," which seemed to please him. He never offered his name, and the residents of Vila Barbosa never asked. When they referred to him among themselves, they took to calling him the Argentine, not because he had revealed the country of his nativity, but because Argentina seemed as likely a point of origin as any. Furthermore, any homeland, even an invented one, lessened the aura of sinister blankness that surrounded the foreigner.

Over time, the Argentine became a fixture at community events, implicitly bestowing his approval on the proceedings through his presence at weddings, funerals, christenings, festivals. Nobody in Vila Barbosa dared make any major decision without first consulting the Argentine. When new squatters arrived in the area, they were told that they needed to secure the Argentine's blessing in settling there, otherwise the consequences could be dire. The new arrivals were told of his history, of the three unfortunate deaths, of the spoken agreement between the Argentine and the residents of the neighborhood. The new arrivals came to fear the man as much as, if not more than, the original residents did. And so, as Vila Barbosa grew, so did the Argentine's power.

CHAPTER 2

When the two missionaries arrived at church the next Sunday morning, they found Bishop Claudemir, the congregation's leader, and his wife, Fátima, setting up a row of folding chairs. Their four children ran back and forth across the room in a game whose apparent object was to transfer all of the dust and grime from the floor and the walls to their faces and their clothes. Elder Toronto and Elder Schwartz each grabbed an armload of chairs and began setting them up in a row behind the first one.

"I appreciate the gesture, elders," said Bishop Claudemir, "but I think a second row of chairs would be overly optimistic."

The elders leaned the chairs back up against the wall. Before they had arrived, Elder Toronto had instructed Elder Schwartz not to mention what he had seen—or thought he had seen—at the market that Thursday. He said there was no reason to worry anyone yet until they knew a little bit more. Marco Aurélio was probably fine, and the little congregation had enough problems already.

The Vila Barbosa ward met in a small rented apartment above a butcher shop in the neighborhood's business center. They held sacrament meeting in the living room, primary in the kitchen, and elders quorum and Relief Society in the two respective bedrooms. The smell of blood and raw meat permeated their meetings from below, and when the butcher got into an argument with a customer, which happened frequently, the church members had to yell to be heard above the shouting from downstairs.

The ward hadn't always been so small. In years past, they had met in a spacious rented dance hall, the last of Saturday night's revelers often still lingering when the church leaders arrived early Sunday morning for their weekly planning meetings. Back then—and this wasn't so long ago—there had been serious talk of growing large enough to have their very own building. The congregation was still a branch then, but growing quickly. Around that time, in an act of overoptimistic generosity, a visiting General Authority had upgraded the branch to ward status, even though the congregation's size didn't quite merit the change. He said it would give them the last push they needed to find just a few more families. Rather than spur a boost to membership, however, this moment marked the beginning of the Vila Barbosa ward's slow decline.

Just when they had been on the cusp of having a large enough congregation to get a building of their own, a counselor in the bishopric—a mousy eyeglass repairman—had absconded with several thousand reaís that he had embezzled from the ward's funds and tithing donations over the past several years. On hearing of the theft, many ward members had become furious at the incompetence that could allow something like that to happen, asking how a church that supposedly functioned by revelation didn't discover one of its own leaders stealing from the congregation. Several people had requested to have their names removed from the records of the church, and they had never returned.

Not long after that, the other counselor in the bishopric had been seen exiting a nautical-themed love motel with a woman who was not his wife, who, as it later came out, was the matriarch of the largest family in the ward. The ensuing fallout—with ward members picking sides, lobbing accusations, and resurrecting past grudges—had resulted in the excommunication of several members, the permanent disillusionment of many others, and ultimately, a decimation of Vila Barbosa's once-promising congregation.

During those dark times, there had been problems with the missionaries working in the ward as well. One set of elders had become so overwhelmed by life in Vila Barbosa that they had spent their days holed up in their apartment concocting convincing but bogus work reports to send in to the mission office each Sunday night, and passing the rest of their time playing two-handed pinochle. Their ruse had been discovered when the mission president, pleased with the progress he saw in their reports, had sent his assistants out to Vila Barbosa to observe the missionaries there and discover the secret to their success. The assistants had found the two elders unshaven, dressed in gym shorts and T-shirts, and disputing whether or not the senior companion had been cheating at pinochle by marking the playing cards to compensate for his massive inadequacies at the game.

Another Vila Barbosa missionary had proposed marriage after church one day to one of the ward's young women, slipping a plastic glitter ring he had bought at a papelaria onto her finger and telling her to think it over. He had been immediately transferred to another area and, after further complications, sent home.

Elder Hanson, the missionary whom Elder Toronto replaced, had suffered a nervous breakdown. One morning he had refused to leave the shower, explaining to his companion, Elder de Assis, through the locked bathroom door that the shower was the only place where he felt safe anymore. Morning had turned to afternoon and then evening, and Elder Hanson still hadn't left the shower. Finally, Elder de Assis had called President Madvig, who, after a couple of hours, had coaxed the distraught missionary out of the shower with assurances that he wasn't in any kind of trouble, that they just needed to talk. Elder Hanson had exited the bathroom, towel around his waist, skin wrinkled from its lengthy soaking, and explained that he had had it, that he was ready to go home. President Madvig had said that seemed like a good idea, and had arranged a flight home for the badly shaken elder later that week.

With so much internal strife, and so many problematic missionaries, the ward had never quite recovered from its various traumas. It was a tough area. However, where most missionaries, Elder Schwartz included, would despair at such a bleak assignment, Elder Toronto relished it.

"You actually enjoy it here?" Elder Schwartz asked on more than one occasion.

"Who said anything about enjoying?" said Elder Toronto with a patronizing frown. "I find the work engaging here. Every day is a challenge. There's something to that."

At eight-fifty, Bishop Claudemir took his seat in the folding chair next to the makeshift podium at the front of the rented living room. He faced the congregation, which at this point consisted of Fátima, his four squirming children, and the two missionaries. Although she often tried to put a cheerful face on things, Fátima seemed to Elder Schwartz to be frustration personified. As a younger woman, she had had a promising career as a singer, performing bossa nova standards and torch songs at some of the city's finest nightclubs. On the strength of her growing reputation, a big jazz label had even offered her a recording contract, but before she had been able to set foot in the studio, her voice had been destroyed by—depending on which account was to be believed—either a horribly botched tonsillectomy or a gruesome car crash. Whatever the case, the loss of her voice had put an immediate end to her singing career, and now here she was in Vila Barbosa with her foiled ambitions, her four rowdy children, and a husband she never saw.

In her raspy voice, she asked, "How many investigators are we expecting this week, elders?"

Elder Toronto shook his head. The same answer as every week. Fátima sighed, and Bishop Claudemir nodded his head at this news, the bags under his eyes seeming heavier with each movement of his head.

"What about Marco Aurélio?" asked Claudemir. "I wanted to talk with him about giving him the priesthood, but I could never catch him at home."

Elder Toronto shot Elder Schwartz a warning glance.

"We haven't had a chance to talk to him this week," said Elder Toronto. "He must be busy."

Bishop Claudemir ran a hand through his prematurely graying hair and mumbled something that neither missionary could quite make out. Everyone in the ward had been so excited when Marco Aurélio was baptized—the first person to join their congregation in ages. They dreaded the day when, like so many others, he might become disillusioned, or discouraged, or angry, and stop coming. Avoiding both church meetings and the missionaries was not a good sign.

Claudemir sighed and said that one of these Sundays he wouldn't be at all surprised if everyone disappeared completely—his wife, his children, Abelardo and Beatrice, the missionaries. He would show up to this stinking room at the same time he did every Sunday, set up a single chair, and hold sacrament meeting, Sunday school, and priesthood meeting all by himself. He said that even then, the stake president wouldn't release him from this calling, that he would be stuck as the bishop of the sorriest ward in the church until the day he died. He shook his head and put his face in his hands.

The two elders looked to Fátima for a clue as to whether her husband was joking or not, but she was so busy untangling the children from one another that she clearly hadn't heard any of it. Elder Toronto said that Marco Aurélio had probably just left town for the weekend. He must be visiting family and would be back as usual next week. Things were going to turn around for the Vila Barbosa ward. Bishop Claudemir didn't respond. With his face still in his hands, he began to snore softly, his shoulders rising and falling with each extended breath.

Claudemir worked as an electrician in a cosmetics factory that was located a couple of hours outside the city. At five o'clock every weekday morning, he boarded the company bus that stopped just a few blocks from his house. The bus made its way through the city, gathering Claudemir's fellow factory workers until it hit the freeway and the hilly countryside that surrounded the city. It delivered the employees to the factory at seven-thirty and then parked in a garage until it was time to take them home. Claudemir spent his twelve-hour shift troubleshooting, repairing, and revamping the intricate electrical systems of the factory's complex machinery. His main human interaction was with his direct superior, and the rest of his attention was given to the various indicator lights, solenoids, thermocouples, limit switches, selsyns, fuses, and circuit breakers that demanded his attention each day.

At seven-thirty every evening, Claudemir and his fellow employees loaded onto the same bus and traveled the same route in reverse, a mirror image of their morning commute. Claudemir usually made it home around ten, ate a light dinner, and sat up talking with Fátima until his eyes closed of their own accord and his body slept.

He was occasionally given a stretch of days or even a week off in an elaborate scheduling system that was never quite clear to the missionaries no matter how many times Claudemir explained it to them. This time off was mostly consumed by household repairs and church business that had been left unattended for weeks.

Once, when the three of them were alone together, Claudemir had told the elders that he had never been unfaithful to Fátima with another woman, had never even considered it, but that he lusted after sleep with an ardent passion. In his daydreaming moments at work, it wasn't his wife that occupied his mind, but the thought of his bed and the deathlike rest it brought him. If sleep assumed a human form, he said, he would take her on as a mistress without a second thought. As was often the case in these conversations, neither of the missionaries was quite sure what to say, so they told Bishop Claudemir that if there was anything they could do to help, they'd be happy to do it.

At eight-fifty-five, Abelardo, Claudemir's elderly second counselor, shuffled in and took his seat at the front of the room, removing the coat and scarf he wore in spite of the morning's already considerable heat. The man survived on the verge of death, fighting off one illness after another. Various conflicting church records put Abelardo's age at somewhere between eighty-five and a hundred-and-two years old.

Based on his rambling conversations with the missionaries when he accompanied them on investigator visits or had them over to his house for lunch, Elder Schwartz knew that as a young man, Abelardo had hastily emigrated from his native land under conditions that he vaguely referred to as his European troubles, and had set out here in the New World on a series of misadventures that had ultimately left him living as an old man in a mildewed shoebox of a house in Vila Barbosa. By his own account, Abelardo had worked as a solitary rubber tapper in the depths of the jungle during the waning days of the rubber boom, had played a key role in a major government overthrow, and had later languished as a political prisoner under the military dictatorship because of that role. He had briefly owned a bakery, had founded a short-lived school for the blind, had worked several years in construction, and had done any number of odd jobs in the times in between. He had been married five times, twice to the same woman, and had fathered, to his knowledge, eighteen children, none of whom ever visited him.

At one point several decades earlier, he had accumulated enough money to retire and had bought a small house at the base of a hill in a small town in the country. He had led a quiet life there, fishing in a nearby stream every morning and evening, and sleeping away the warm afternoons in a hammock stretched between two shady trees. Then, one day in the rainy season, a mudslide from the hill buried Abelardo's house and all of his worldly possessions. He'd had a little bit of money left, and so he had moved to Vila Barbosa, a burgeoning slum at the time, because he knew he could live cheaply there and stretch his remaining resources as far as possible.

Soon after moving, he had met a pair of missionaries who had told him a story about God appearing to a young farm boy and telling him to restore the true church to the earth. Abelardo had told the missionaries that he had seen enough crazy things in his life that the story seemed plausible to him. He had read the Book of Mormon, had prayed to God about their church, and had decided to be baptized, becoming one of the first members of the Vila Barbosa branch. In the intervening years, Abelardo had briefly served as branch president, managing in that small period of time to alienate several new converts with his stern interpretations of church doctrine and his propensity for calling individual members of the congregation to repentance over the pulpit every Sunday. Not long after his baptism, he had also married his current wife, Beatrice, a long-suffering woman now in her sixties who, not long after joining the church, had had a dream—whose provenance the missionaries privately questioned—that she needed to marry Abelardo.

Beatrice came into the makeshift chapel a few moments after her husband, smiling at the missionaries and taking a seat next to Fátima. The missionaries knew far less about Beatrice than they did about her husband. When she talked about any period in the last twenty years of her life, it was always in terms of whatever illness Abelardo had been suffering at the time—the era of his edema, the time of the terrible shingles, or the age of the great pneumonia scare. In spite of his near-constant state of illness, the man seemed incapable of dying. At some point in every conversation the elders had with him, Abelardo shook his head and bemoaned the fact that with health like his, he couldn't be much longer for this life. And yet he soldiered on, conquering—

just barely—one illness after another, sapping the vitality from his attentive wife with each bout of chilblains, each flare-up of gout, each massive constipation. Whenever the missionaries asked Beatrice how she was doing, they received a detailed account of the state of Abelardo's body.

"But how are *you* doing, sister?" Elder Toronto would say, and she would always reply that she was persevering, that she couldn't complain because there were others in this world far worse off than she was. No matter what questions Elder Toronto asked her, Beatrice never disclosed any information about her own interests, her own past, her own thoughts and desires. Her answers always veered inevitably back to the illnesses of Abelardo and the suffering endemic to the world at large.

After she had arranged herself in her seat, Beatrice leaned over Fátima and asked the missionaries what was going on with Marco Aurélio. Elder Toronto said that they hadn't seen him in a few days, that he must be busy. He didn't mention the incident at the street market. Beatrice said it was strange because ever since he was baptized, Marco Aurélio had been almost a bother to her and Abelardo, stopping by their house at odd hours to chat, often keeping Abelardo up late into the night. She said she didn't mind the company, it was the potential threat to Abelardo's delicate health that worried her. Elder Schwartz watched Elder Toronto's brow furrow in surprise.

"That doesn't sound like Marco Aurélio," said Elder Toronto. "He never leaves his house."

"No," said Beatrice, "he visits us nearly every night. At least until this past week."

"What does he talk about?"

Beatrice shook her head and said they'd have to ask Abelardo.

"Are you talking about that Marco Aurélio?" said Abelardo on hearing his name.

"Yes," said Beatrice, "I told them we're concerned about him."

"He's a shifty one," said Abelardo.

"Shifty?" said Elder Toronto. "How so?"

He was leaning forward now, rapt.

"He's not shifty," said Beatrice, shaking her finger at her husband. "He has a good heart."

"He's up to something," said Abelardo.

"Why do you say he's shifty?" said Elder Toronto.

"He's up to something," said Abelardo.

"Like what?" said Elder Toronto.

Abelardo waved an angry hand at the elder.

"It's not something for missionaries to worry about," he said, and folded his arms, the matter closed.

Elder Toronto, who, truth be told, couldn't stand Abelardo and disregarded every word that came out of the old man's mouth, leaned over to Elder Schwartz and dropped his voice low. "Abelardo thinks everyone's shifty. It's probably nothing."

Elder Schwartz nodded, unsure.

Throughout the previous exchange, Bishop Claudemir sat hunched over and snoring next to Abelardo. The clock on the wall now read five after nine. Fátima asked Abelardo to wake her husband up so they could get started. Abelardo elbowed Claudemir in the ribs, causing him to sit up with a snort, blinking his bloodshot eyes. He looked at the clock and at the congregation of eight that sat facing him.

"All right, then," he said, and stood up to the podium. "I'd like to welcome you all to sacrament meeting this morning. We'll start by singing a hymn, whatever hymn Sister Beatrice has chosen for us to sing, and then we'll have an opening prayer by one of the missionaries. It doesn't matter which one."

He sat down and rubbed his eyes. Beatrice stood up, hymnal in hand, arm raised.

"Hymn number one-ninety-six," she said. "'Nas Montanhas de Sião.'"

She waited for everyone to open their hymnbooks and then they all began to sing, approximating the tune as nearly as they could without accompaniment, Beatrice's hand waving in four-four time in a vain attempt to get them to sing in something like unison. When they had finished singing, and Elder Schwartz had said the opening prayer, Bishop Claudemir stood up at the podium again, fully awake now.

"There's no ward business that I'm aware of, so we'll now prepare for the sacrament by singing hymn number one-oh-six."

They all opened the hymnbooks they had just closed and, at Beatrice's signal, began to sing again. Halfway through the first verse they heard the door at the back of the room open and someone step inside.

"Excuse me."

Everyone but Abelardo stopped singing and turned around. The man standing at the back of the room was tall and thin. He wore a faded brown suit that was several inches too short for him in the legs and arms. He had a short, thick scar under each of his eyes.

"I don't mean to interrupt," he said, "but is this where the Mormons meet?"

Bishop Claudemir said that it was, and that the man was welcome to join them if he'd like. The man said that he appreciated the offer, but actually just wanted a word with the missionaries. Elder Schwartz and Elder Toronto looked at each other. They had never seen this man before. They stood up from their seats and the rest of the minuscule congregation rejoined the hymn with Abelardo, who hadn't stopped singing through the exchange with the tall stranger.

The missionaries walked to the back of the room where the tall, thin man stood waiting for them, his hands clasped politely in front of him. Elder Schwartz and Elder Toronto each introduced themselves. The man said it was nice to meet them but didn't offer a name of his own. He smelled like fried food and cigarettes.

"So you're the missionaries?" he said.

"That's right," said Elder Toronto.

"You're just kids," said the man.

"We're old enough," said Elder Toronto. "How can we help you?"

The man in the brown suit turned so his back was to the front of the room.

"Listen," he said, his voice low, drawing the elders closer. "This isn't the right time or place, but I didn't know how else to get in touch with you. We need to discuss your friend Marco Aurélio."

"How do you know Marco Aurélio?" said Elder Toronto, his voice high with interest, a crack in his usual detached demeanor. He quickly composed himself. "Are you a friend of his?"

"I can't talk now," said the man. He reached into the pocket of his faded brown suit coat and pulled out a small black notebook and a pen. He opened the notebook and wrote something down. He tore out the paper and handed it to Elder Toronto.

"We can talk at eight o'clock tonight at this address," he said.

The man replaced the notebook in his jacket pocket, lifted a hand in farewell to Bishop Claudemir, who had been watching the whole conversation, and slipped out the door.

After sacrament meeting, Bishop Claudemir pulled the missionaries aside and asked what the tall, thin man had wanted.

"He said he just had a few questions about the church and wanted us to come by later," said Elder Toronto.

Elder Toronto was not in the habit of lying. Elder Schwartz, who had been picking at a thread in his tie, looked up at his companion in surprise. If Bishop Claudemir had seen the expression on his face, the game would have been up. But Claudemir didn't notice, as Elder Schwartz, in his incompetent silence, remained essentially invisible to the members of the ward.

"Really?" said Bishop Claudemir.

"Yeah," said Elder Toronto, "which is great because we could definitely use some new investigators right now."

Bishop Claudemir nodded, squinting his bloodshot eyes.

"Is that all he wanted?" he said.

"Yeah," said Elder Toronto, "as far as I could tell."

Bishop Claudemir rubbed his eyes. He told the elders that he appreciated all the work that they did—he could tell that they really cared about the ward here and wanted things to go well.

"Absolutely," said Elder Toronto.

Bishop Claudemir looked the two missionaries in the eyes.

"Elders," he said. "You two are the most reliable missionaries this area has had in a while. Please don't do anything that we'll all be sorry about later."

He clapped Elder Toronto on the shoulder and the three of them crossed the room to take their seats in the Sunday school class that Beatrice had already, at Abelardo's insistence, begun to teach.

CHAPTER 3

The elders couldn't find the tall, thin man's address anywhere on their map. Of course, many addresses in Vila Barbosa couldn't be found on their map. The government cartographer who had designed it had chosen to represent the neighborhood's favelas—with their guerrilla architecture, their makeshift dirt roads, their unofficial addresses—as empty patches of green, giving the false impression that Vila Barbosa consisted of a few small clusters of neatly ordered streets surrounded by acres of green, rolling hills, a pastoral fantasy that glossed over the crowded, tangled reality of the neighborhood's physical space. Over the years, various missionaries had attempted to remedy this incongruity, drawing the streets they traveled and the houses they visited onto the map's green areas. However, the favelas had such a dramatic tendency to mutate, even from one month to the next, that the missionaries' ongoing cartographic efforts were continually rendered irrelevant.

So Elder Toronto and Elder Schwartz did what they always did when they couldn't find an address: They asked at every bar or padaria that they passed. Unfortunately, this, too, proved fruitless; it seemed that nobody had heard of the street where they were supposed to rendezvous with the man in the brown suit.

"What time is it?" asked Elder Toronto as they walked down the wildly uneven sidewalk, unsure of where to go. The sun was low on the horizon, the sky a burnt orange over the red-brick sprawl of the city.

"My watch was stolen, remember?"

Elder Toronto said he had forgotten. The previous week they had been mugged an unprecedented three times in four days. After the first two muggers had deprived them of, respectively, their dummy wallets—containing just enough cash to satisfy a mugger—and their actual wallets—containing, in addition to some cash, their government-issued identification papers—the third mugger had found a greatly diminished profit to be had from his two intended targets. Elder Toronto had apologized for their lack of cash and had offered up Elder Schwartz's watch as compensation—it wasn't a new watch, or even a very good one, but it did keep very accurate time. After making sure that their pockets and their bags truly contained no cash, the mugger had settled for Elder Schwartz's watch and, almost as an afterthought, his tie, before running off down a nearby alleyway.

"It's probably close to eight," said Elder Schwartz. "I don't think we're going to make it."

He hoped that Elder Toronto would nod his head in response, throw away the address, and choose a nearby street where they could knock a few doors until it was time to call it a day. All Elder Schwartz wanted out of his mission experience, out of life, really, was to keep his head above water; he didn't want any trouble, and this business with the man in the brown suit seemed certain to bring just that.

"No," said Elder Toronto, "we're going to make it."

If it had been a week earlier, with his senior companion in much different spirits, there might have been a ghost of a hope of Elder Toronto giving up on the venture.

Although his fellow missionaries had told Elder Schwartz plenty about his current companion's odd and frustrating behaviors, no one had warned him of the dramatic, unexpected shifts in mood. Much of the time, Elder Toronto behaved more-or-less exactly as might be expected. If Elder Schwartz ever made even a glimmer of an assertion, Elder Toronto latched onto it, pointing out its flaws and demanding that his junior companion defend the idea, thus providing further argumentative fodder. If Elder Schwartz refused to play along, Elder Toronto subjected him instead to a pedantic, over-detailed lecture on whatever topic came to mind: the importance of dedicated language study, the merits of a robust space program, the pitfalls and advantages of continental philosophy.

In these moods, Elder Toronto attacked missionary work with a similar vigor. He knocked on door after door after door with a constant, assured energy, and on the rare occasion when somebody invited them inside, the lessons he taught effervesced with perfectly crafted bubbles of basic Mormon doctrine.

Then, each evening, Elder Toronto addressed, in a concise and stinging summary, any flaws in Elder Schwartz's speech, behavior, or person that had been left unexamined throughout the day.

All this behavior was to be expected, but what surprised Elder Schwartz was his companion's occasional tendency to, apropos of nothing, shut down, completely disengaging from the world around him. Elder Toronto might spend hours or even days in one of these dark, reserved moods. He spoke only when necessary, responding to Elder Schwartz's questions with halfhearted monosyllables. His junior companion could make whatever ridiculous assertion came to mind, the more outrageous the better, and Elder Toronto wouldn't even bat an eye. He allowed Elder Schwartz—disastrously—to teach all of the lessons, to the complete bafflement of their investigators. During these times, Elder Toronto went to bed early and got up late, eating only sporadically. As they walked to appointments or knocked on doors, he always lagged a step or two behind Elder Schwartz.

Then, just as suddenly as it had arrived, the mood would pass, instantly transforming Elder Toronto back into his energetic, condescending self. Whenever Elder Schwartz broached the subject of these drastic shifts, asking what caused them or what ended them, Elder Toronto refused to acknowledge that his mood was anything but constant and predictable.

The past twelve days had brought an especially intense bout of this chilly disengagement, and Elder Schwartz had begun to worry. Even the previous week's muggings had left Elder Toronto gloomily unruffled. But the visit of the man in the brown suit had flipped a switch. Elder Schwartz could see the gears picking up speed, his companion reanimating at the prospect of this meeting. He wasn't going to let it go.

"We're going to find this place," Elder Toronto said.

Just then, a battered, unlicensed cab rolled down the street toward the two missionaries. As it approached, the driver yelled through the open window asking if they needed a ride—he had the lowest fares in town. Elder Toronto stepped forward and said they didn't need a ride but they could use some directions. The pirate cab rolled to a stop. The driver, a young guy with a halfhearted beard, said he also had the best price in town on directions. Elder Toronto told him they didn't have any money.

"Then maybe I don't have any directions," said the driver.

Elder Toronto reached into his pocket. He had found a ten-real note in one of his desk drawers, which had served as the missionaries' food and transportation budget for the past few days. But the money, scarce to begin with, had nearly run out. Elder Toronto pulled the two remaining bills from his pocket.

"I've got two reaís," said Elder Toronto.

The driver looked at the bills and shook his head.

"Seriously," said Elder Toronto, "this is all I've got."

After a moment of deliberation, the driver scratched at his wispy beard and said that two reaís was better than nothing. He reached out and took the bills. Elder Toronto told the driver the name of the street.

The driver said, "Yeah, I know where that is." He said he had a friend who had lived there for a while, and it could barely even be called a street. It was really just a little row of shacks on a strip of land between the train tracks and the river.

"By the tracks?" said Elder Toronto.

"Yeah," said the driver. "Is that a problem?"

"What time is it?" said Elder Toronto

The driver looked at a small digital clock taped onto the dashboard of his car.

"It's seven-fifty," he said.

The elders stepped back from the window of the car.

"It's too far," said Elder Schwartz. "We're not going to make it."

"We're going to get there," said Elder Toronto, and Elder Schwartz could see, much to his dismay, that his companion's pugnacious spark had returned, that he wouldn't be talked out of this.

"Hey," said the driver.

The missionaries looked at him.

He said, "You guys are like priests or something, right?"

"Kind of," said Elder Toronto. "We're missionaries."

"Right, right," said the driver. "I'll tell you what. You guys hop in and I'll drive you there for free. We'll call it my good deed for the day, and you put in a nice word for me next time you say one of your prayers or whatever."

The missionaries said he had a deal and got into the car.

As they drove along the neighborhood's twisting dirt roads, teetering stacks of makeshift houses towering on either side of them, the driver regaled the two missionaries with the story of how he had acquired his car. In short, over the course of six months he had engineered a succession of shrewd exchanges, trading a pair of leather dress shoes he found on a curb for a seven-speed blender, which he had traded for a nail gun, which he had traded for a sewing machine, which he had traded for an amethyst ring, which he had traded for a lightly used leather armchair, which he had traded for a pool table, which he had traded for a motorcycle, which he had traded, ultimately, for this car, which had needed a few repairs, but was now running like a top. As his story reached its conclusion, they came to the end of the narrow dirt and cobblestone road they had rattled along for the past few blocks. When the dust settled, the elders could see the banks of the river just a few yards in front of them.

"This is as far as I can take you," said the driver. He pointed out a ramshackle footbridge that spanned the dirty river and told the elders they'd have to cross there. The missionaries thanked him and said that they really appreciated the ride. The driver said it was his pleasure and handed Elder Toronto a grimy square of cardstock with a name and phone number handwritten on the front.

"Next time you have some money and need a ride somewhere, give me a call," said the driver. "My name's Wanderley. It's on the card."

The missionaries thanked him again. He waved to them and then drove off, his little car jostling over the rutted dirt road and then disappearing into the mountain of dusty brick houses.

The two elders stepped tentatively onto the narrow bridge, really just a ragtag collection of worm-eaten boards nailed precariously together, and began to cross. Beneath them, the river carried a miscellany of garbage on its filthy surface—candy wrappers; used condoms; a hairbrush; toilet paper; a lampshade; rats, living and dead; bloated scraps of cardboard; broken toys; rotten vegetables; the arm of a sofa. Elder Toronto claimed that, during the rainy season, he had even seen the stiff, dead body of a horse floating by a couple of miles downstream.

As the two of them walked across the makeshift bridge, the boards rocked from side to side.

"Maybe we should have crossed one at a time," said Elder Schwartz.

"Just keep moving," said Elder Toronto from behind him, his arms held out like a tightrope walker's.

"How do we know this guy isn't luring us here to kill us or something?" said Elder Schwartz.

"Well, Elder Schwartz, we don't," said Elder Toronto, his powers of condescension now back in full force. The boards creaked dangerously and they started walking faster.

"No, really," said Elder Schwartz. "Is this some kind of ambush?"

Elder Toronto allowed that this was a possibility, but there were much easier ways to kill them. Furthermore, he figured the guy wouldn't come to a semi-public place with a handful of witnesses to make an appointment with his intended murder victims. Elder Schwartz said he guessed that made sense. He jumped the remaining couple of feet from the end of the bridge to the muddy riverbank, inadvertently jouncing the boards.

"Careful," said Elder Toronto, balancing on the wobbling bridge.

After a moment of regaining his balance, he joined Elder Schwartz on the riverbank. They found the street, such as it was, just as Wanderley had described it—a narrow strip of land between the river and the train tracks. A series of plywood shacks occupied the land's middle ground, presumably far enough away from the tracks to avoid being whisked away by the sucking wake of the train, and far enough from the river to avoid being carried off when the water level rose. A few yards away from the missionaries, a pack of bony stray dogs tussled over a discarded scrap of food. As the elders picked their way across the muddy ground, they were careful not to make eye contact with any of the snarling dogs. In front of the nearest shack, a middle-aged woman stood sweeping the dirt off of the mat in front of the door.

"Evening," said Elder Toronto.

The woman looked up at him and greeted them quietly. The missionaries introduced themselves and said they were looking for house number twelve—did she know where it was? The woman nodded and said that it was the house five doors down from here. The missionaries thanked her and asked if they might stop by the woman's house later and talk with her and her family about God's plan of happiness. The woman shook her head and stepped inside, leaving the broom leaning against the door frame.

They found the address just where the woman had said they would, a flimsy shack identical to the rest. The door—adorned with a hand-painted number twelve—hung crookedly in its frame.

"I'm not sure this is a good idea," said Elder Schwartz.

"It's fine."

Elder Toronto knocked. The door was slightly ajar and swung in a couple of inches. The flickering of a candle lit the inside of the shack. Elder Toronto took a step back, waiting. The sun had gone down completely now, but some rusty light still lingered in the sky. No one came to the door. Elder Toronto knocked again. A few dirt-caked children kicked a ball around in front of the shack next door.

"Hey," said Elder Toronto, waving to the kids, "any of you all know the guy who lives here? Is he home?"

The kids giggled and continued their kicking of the ball.

"I think we should go," said Elder Schwartz.

Elder Toronto said, "He's probably just running a little late. This place is pretty out of the way."

"What could this guy even know about Marco Aurélio?" said Elder Schwartz.

"That's what we're here to find out," said Elder Toronto.

They stood there for a few minutes watching the dogs back by the bridge. The tussle had escalated into a nasty fight with two of the dogs scratching and biting at each other, jumping and snarling, tearing into whatever chunk of their opponent's flesh they could get their jaws around. A few people had stepped out of their homes to watch the scuffle. When the fight died down, the people went back inside. By this point, the color had drained out of the sky, leaving the small row of shacks by the river in darkness.

"Let's go," said Elder Schwartz, who, with the setting of the sun, had gone from being broadly uncomfortable with the situation to being certain they were about to pass a point of no return. He tapped Elder Toronto on the shoulder. "Please?"

"Hang on," said Elder Toronto.

He stepped up to the crack in the door and peered inside. He turned back to Elder Schwartz and whispered that somebody was in there.

"Well, it seems like they don't want to answer the door," Elder Schwartz whispered, turning to go and hoping his companion would follow suit. He didn't, and Elder Schwartz remained in place.

"Excuse me, sir," said Elder Toronto, pushing the door open cautiously. He stepped inside. Elder Schwartz followed reluctantly.

"Sir?" said Elder Toronto.

The candlelight revealed the tall, thin man in the brown suit lying on a cot against the plywood wall. A small table, the only other furniture in the room, held the remains of a candle that provided light to the tiny shack. The man's feet hung over the end of the cot, exposing the pale skin between his drooping gray socks and his too-short suit pants. His brown suit was rumpled and torn at the seams, but it was the thing above his shirt collar, the thing that used to be the tall, thin man's head—now a smashed, pulpy mess of grays and purples and reds—that sent both missionaries sprinting out of the shack, running toward the dubious safety of the bridge.

CHAPTER 4

Two months earlier, the train jostled along the tracks, carrying Elder Schwartz toward his new, dreaded assignment in Vila Barbosa. He crouched on the gritty train car floor with his arms wrapped tightly around his luggage, a squatting embrace that had proved the only effective method in preventing his unwieldy suitcase from toppling over and banging the shins of a fellow passenger on the overcrowded car. He had tried to pack well this time, tried to make the process of hauling all his belongings via the city's busy public transportation system as painless as possible. It seemed, however, that he had failed. Among other things, he had accidentally packed all of his books at the top of his suitcase, realizing his mistake too late to remedy it. He couldn't have made his luggage harder to handle if he had tried.

The train lurched to a dramatic stop, toppling Elder Schwartz onto his back with his suitcase crashing down on top of him. His fellow passengers, trying to keep their own balance, glared down at him. Elder Toronto leaned over, righted the fallen suitcase, and helped Elder Schwartz stand up.

"Let me help you with that," said Elder Toronto.

"It's fine," said Elder Schwartz. "I can handle it myself."

• • •

Earlier that day, their partnership got off to a rocky start. After the transfer meeting, they left the mission office and walked to the nearest train station, Elder Schwartz dragging his suitcase behind him.

The station, a modernist work of concrete and glass, bustled with crowds, even though rush hour had long passed. People had places to go. The commuters milled around the platform, some of them jockeying for spots at the edge so they could be first to board. The missionaries hung back, standing next to a concrete column as part of Elder Toronto's strategy to get the luggage on the train as painlessly as possible. His plan involved jumping into the flow of people at just the right angle and just the right moment to take advantage of the force of the moving crowd rather than fight against it. The whole thing sounded dubious to Elder Schwartz, but he agreed to go along with it. As they stood there, Elder Toronto alternated between carefully observing the jostling crowd of commuters, and glancing down the dark tunnel where their train would eventually emerge.

Elder Schwartz looked around at the clean, almost sterile architecture of the station. On a wall to his right, he noticed a plaque with a masonic symbol on it. He pointed it out to Elder Toronto, just to get some conversation going.

"See that?" said Elder Schwartz.

"The masonic symbol?" said Elder Toronto.

"Yeah," said Elder Schwartz. "Elder Pelourinho told me that his trainer, Elder Brands, once met a guy and saw that he was wearing a ring with the mason symbol on it. And you know how sometimes, the mason symbol has a G in the middle of it? Well, Elder Brands asked the guy if he would tell him what the G stood for, and the guy laughed a little and said no. But then Elder Brands asked, *Does it stand for Gadianton?* And as soon as Elder Brands said that, the guy jumped out of his seat, and his face was all red, and he kicked the elders out of his house and told them never to come back. Isn't that crazy?"

"It never happened," said Elder Toronto, looking down the tunnel for an approaching train.

"No," said Elder Schwartz, "Elder Brands told me, and he says—"

"That's the stupidest thing I've ever heard," said Elder Toronto, looking back now at the crowd of commuters.

"But don't you think that—"

"No," said Elder Toronto. "It's so stupid it makes my head hurt. It's not even worth discussing."

He looked back at the train tunnel. Even though Elder Schwartz had been warned about his companion, Elder Toronto's response still stung. He wanted to get off to a good start, though, so he tried a new gambit.

"Did you pick up any letters from your family this morning?" he asked.

As soon as he said it, he realized his mistake.

Every missionary knew what had happened to Elder Toronto's family. This was back at the beginning of his mission when he was still in the training center, the CTM. Apparently, one icy Idaho evening, Elder Toronto's family—his mom, his dad, his two younger sisters—were driving down the highway to visit some friends in the next town over. Nobody saw it happen, but the first people to arrive on the scene found a semi-truck jackknifed across both lanes of the highway and the Torontos' car upside down in a ditch, all four passengers dead inside.

As soon as he was notified of this, the president of the CTM called Elder Toronto into his office, gave him the news, and told him he could interrupt his mission to fly back to the States for the funeral—the church would cover all his travel expenses. In fact, he could fly back for the funeral and then take as much time as he needed. He shouldn't feel any pressure to come back to the mission until he was ready.

But Elder Toronto turned down the opportunity to go home, and when the CTM president insisted, Elder Toronto dug in his heels. He refused to leave the mission. He said he didn't see the point. And so, on the morning of his family's funeral, he sat in his Portuguese class singing songs about the difference between *ser* and *estar*, a rictus grin plastered to his face.

Of course, all of this only made Elder Toronto less approachable, his fellow missionaries unsure how to act around that kind of trauma.

Elder Schwartz braced himself for the inevitable backlash.

"Nope," said Elder Toronto, his expression steady. "No letters."

The horn of an approaching train sounded and he turned to Elder Schwartz.

"Pick up your bags," he said. "This is us."

• • •

Now, on the train, Elder Schwartz scrambled to keep his luggage from spilling across the car.

"Are you sure you don't want help?" said Elder Toronto.

"I'm fine," said Elder Schwartz.

He didn't argue, though, when Elder Toronto placed the suitcase between them so they could stabilize it with their legs. Just before the train began to move again, a young man clutching at his side boarded their train car. When the doors closed, the young man squeezed his way to the middle of the car. He raised his free hand in the air and yelled that if he could have a few minutes of everybody's time, he would really appreciate it. A few people turned to look, but most of the car's passengers kept their eyes fixed on their newspapers, their windows, or their hands. The young man continued, his hand gripping his abdomen.

"To those of you who have good health," he began, in an over-the-top preacherly tone, "I recommend that you treasure it. Since I was a small child, I have been afflicted with constant illness and suffering. My mother remembers many nights that I cried myself to sleep with pain. We come from humble circumstances and my poor mother was forced to watch me suffer, as she couldn't afford adequate medical treatment."

As the young man's speech progressed, a distinct rotting smell permeated the car. Elder Toronto leaned toward Elder Schwartz.

"Have you ever seen one of these before?" he said.

Elder Schwartz shook his head.

"Keep watching," said Elder Toronto.

The young man had paused, apparently to compose himself, and then continued.

"Like I said, I've been suffering since I was a child. Nobody could figure out what was wrong with me. Then, a few weeks ago, I met a doctor who said he knew what afflicted me and that he was willing to treat me. He was aware of my circumstances and offered his services for free. At the time, I thought this man must be a saint, but he has since turned out to be a wolf in sheep's clothing, a demon in human form."

The young man looked around the car, allowing the drama— and the pungent rotting smell—to build for the few people who were paying attention.

"He said he could cure me with a simple surgery. My mother and friends were overjoyed. We made an appointment, I came in to his office, and he anesthetized me. When I woke up, several of my vital organs were dangling—yes, dangling—from a hole in my belly."

The young man lifted up his shirt, revealing the source of the sharp rotting smell. A large plastic bag, its opening attached with duct tape to the young man's abdomen, held what looked to be an assortment of organ meat floating in a yellowish liquid.

"This thief of a doctor, this demon from hell, said that until I raise two thousand reaís, he refuses to put my organs back inside my body where they belong."

A man standing near the elders laughed and shook his head.

"This is serious," said the young man. "A small contribution from each of you of just one real would put me that much closer to meeting this so-called doctor's demands. As you can probably imagine, I don't have much time."

As he walked around the train car, a few people pressed coins and small bills into his hand, just to get him to move his stinking bag of meat away from them. He stopped in front of one woman who shook her head and told him to keep practicing—if she was going to pay for a show, it had better be well-performed. The train stopped and the doors of the car opened. The young man thanked everyone who contributed, and hopped off onto the platform.

"The lady's right," said Elder Toronto. "This kid was okay, but I've seen better. The first time I saw someone do that, the guy was so convincing that I bought the whole story for a few seconds. Until I thought about it, you know?"

Elder Schwartz nodded, relieved at the easy tone of the conversation. The doors closed and the train started moving again.

"You're coming to Vila Barbosa at a good time," said Elder Toronto. "We actually have a baptism scheduled for this Sunday. First one in a long time. The ward's really excited."

Elder Schwartz said that was great. He asked who was getting baptized.

"His name's Marco Aurélio," said Elder Toronto. "You'll meet him later today. He's a fascinating guy."

Elder Toronto pointed out the window.

"This is where our area starts," he said.

Elder Schwartz looked out the window at the rolling hills of houses built on houses built on houses, a vast landscape of red ceramic brick and corrugated tin, accented by a faded blue water tank here, a lonely stand of palm trees there. In the tobacco-colored sky above the hills of houses, little flecks of color jerked and darted—paper kites flown by earthbound boys of all ages. Occasionally, one of the kites fluttered out of the sky, cut down by the glass-coated string of one of the other kites.

Elder Schwartz looked away from this first sight of the neighborhood and closed his eyes. As long as he was on this train, he could put off the inevitable discomfort of getting to know a new area. On the train, he didn't have to meet the local church members, who would squint at the missionary tag on his shirt pocket and tell him his name was completely unpronounceable and that they were sorry but they would just have to call him "Elder." And then they would ask him where he was from, how big his family was, and when he answered their questions they would ask him to repeat himself. They would tell him his tongue was still too slow, too American, and they could hardly understand a word he said. They would say that this must be his first area, and that Portuguese was a difficult language but he'd get the hang of it soon. When he managed to communicate how long he had actually been out, how many other areas he'd served in, they would look at him with pity and say that it just takes some missionaries a little longer than others. And then they would avoid talking to him from that point on, put off by the awkwardness of having to ask him to repeat himself again and again, to no avail.

Here on the train, he could put off the constant feeling of disorientation; of walking down unfamiliar streets through unfamiliar neighborhoods; of knowing that if anything were to happen to Elder Toronto and he were forced to find his own way home that he would be completely at the mercy of strangers, asking for directions at every turn, loudly broadcasting the fact that he was a lost, confused foreigner with a growing sense of panic.

On the train, he could put off the unpleasant surprises that were sure to come with every moment spent in his new area—the attacks by stray dogs, the belligerent drunks, the tripping and falling over broken sidewalks, the irate pastors, the freak rain storms—surprises that were bound to be exacerbated by the fact that this was Vila Barbosa. So he gripped his luggage, eyes closed, dreading the coming hours and days.

"Here we are," said Elder Toronto, and as the train slowed to a stop, Elder Schwartz opened his eyes.

• • •

Later that afternoon, after hauling his luggage across the hilly streets of Vila Barbosa and settling into the musty downstairs apartment he'd now call home, Elder Schwartz met Marco Aurélio for the first time. The two missionaries met up with him at a little lanchonete tucked into an alleyway at the edge of the neighborhood's business district. He sat reading a newspaper on one of the tall stools at the counter, so intent on what he was reading that he didn't notice at first when the two elders walked in.

"Marco Aurélio," said Elder Toronto.

He looked up from his newspaper.

"Hey," he said.

He folded the newspaper and tucked it under his arm as he got down from the stool. He wore khaki slacks and a plaid button-down shirt that had both seen better days. His dark hair was thinning at the temples and crown, and the beginnings of wrinkles bracketed his eyes. Later that day, Elder Schwartz would have trouble remembering Marco Aurélio's face. In fact, every time he saw Marco Aurélio after that, Elder Schwartz would think, *Right, that's what he looks like.* There was just something indistinct about his features. His eyes, nose, mouth, ears, jawline—they were all nearly impossible to commit to memory.

"Let's sit at that table," he said, pointing with the newspaper.

They sat down in the corner at a metal folding table with a beer logo printed across its top. Marco Aurélio reached out and shook Elder Schwartz's hand.

"You must be the new missionary," he said. "I'm Marco Aurélio."

"It's nice to meet you," said Elder Schwartz. "I look forward to getting to know you."

"I'm sorry, I didn't quite get that," said Marco Aurélio. "One more time?"

"You really can't speak Portuguese, can you?" said Elder Toronto, staring in wonder at Elder Schwartz.

"Hey!" said Marco Aurélio, his eyebrows furrowed. "What kind of thing is that to say to your new partner?"

"Well, am I wrong?" said Elder Toronto.

Marco Aurélio turned back to Elder Schwartz.

He said, "One more time, please. You said it fine. It's just noisy in here."

"I said, 'It's nice to meet you,'" he said.

"Likewise," said Marco Aurélio. "And your name?"

"I'm Elder Schwartz."

"Schwartz?" said Marco Aurélio.

"Yes," said Elder Schwartz.

"Is that German?"

"Yes," said Elder Schwartz.

"But you're another American, right?"

Elder Schwartz said that was right. Marco Aurélio nodded. He rolled back the fraying cuffs of his shirt and asked the elders if they'd eaten lunch yet. Elder Toronto said they hadn't.

"What'll you have?" said Marco Aurélio.

Elder Toronto said that they could take care of their own orders. Marco Aurélio shook his head. He said lunch was on him today. The elders thanked him and told him what they wanted. Marco Aurélio got up from the table.

The woman behind the counter—who had been watching their table with a more-than-businesslike interest—looked at Marco Aurélio warily and asked if he was ready to order. She looked to be somewhere in her forties, wiry and tough. She acted like she owned the place, which they later found out she did. In her interactions with the other patrons of her lanchonete, she eschewed the eager, polite subservience demonstrated by so many in customer service positions. There was no illusion between her and her customers that theirs was anything but a business transaction, that she got any pleasure from the exchange. They would give her money, she would give them food, and that was that.

Marco Aurélio approached the counter and she flipped her little notebook to a fresh page. He said they wanted two x-calabresas and a misto quente. Also a passionfruit juice, a guaraná, and a papaya vitamina. She wrote the order down on her notepad and asked if that would be everything. He said it would and handed her a few bills. She gave him his change and said that the drinks would be right out. As she turned away, Marco Aurélio leaned over the counter and said something the two elders couldn't quite make out. Whatever he said, the woman didn't acknowledge it. She handed the slip of paper with the order on it to the young man cooking at the grill. Marco Aurélio waited for a response to whatever it was he had said to the woman, but she kept her back to him and after a moment, he sat back down at the table.

"Do you know her?" said Elder Toronto.

Marco Aurélio shook his head. "I wish I did."

He smiled.

Elder Toronto said, "I talked to Elder J. da Silva, and he said that they're free tonight at seven-thirty."

"Over at the church?" said Marco Aurélio.

"Yeah," said Elder Toronto.

"And remind me what he'll be asking me."

Elder Toronto told him not to worry too much about the interview. Elder J. da Silva would ask him if he believed in God and Jesus Christ, if he believed that they restored their church through Joseph Smith, if Marco Aurélio was willing to obey the principles he had learned in the missionary lessons—keeping the Word of Wisdom, obeying the law of chastity, things like that. Elder J. da Silva would ask if he felt like he had repented of all past sins, if he had ever committed a serious crime, and if he felt ready to be baptized. It was all stuff they had talked about before.

Over behind the counter, the woman turned on a pair of blenders, bringing the conversation to a temporary halt. When the blenders stopped, they sat in silence for a moment until the woman brought their drinks over on a tray and said their sandwiches would be right out. Marco Aurélio flashed her a smile, but she returned it with a chilly stare—the intensity surprising—before walking back behind the counter.

"What did you say to her earlier, when you were ordering?" said Elder Toronto.

"What do you mean?" said Marco Aurélio.

"To offend her? She looked furious just now. What did you say?"

"I just gave her our order. I'm not sure what her problem is."

"No," said Elder Toronto, "after she took your order, you said something, and it looked like it really upset her."

"You must have misheard," said Marco Aurélio.

"No, I didn't hear it, I saw it," said Elder Toronto. "She took your order and then you said something else to her."

Marco Aurélio shook his head, a look of confusion on his face. Elder Toronto looked to Elder Schwartz for confirmation.

"I saw it, too," he said.

Marco Aurélio either didn't understand, or pretended not to.

"How was your train ride this morning?" he asked.

Elder Toronto played along, dropping his line of questioning to presumably pick it up again at a more opportune moment.

"Fine," he said. He told Marco Aurélio about the guy with the bag of organ meat strapped to his torso.

"That act is getting old," said Marco Aurélio. "There used to be a guy—maybe three, four years ago—who had mastered it. You'd listen to him talk and you knew it was all completely ridiculous—

you know, the corrupt doctor, the organs hanging out of his body, all that—but you completely bought it. He was just that good. It's a shame—now the kids who do it practically play the whole thing for laughs."

"At a park once, I saw a guy do a pretty good job of it," said Elder Toronto.

"With an act like that, pretty good isn't good enough," said Marco Aurélio. "The people have to really believe."

The woman who owned the lanchonete called out their order number and Marco Aurélio got up to retrieve their sandwiches from the counter. He brought them back to the table—a misto quente for Elder Toronto and an x-calabresa each for himself and Elder Schwartz—and the three of them began to eat.

Between bites, Elder Toronto asked how the job hunt was going. Marco Aurélio shrugged.

"Same as always," he said.

Elder Toronto told him he should talk to Bishop Claudemir, see if he knew of any good opportunities. Marco Aurélio said that would probably be a good idea. Elder Toronto said he was sure he'd find something soon. Like many people in the neighborhood, Marco Aurélio hadn't been able to find regular work in months.

"How are you liking Vila Barbosa so far?" said Marco Aurélio to Elder Schwartz.

"Good," said Elder Schwartz.

"You should have seen him on the train," said Elder Toronto, and launched into an exaggerated account of Elder Schwartz's struggle with his bags—the awkward crouching; the dirty looks from other passengers; the tumble to the floor; the sweaty, panicked expression on Elder Schwartz's face. If Elder Toronto had told the same embarrassing story ten minutes earlier, Elder Schwartz may have stood up from his chair and punched his companion in the face, or at least considered it, but the x-calabresa sandwich and the papaya vitamina were having a soothing, almost redemptive effect on his general state of mind, a warm pleasantness spreading from his mouth, to his legs, to his arms, to his head. It spread to his mouth and he laughed, jumping into the telling of the story and adding his account—in his garbled Portuguese—of the perilous trek over the hills of Vila Barbosa from the train station to the apartment. By the time he finished, all three of them were laughing, their plates empty, their stomachs full.

Elder Toronto said, "The food here's really good. Do you come here a lot?"

Marco Aurélio, who had been watching the woman behind the counter as she took the order of another customer, turned back to Elder Toronto.

"My first time," he said. "Apparently it's one of the neighborhood's best-kept secrets."

Elder Toronto said he had walked right by it dozens of times without ever noticing it was there—they ought to move it to someplace a little less tucked away and they'd probably do much better business. Marco Aurélio agreed. Elder Toronto looked up at the clock on the wall. He said they should get going so Elder Schwartz would have time to unpack before they started working tonight. The three of them stood up and the two missionaries thanked Marco Aurélio for the meal. He shook his head and told them it was a small token of his great appreciation for everything they had done for him.

On their way out of the lanchonete, Marco Aurélio stopped and said he had left his newspaper at the table. He said he'd be right back—they could go on without him and he'd catch up in a minute. The missionaries stepped outside of the lanchonete and then paused, looking back. They saw Marco Aurélio standing at the counter, talking to the woman who ran the place. He gestured dramatically with his hands and she looked like she was trying not to get upset. She shook her head and walked to the other end of the counter. The missionaries moved out of the entryway and walked quickly through the alley to the connecting street.

Marco Aurélio joined them a few seconds later. He said that someone must have thrown his paper away, it wasn't in there anymore. Elder Toronto said that was too bad, and then they started walking. As the three of them made their way through the sweaty chaos of the street—the honking, stinking cars; the shouting street vendors; the skittering stray dogs—the pleasantness of lunch dissipated out into the thick, brown smog that covered the city.

CHAPTER 5

Fueled by the shock of finding the dead man in the shack, the two missionaries ran and ran until they came to a payphone several blocks away. Elder Schwartz would have kept running, but Elder Toronto grabbed his arm, stopping him, and said they needed to call the police. Elder Toronto ducked his head under the cracked, yellow dome of the payphone and told Elder Schwartz to keep an eye out. Elder Schwartz nodded, panting. He looked around the dark street. A group of old men played dominoes in the lighted entryway of a bar. A few doors down from there, a young man sat against a wall, strumming a guitar absent-mindedly. Two middle-aged women walked by carrying two-liter soda bottles filled with homemade cleaning solution. The sounds of a telenovela echoed from an open window somewhere.

Elder Schwartz's ears began to buzz and his vision clouded with the overexertion of his sprint from the little shack. He sat down on the curb next to the payphone and put his head between his knees. At the phone, Elder Toronto dialed the emergency number and said he had a murder to report. As he described their location and explained what had happened, Elder Schwartz leaned forward and vomited, trying not to get any on his shoes. A nearby dog trotted over to investigate. Its yellow hide was mangy and scabbed, its shoulders and ribs visible through the skin. The dog sniffed at the puddle of vomit and then began to lap it up. Elder Schwartz vomited again, the dog stepping back in momentary alarm before returning to its task.

Elder Schwartz stood back up and stepped away from the puddle of vomit. He pulled his handkerchief from his pocket and wiped at his watery eyes and running nose. Elder Toronto hung up the phone. He said that the police had never heard of the address where the man was murdered, so they were going to come here so the missionaries could show them where it was. Elder Toronto looked at the dog, the puddle of vomit, and Elder Schwartz.

"Why did you do that?" said Elder Toronto.

"What do you mean?" said Elder Schwartz.

Elder Toronto nodded at the puddle of vomit, which had attracted a second dog.

"What kind of question is that?" said Elder Schwartz. "It's not like I could help it."

"Still," said Elder Toronto.

He turned away from the dogs and the vomit.

"Are you okay?" he said, his profile to Elder Schwartz.

"I'm fine," said Elder Schwartz, wiping his nose, an acidic tingle at the back of his throat.

As the puddle diminished, the two dogs began to scuffle. Elder Schwartz turned away as well.

"What did the police say?" he said.

"They said to wait," said Elder Toronto.

So, moving well away from the vomit, they started to wait.

A few weeks earlier, the missionaries had been eating lunch at Bishop Claudemir's house when the subject of the police had come up. They had been sitting there around the scratched wooden table, finishing their meal of rice, beans, and panquecas, Claudemir nodding off in his chair, when Fátima had mentioned that the police had stopped her on her way home from church today, asking her if she could identify a man depicted in a vague police sketch. Elder Schwartz had said that it was good to hear about police officers doing their job, doing what they could to reduce crime in the area. Fátima had shaken her head.

"The police in our city are useless," she had explained in her thin, raspy voice. "Worse than useless."

Elder Schwartz had asked why.

"It's complicated," Fátima had said. "We have a joke around here that goes like this. One day an eccentric billionaire decides to hold a contest to find the world's best tracker. He does some research, asks around, and finally decides who to invite—a bounty hunter, a safari guide, and, surprisingly, a policeman from our city. So these three contestants all meet up at the billionaire's mansion and the billionaire explains the rules. He will release a rare and elusive bird into the jungle and each contestant will take a turn tracking the bird down and capturing it. Whichever contestant can capture the bird the fastest, wins. And they have to bring the bird back alive.

"The bounty hunter goes first. The bird is released, given a twelve-hour head start, and then the bounty hunter begins his hunt. Three weeks later he comes back, muddy and thin, holding a canvas sack. The billionaire looks inside the sack and sure enough, there's the bird, alive and well.

"The safari guide goes next. The bird is released again, given the same head start, and then the safari guide goes after it. Three days later, he comes back, a little bit muddy, a little bit tired, holding a canvas sack. Once again, the bird is inside, alive and well.

"Now it's the policeman's turn. The bird is released, given its head start, and our policeman goes after it. Three hours later, he comes back, canvas sack in hand. 'I got it,' says our policeman. The billionaire, the bounty hunter, and the safari guide are very impressed. The billionaire's getting out the trophy and polishing it up to give to our policeman. Then he looks inside the policeman's canvas sack. Instead of a bird, the billionaire finds a large monkey covered in blood, shot several times in the head and the chest."

Elder Toronto and Elder Schwartz had both laughed a little.

"It's not a very funny joke," Fátima had said, "because that's really how they work."

Now, sitting on the curb next to the payphone, Elder Schwartz wondered out loud how much longer they would have to wait for the police.

"They're clearly not in a hurry," said Elder Toronto.

"What do you think they'll do when they get here?" said Elder Schwartz.

"That's a good question," said Elder Toronto. "The person I talked to on the phone sounded more annoyed than anything else."

As neither of them had a watch, neither of them knew exactly how long they had been waiting. The game of dominoes had broken up, the old men dispersing to their homes, and the young man a few doors down had wandered off, guitar slung over his shoulder. The two missionaries sat alone on the empty street. Elder Schwartz began softly humming a hymn. Elder Toronto looked at him.

"Could you stop humming, please?" he said.

"Why shouldn't I hum?" said Elder Schwartz, the absurdity of their situation beginning to sink in. "I mean, what are we even doing here? The police obviously don't care enough to show up, and it's definitely not safe for us to be out here right now. We're out past curfew, and someone got killed tonight"—his voice rose in pitch—"and we found the body, and we're just sitting here in the dark? Seriously—what are we doing here?"

"Settle down, Elder Schwartz," said Elder Toronto, his chin resting on his knees.

A few streets away, a dog barked.

"No," said Elder Schwartz. "We need to leave. Come on."

He stood up.

"I'm going to wait for the police," said Elder Toronto.

"Come on," said Elder Schwartz. "Do you know how many rules we've already broken? We need to get back to the apartment."

Elder Toronto didn't budge.

"I refuse to stay here," said Elder Schwartz. "I refuse."

"All right," said Elder Toronto.

Elder Schwartz started walking away. He crossed the street, walked up the sidewalk, and turned left onto the cobblestone road they had come in on earlier that evening. Chaotic stacks of dark houses loomed over him on either side. The street was eerily empty. It was too late for the daytime crowd, and too early for the neighborhood's nightlife. Elder Schwartz hadn't been this alone since before his mission. Sans companion, he had that unsettling, dreamed feeling of showing up at school completely naked. He whistled a hymn as he walked.

He hadn't gone far when he came to a fork in the road. He stopped and considered it. He looked around for any familiar landmarks. During the cab ride earlier that evening, his mind had been on other things and he had paid only scant attention to the route they had taken. He vaguely remembered coming downhill at some point. Unfortunately, both branches headed up a steep hill. Elder Schwartz realized he had no idea how to get back to their apartment.

It was very dark out. Elder Schwartz took a deep breath, the scent of vomit still in his nose. He took one last look around, halfheartedly hoping for some divine sign to point him in the right direction. He saw nothing. Bracing himself for humiliation, he turned around and walked back the way he came, cursing his incompetence with every step.

When Elder Toronto—still sitting by the payphone—saw him round the corner, he patted the spot next to him on the curb.

"I'm not sitting next to you," said Elder Schwartz, and stood a few yards away. After a while, though, his legs got tired, and he sat down next to Elder Toronto.

They waited and waited and waited. Faint laughter echoed from somewhere down the street. A cockroach scurried past their feet. Elder Toronto stood up, quickly enough to startle Elder Schwartz. For a brief moment, he thought that maybe he had finally managed to talk some sense into his companion.

"Are we leaving?" said Elder Schwartz, standing up himself.

Elder Toronto ignored him and began pacing back and forth on the craggy sidewalk.

"Here are the salient questions," he said. "Is it a coincidence that this man was murdered on the evening we were supposed to meet with him? It's possible, although I doubt it. So if it's not a coincidence, how does it relate to our meeting?"

Elder Schwartz sat back down. Elder Toronto, still pacing, went on:

"Did someone want to keep him from telling us something? Or are they sending us a message, trying to scare us off? Or a little of both? If it's the former, what could he have had to say to us? And if it's more the latter, what are they trying to stop us from doing?"

He paused here and looked down at Elder Schwartz.

"Any thoughts?" said Elder Toronto, but before Elder Schwartz could answer, he continued. "Clearly Marco Aurélio's disappearance relates to all this. Which raises further questions. Is, or rather, *was* the dead man a friend of Marco Aurélio's? An enemy? A disinterested third party?"

He paused.

"At this point we have so little information. My hands are tied—I can only make suppositions." He kicked at a loose chunk of cement, sending it skittering into the street. "We'll just have to wait for the police."

He sat back down next to Elder Schwartz, his chin resting on his knees. They waited for what felt like another hour, Elder Toronto in contemplative stillness, Elder Schwartz in twitchy discomfort.

Finally, a police cruiser turned the corner and pulled up next to the curb where the missionaries sat. The elders stood up. The passenger-side window of the cruiser rolled down and an officer with a thin moustache leaned out of it, the barrel of his M4 aimed at the missionaries. The elders put their hands in the air.

"Did you report a murder?" said the officer.

"Yes, sir," said Elder Toronto.

"You boys put your hands down and get in the car," said the officer.

The two missionaries looked at each other.

"Come on," said the officer, pointing with his gun.

They got into the back seat.

"Where is this place?" said the officer in the driver's seat, a bald man with a square, unreadable face.

Elder Toronto gave him directions and they started driving. The few people lingering in the street at this hour of the night casually disappeared as the police cruiser drove by them, not running, not acting panicked or guilty, but drifting deliberately into the protective shadows of alleyways and storefronts. The officer with the moustache looked at the two elders from the rearview mirror.

"You're missionaries," he said.

"We represent the Church of Jesus Christ of Latter-day Saints," said Elder Toronto.

"I know who you are," said the officer with the moustache.

Elder Toronto said that was great and asked if he'd ever received visits from the missionaries in his home.

"No."

Elder Toronto asked if he had ever wondered about things like where we came from before we were born, or where we were going after we died.

"I'll tell you what I know about your church," the officer with the moustache said. "I grew up next door to some Mormons. They had a son a few years older than me. He beat me up every chance he got. Real mean kid. If I ever had anything he wanted, a kite or maybe some ice cream, he'd punch me in the gut and take it right out of my hands. Didn't think twice about it. And the whole neighborhood thought he was this model child—going to church in his little white shirt and tie, singing his hymns, all that garbage. He once told me that if I ever ratted on him, he'd sneak into my house and strangle me in my sleep. And I think he would have done it."

The officer with the moustache stared at the missionaries from the rearview mirror. Elder Schwartz couldn't see the man's mouth, but he imagined it must be sneering.

"I'm sorry to hear that," said Elder Toronto.

"I bet you are," said the officer with the moustache.

The car stopped at the rickety footbridge that spanned the river.

"What's the address?" said the officer with no hair.

"Number twelve," said Elder Toronto.

The two officers got out of the car, their assault rifles hanging at their sides, their flashlights drawn, leaving the two missionaries locked up in the back seat of the cruiser. The elders watched the bobbing gleam of the flashlights cross the bridge and then disappear behind the row of shacks on the other side of the river.

"Are they going to arrest us?" said Elder Schwartz.

"I don't think so," said Elder Toronto. "Although I guess they could."

They sat there in the cruiser listening to the steady white noise of the river. Elder Schwartz reached over and tried opening his door. It was locked.

"It's locked," he said.

"Yeah," said Elder Toronto. "This is a police car."

Dim moonlight, streaming in through the window of the car, illuminated the left side of Elder Toronto's face, making him look like a smaller, smugger version of the waning moon itself.

"I told you this was a bad idea," said Elder Schwartz.

"You did say that earlier," said Elder Toronto. "But you were wrong then, and you're wrong now."

"How am I wrong?" said Elder Schwartz.

Elder Toronto interlaced the long, thin fingers of his hands and rested them on his knee.

"Isn't this all just a little bit fascinating to you?" he said, his face half in shadow. "Don't you feel like we're on the cusp of something exciting?"

"Really?" said Elder Schwartz. "Really?"

"Yeah," said Elder Toronto. "Really. I wish you could see it."

"I bet you do," said Elder Schwartz, and turned to look out the window.

"Hey," said Elder Toronto. "Listen. I understand you're scared, but we're going to be fine."

Elder Schwartz looked out at the dark gleam of the river.

"Elder Schwartz?" said Elder Toronto. "Would you look at me?"

Elder Schwartz didn't turn around.

"You're going to be fine," said Elder Toronto. "Okay?"

"Sure," said Elder Schwartz, trying to make out any movement in the little row of dwellings on the other side of the river.

After a minute, the bobbing lights reappeared from behind the shacks and crossed the river toward them. The officer with the thin moustache opened the back-seat door and told the missionaries to get out. He still held the gun and the flashlight, and aimed both in the general vicinity of the missionaries' faces. The officer with no hair stood a few feet away, a bored look on his face, his gun also trained on the missionaries.

"Follow my lead," Elder Toronto said quietly.

The elders got out of the car, their hands held in the air.

"Is this supposed to be some kind of joke?" said the officer with the moustache to Elder Schwartz.

Elder Schwartz didn't respond, didn't know how. The officer raised his assault rifle.

"Huh?" he said, pointing the gun at Elder Schwartz. "Are you going to answer me, kid?"

He fingered the trigger guard and Elder Schwartz flinched.

"Did I tell you to move?" said the officer with the moustache.

Elder Schwartz shook his head.

"That's right," said the officer. "I didn't. I didn't even tell you you could shake your head, so don't. What I told you to do was answer my question. Is this supposed to be some kind of joke?"

Elder Toronto responded, rescuing his companion.

"I'm not sure what you're talking about," he said.

The officer turned to Elder Toronto, who squinted into the glare of the flashlight.

"Don't play games with me," said the officer, waving his assault rifle.

The bald policeman smiled at this.

"You boys think it's fun to mess around with the police?" The officer with the moustache was yelling by this point. "You think we don't have better things to do?"

"I'm sorry, but I don't know what you mean," Elder Toronto said, his voice steady in spite of the gun aimed at his head.

"Are you saying I'm a liar?" said the officer.

"I'm just very confused," said Elder Toronto.

"Maybe your friend can explain," said the officer, shifting his aim back to Elder Schwartz.

Elder Schwartz shook his head.

"What did I tell you about shaking your head?" said the officer.

Elder Schwartz couldn't think of the words to answer.

"What are you, mute?" said the officer.

Elder Schwartz shook his head, and then flinched, his body trembling visibly. The officer with no hair chuckled.

"Let's go," said the officer with the moustache.

Elder Toronto moved to get back inside the car.

"No," said the officer with the moustache. "To the bridge."

The elders looked at him. He gestured with his gun barrel.

"Move," he said.

The missionaries started to walk, the two police officers following close behind with their guns and their flashlights pointed at the elders' backs, casting long, missionary-shaped shadows in front of the small party. They crossed the bridge and walked to shack number twelve.

"Now go inside and tell me what you see," said the officer with the moustache.

Elder Toronto opened the door and the two missionaries stepped into the shack. The candle had burned out, but the light from the officers' flashlights illuminated the small space. The room was empty except for the small table and the burned-out candle. The body and the cot it had lain on were gone.

"Pretty gruesome murder scene," said the officer with no hair, speaking for the first time.

"There was a dead body in here," said Elder Toronto.

He got down on his hands and knees.

"Hey—what are you doing?" said the officer with the moustache.

"Looking for blood," said Elder Toronto. But the wall and floor were clean, free from any trace of a murder. He crawled toward the small table.

"Hey, get up," said the officer with the moustache.

Elder Schwartz watched Elder Toronto bump the bottom of his shirt pocket with his hand, sending his ballpoint pen skittering under the table.

"I dropped my pen," he said.

"Then pick it up," said the officer with the moustache.

Elder Toronto crawled under the table, his torso momentarily lost in shadow. He emerged a moment later, pen in hand, and stood up.

"Someone must have moved the body," said Elder Toronto, seemingly unbothered by the gun pointed at his face. "Do you want us to come in to the station and make a statement?"

The officer with the moustache muttered something under his breath. He stepped forward and pushed his index finger into Elder Toronto's chest. He held the barrel of his assault rifle against the missionary's cheek, the metal pressing into this skin.

"I want you to stop wasting our time," said the officer with the moustache, his voice low, "and trying my patience. Do you understand?"

Elder Toronto said that he did and that he was sorry for the inconvenience. His voice remained steady and calm. The officer with the moustache lowered his gun.

"Let's go," he said to his bald partner.

"Shouldn't we ride back with you?" said Elder Toronto.

"Do we look like a taxi service?" said the officer with the moustache, pointing his gun in the elder's face one last time.

"No," said Elder Toronto, still unruffled. "I guess not."

"Idiots," said the officer with the moustache. "Wasting my time."

Then he and his partner, guns and flashlights in hand, walked backward out of the shack, leaving Elder Toronto and Elder Schwartz alone in the darkness.

THE ARGENTINE

They say that as Vila Barbosa grew and the Argentine's power increased, his personal interactions with the people of the community diminished. He no longer attended their weddings, their funerals, or their christenings. Instead, he confined himself to the little general store, or rather, its front steps, where he held court with his growing number of deputies.

This wasn't to say that the Argentine's presence was no longer felt throughout the neighborhood. If anything, the hold he maintained over the general consciousness of Vila Barbosa had only strengthened. His commercial interests had expanded from the general store to include a broad assortment of ventures—clothing sales, prostitution, small loans, cafés, gambling, commercial construction, produce stands, landscaping. It was understood that competing businesses were not to be established, and when they were, usually by newcomers who disbelieved the stories they heard about the Argentine, the unfortunate entrepreneurs were made to serve as examples for the community at large.

For instance, a man from the North who opened a general store offering lower prices than the Argentine's ended up lying in a pool of blood on the floor of his little shop with his eyes gouged out and a garden spade between his ribs. In another case, an old woman started an independent flower stand in the heart of the neighborhood, choosing to forego the patronage of the Argentine. After several warnings, the stand was smashed to bits and the woman ended up falling down a flight of stairs at the bus station, sustaining fatal injuries. One memorable spring, a big shot from another neighborhood tried to horn in on the gambling scene in Vila Barbosa and take a little control from the Argentine. On his way home one night, he was grabbed from behind, a pungent cloth held to his face until he passed out. He regained consciousness handcuffed to a street sign and drenched in motor oil. In the darkness, someone lit a match and held it to his shirt, setting him on fire. Any time the flames threatened to die down, more oil was added, until there was nothing left of the man but a charred, kneeling corpse. You could hear him screaming that night from everywhere in the neighborhood.

The Argentine reigned supreme.

They say that around this time, the Argentine grew bored with his power. He controlled Vila Barbosa so completely that his day-to-day life posed no new challenges, no surprises. Every day, sitting on the steps of his general store, he had the same conversations with the same group of people about the same tired subjects—torch this or that competing business, pay off such-and-such police officer, cut out so-and-so's heart. None of it excited him anymore.

To address this issue, he called a meeting of his most trusted deputies. After he had closed up shop one evening, they gathered inside his store, the half-dozen men sitting in a circle on overturned crates that had once held rice, beans, and laundry soap. The Argentine stood before them, dressed in the same three-piece suit he had worn on the day of his arrival in Vila Barbosa. Pacing in front of the counter, he laid out his problem to the deputies—he was bored with his power and wanted their advice on how he might remedy the situation.

For several minutes, the men contemplated the problem in silence. Finally, a heavily tattooed deputy spoke up.

"What if we leave Vila Barbosa," he said, "and start out someplace else?"

A few of the other deputies nodded cautiously. The Argentine shook his head.

"That would be fine for a while," he said, "but ten, twenty years down the line, we'll be in exactly the same position we are now. It's a dead end."

The tattooed deputy nodded, head lowered.

"What other ideas do you have?" said the Argentine.

The deputies studied their feet and their hands, mulling it over.

"What if we expand?" said the deputy with glasses. "We could spread out over more neighborhoods."

The Argentine's face remained noncommittal.

"What do the rest of you think of this idea?" he said.

The deputies shrugged, mumbled, avoided eye contact. The Argentine waited.

The bearded deputy said, "It would be a challenge, if that's what we're looking for."

The sickly looking deputy said, "I think it's a good idea."

The tall deputy said, "I do, too."

The Argentine grimaced, flashing his square, white teeth.

"No," he said. "It's the same problem as moving someplace else. Once I take over, say, three neighborhoods, I'll grow tired of that. So I'll take over four, five, six neighborhoods, then the entire city. Then the state, then the country, then the hemisphere, then the world. And would I be satisfied with that?"

The deputies looked at their hands.

"Somehow I doubt it," said the Argentine.

He looked at his deputies, who avoided his gaze. Shaking his head, he kicked the crate out from under the bearded deputy and told them all to get out, he needed to think.

Over the next several months, the Argentine consecrated himself to the task at hand. He studied the writings of ancient kings and emperors. He pored over dense philosophical tracts on the nature of power. He read the sacred texts of world religions. He wandered the neighborhood, observing the quotidian activities of Vila Barbosa's residents. He stopped strangers on the street and demanded they explain to him what, if anything, they found fulfilling in their own particular lives. He sat alone on the steps of his store in quiet meditation. He thought and thought and thought.

Nearly a year after their previous meeting, the Argentine gathered his deputies once again in the dimly lit interior of his little general store. Standing before them, he said that he had good news to report. He said that based on careful study and contemplation, he had decided to forego his career as a criminal administrator to become a taxonomist of sorts. From this day forward, he would devote himself to the compilation of a universal catalog of human cruelty.

On making this announcement, he grinned at his deputies, a sinister smile that bared each of his square, white teeth. The deputies looked at each other, unsure of how to react. The bald deputy nudged the tattooed deputy who nudged the bearded deputy, who spoke up for the group.

"What exactly does that mean?" he said.

The Argentine smiled at the bearded deputy.

"That's a good question," he said. "First—I will be ceding control of my business interests to the six of you. Ultimately, you'll still answer to me, of course, but on a day-to-day basis, you will be running things. Second—I myself will be observing and recording every instance of cruelty I can find in Vila Barbosa. I will compile my findings, catalog them, classify them, and study them."

The deputies looked at him blankly. They nudged the bearded deputy.

"Speaking on behalf of all of us," said the bearded deputy. "I'd like to say that we support you completely. What still isn't clear to me, though, is what you hope to accomplish with this catalog."

The Argentine smiled. He said he wasn't sure what he might learn from this catalog, or where it all might lead. That's what he found so compelling about the project—its potential to surprise him.

The deputies shifted in their seats.

"But enough chit-chat. We all have so much to do," said the Argentine, and with that he dismissed his deputies and set to work.

CHAPTER 6

By the time they made it back to their apartment, the sun had risen and it was light out. Elder Toronto sat down at his desk, loosening his tie. Elder Schwartz sat down in his own chair and closed his eyes. The next thing he knew, Elder Toronto was shaking him by the shoulder.

"Come on," he said. "I almost forgot. We're going to be late to district meeting."

In a bleary haze, Elder Schwartz got up from his chair, grabbed his bag, and followed Elder Toronto out the door. They had to run the whole way, but they caught their bus. Sweaty and out of breath, they walked down the length of the aisle until they found two seats with no one nearby. They sat down.

As Elder Schwartz caught his breath, Elder Toronto pulled a graying handkerchief from his bag and wiped at his sweaty face.

"So when are we going to call President Madvig?" said Elder Schwartz.

"About what?" said Elder Toronto, slipping the handkerchief back into his bag.

"What do you mean, about what? About finding a dead body last night."

Elder Toronto shook his head.

"We're not bringing President Madvig in on this one. And we won't be mentioning it to anyone at district meeting either."

Elder Schwartz shouldn't have been surprised. Still, the reaction upset him.

"Elder Toronto, we can't just not tell people about it. This is a huge deal—Marco Aurélio is missing and somebody got murdered because of it."

"Right," said Elder Toronto. "This is a big deal, and we're going to do everything we can to help. Which is why we can't tell President Madvig what's going on."

"That doesn't even make sense," said Elder Schwartz.

"Yes it does," said Elder Toronto. "Look—Marco Aurélio is clearly in some serious trouble. If we don't go looking for him, who will?"

His round forehead creased. He avoided Elder Toronto's expectant gaze, scrambling to form a coherent counterargument.

"But what I'm saying is," said Elder Schwartz, "this is none of our business. We're not allowed to do this kind of stuff, and we don't know how to do it."

"That doesn't answer my question," said Elder Toronto.

"Missionaries don't handle missing persons cases."

A few rows up, a baby started to cry.

"Okay," said Elder Toronto, nodding patiently, "so who should handle this? And don't say the police."

"I think it's wrong not to tell President Madvig," said Elder Schwartz. "He needs to know."

"So let's say we tell President Madvig. What's he going to do about it?"

"Well," said Elder Schwartz. He paused. "We could tell him what happened and he could talk to—" He stopped himself.

"The police?" said Elder Toronto. He raised an eyebrow. "He could talk to the police? Like those two nice officers we met last night?"

The mother of the crying baby had started walking it up and down the aisle of the bus. As she passed the elders, she smiled at them. The missionaries paused their conversation to smile in return. The baby kept crying. When the woman turned and headed back the other way, they resumed their discussion.

"Not them," said Elder Schwartz. "Obviously. But maybe he could talk to a different department or something. And he's an important person. The police would listen to him, and they'll take care of it."

"Is that what you think?" said Elder Toronto.

"Yeah."

Tim Wirkus

Elder Toronto rested a hand on Elder Schwartz's shoulder. "I want you to look me in the eye," he said, "and tell me that you honestly think the police will conduct a substantive investigation into the disappearance of Marco Aurélio and the murder of the man in the brown suit."

The mother with the baby—still crying—passed by them again, smiling apologetically. The missionaries smiled back, waiting again for her to leave.

"Fine," said Elder Schwartz after she had left. He brushed Elder Toronto's hand off his shoulder. "Maybe they wouldn't. But we still need to tell President Madvig. He'll have a better idea of what to do than we will."

The bus stopped and the woman with the baby sat back down. With a hiss of hydraulics, the doors opened.

"Do you know what President Madvig will do?" said Elder Toronto. "I'll tell you what President Madvig will do. First thing, he'll tell us to pack our bags and come down to the mission office because Vila Barbosa may not be safe for us anymore. Then he'll sit us down and tell us he's sorry to hear about what's happened to the man we baptized. He'll tell us that the world's a complicated place, and understanding that is part of growing up, and we don't always understand why bad things happen to good people, blah blah blah blah blah. And then he'll call the police, and—since he's an incredibly well-intentioned person, and I mean that sincerely— he'll even follow up with them, possibly multiple times. But as we know, nothing will come of working with the police. Then President Madvig will reassign us both to new areas, and if he ever sends new missionaries to Vila Barbosa, all of this will be old, forgotten news. It will be like Marco Aurélio never existed. That's why telling President Madvig—at least at this point—is not an option. So try again."

"What?"

"I asked you who will go looking for Marco Aurélio if we don't. Clearly, the answer is not President Madvig. So try again."

The turnstile at the front of the bus cranked loudly with each paying passenger. Elder Toronto folded his arms, awaiting his companion's reply.

"We could talk to Bishop Claudemir," said Elder Schwartz.

"Bishop Claudemir?" said Elder Toronto. "The same Bishop Claudemir who works a zillion hours a week? The same Bishop Claudemir who, on the rare occasions when he's not at work, can barely stay awake on his feet? The man couldn't help us if he wanted to. Try again."

"Maybe Fátima—"

"Fátima has four kids to deal with and a husband who's never home," said Elder Toronto. "Try again."

An elderly bearded man wearing a slouchy fedora sat down in the row across from the missionaries. He nodded to the elders and glared up at the baby a few rows in front of them, who was only whimpering at this point.

"Fine," said Elder Schwartz after a minute. "Maybe you're right. Maybe if we don't go looking for Marco Aurélio, no one else will. But I still think it's a bad idea."

Elder Toronto sighed. The bearded old man in the slouchy fedora looked over at them but said nothing.

"Good morning, sir," said Elder Toronto, catching the old man's eye, his voice raised to be heard from across the bus. "How are you today?"

"I'm fine, son, how are you?" said the old man.

"I'm doing well, thank you, sir," said Elder Toronto. "Are you off to work this morning? Or visiting friends?"

"I'm minding my own business," said the old man.

"Of course," said Elder Toronto. "I didn't mean to be too forward."

The old man grunted and turned away.

"Just one more thing, sir, if I may," said Elder Toronto. "My name is Elder Toronto and my partner and I are representatives of the Church of Jesus Christ of Latter-day Saints. It's also known as the Mormon church. Have you heard of us?"

"I'm not interested," said the old man.

"All right," said Elder Toronto. He gave the man a wide smile. "Have a nice day, sir."

"I'm not interested," repeated the man.

"That's fine," said Elder Toronto and turned back around.

As the bus bumped its way along, he picked at a flaking bit of plastic on the seat in front of him. Elder Schwartz watched him, waiting with his muscles tensed, bracing for the next volley.

Finally, Elder Toronto said, "Can I ask you a question, Elder Schwartz?"

"I think you will whether I want you to or not."

"That's probably true," said Elder Toronto, and paused.

The bus jostled its way down the street.

"So?" said Elder Toronto.

"So what?" said Elder Schwartz.

"Can I ask you a question?"

Elder Schwartz braced himself.

"Go ahead," he said.

"What are you doing here?" said Elder Toronto.

The question seemed innocuous enough, but Elder Schwartz could sense his senior companion laying the groundwork for a larger, more cunning argument.

"I'm on a bus to district meeting."

"No, I mean on the mission."

Elder Schwartz adjusted the knot of his tie, thinking.

"I'm here to preach the gospel," he said.

"No, seriously," said Elder Toronto.

"I am being serious."

"Okay, fine," said Elder Toronto, "you're here to preach the gospel. But why?"

"Why does it matter?" said Elder Schwartz.

Maybe this would force Elder Toronto's argument out into the open. Unless that was what he wanted. Either way, Elder Schwartz could tell he was being cornered.

"It's just, I can't figure you out," said Elder Toronto. "Can I speak freely here?"

"Fine," said Elder Schwartz, wanting to get it over with.

"Okay," said Elder Toronto. "From my perspective as an older missionary—"

"We're the same age," said Elder Schwartz.

"I've been a missionary a full year longer than you have," said Elder Toronto. "And I'm nearly a year older than you."

"That's nothing," said Elder Schwartz.

"Actually in terms of cognitive development, especially at this point in our lives, a year in age can make a significant difference," said Elder Toronto.

"Please," said Elder Schwartz.

"Fine," said Elder Toronto. "I'll come to the point. This is kind of a delicate topic, but I'm going to jump right in. You probably don't realize this, but I can hear you crying every morning before your alarm goes off."

"I have allergies," said Elder Schwartz, louder than he intended to. The old man across the aisle looked over at them. Elder Schwartz dropped his voice. "I think something in the pillow makes me—"

"It's fine," said Elder Toronto. "What we do is hard. I don't think any missionary in his right mind finds this easy. But still. I mean, a greenie might cry every morning, but you've been out nearly a year, and I wonder—"

"I said I have allergies."

The bus hit a bump and the baby a few rows up started yelling again.

"Okay," said Elder Toronto. "But even generally, you seem pretty miserable. And I wonder, if you're that miserable all the time, why you don't just go home. It really doesn't make sense to me. I mean, what driving force gets you through the day?"

Elder Schwartz was reminded suddenly of a lazy summer day back home in Arizona a couple of years before he left for his mission. His sister Karen was home from college and had been fighting with their parents for days—he couldn't remember what about, only that things were tense. It was morning, and he was at the kitchen table eating breakfast. Karen and their mom were both at the table as well, ignoring each other.

"Hey, Mike," said Karen in a stagy voice. "Have you been thinking much about what you're going to do after high school?"

"I don't know," said Mike, mouth full of frosted flakes.

"No, really," she said. "How are you planning on disappointing Mom and Dad?"

Their mom glanced up from the paper but didn't take the bait.

"Seriously, though," said Karen. "What are you planning on doing?"

"I don't know," said Mike. "I'll go on a mission, I guess. Then come home and go to ASU if I can get in. Probably study accounting. Something safe."

"That's your greatest dream," she said.

"It's my plan," he said.

"You don't have any sort of grand, secret hopes for your future?" she said, her voice tenser.

"I guess I'm just a pretty sensible person," he said.

This set Karen off.

"You have no ambition whatsoever," she said, or rather yelled at him. "It's pathetic."

"You leave him out of this," said their mom, taking the bait this time. She threw down the newspaper, and a new argument began. Mike left the room.

Karen wasn't completely wrong. He disagreed about the pathetic part, but it was true that he had no great aspirations. Generally speaking, he found the path of least resistance to be the path to contentment, and his lifestyle to date reflected that philosophy. In school, his grades were good, but unremarkable. He played tennis and sang with the Mesa View High Singers, neither distinguishing nor embarrassing himself in either venture. He was well-liked but not especially popular among his peers. When he needed money, which wasn't often, he did light landscaping work for his neighbors, waking just after dawn to beat the punishing Arizona sun. With the exception of Karen, he got along well with the other members of his family. All things considered, his life to that point had been mildly, persistently pleasant, and if he had any ambition, it was to keep that easy contentment going. Sure, he had no grand plans, but the less he asked from life, the more likely he'd be to find satisfaction. Was there anything wrong with that?

The mission proved to be the first major hiccup in this plan. He had never given much thought to being a missionary. Which is to say, he had always planned on going on a mission—it's what you did after high school—but he hadn't given much thought to what the on-the-ground experience of missionary work might be like. In any case, he figured a well-mannered, well-meaning boy like himself would do just fine.

He couldn't have been more wrong. If his life before the mission had been a steady stream of mild contentment, his life on the mission was a constant barrage of acute discomfort. Each new day brought a fresh, overwhelming batch of humiliations and perils, and each night he went to bed unsure of how he'd manage to survive the next day. He couldn't remember the last time he'd felt comfortable.

Although calling it quits and flying back home seemed like a reasonable solution, Elder Schwartz never considered it a viable option. If he went home early, his reasoning ran, this gnawing discomfort might never leave him. His uncompleted mission would be an open sore, festering away for the rest of his life and contaminating any source of contentment that might otherwise await him. If, on the other hand, he stuck it out for the full two years, he could go home and forget about the whole thing. It would be like none of this ever happened. *That* was what got him through the day, and what business was it of Elder Toronto's?

"I'm asking as a friend," said Elder Toronto when Elder Schwartz didn't respond. "I just want to know."

"All I want is to keep my head above water," said Elder Schwartz, "until my two years are up."

"And that's how you get yourself through the day?"

"That's right," said Elder Schwartz.

Elder Toronto shook his head, lips pursed in concern.

"See, that's what worries me," he said. "You've told me that before, and when you say it, you make it sound like it's a brave way to think. But the thing is, it's actually an incredibly selfish approach to missionary work. And to life, really."

"Hey, listen," said Elder Schwartz, louder, once again, than he intended. The old man across the aisle glared at them until the wails of the baby drew his attention away.

"No, just a second," said Elder Toronto. "Here's what I'm saying: If you wake up crying every morning, that may be a good indication that your current approach isn't working. So what do you have to lose by trying something new, a different approach?"

Elder Toronto paused, waiting for him to respond. As much as he wanted to, Elder Schwartz knew he couldn't disagree; he had walked right into the trap. He said nothing, and Elder Toronto continued.

"What I'm proposing is that you try a different strategy and focus on helping somebody else. Because that's exactly what this is—a chance to help somebody. Right?"

By this point, Elder Schwartz was too tired to resist.

"I guess so," he said.

"Right," said Elder Toronto. "And like I explained earlier, this is something we have to do ourselves. So we're not going to tell anyone at district meeting what's going on, and we're not going to call President Madvig, right?"

Elder Schwartz nodded.

"Right?" said Elder Toronto.

"Right," said Elder Schwartz, and a wave of exhaustion swept over him.

"Great," said Elder Toronto, and patted him on the shoulder. "I'm glad you're on board with this."

Elder Toronto grinned and Elder Schwartz smiled weakly in return.

"So, let's review what we know," said Elder Toronto. "And, by the way, I'll have to apologize for doubting you last week—it seemed unlikely at the time, but the evidence we've come across since then suggests otherwise. Now tell me again what you saw that morning at the market."

"I've told you already."

"I know, but I'd like to hear it again."

"Okay," said Elder Schwartz. He had no remaining energy to slow his companion's momentum. "You were talking to that woman, and I was just kind of looking around, and then I saw Marco Aurélio. I yelled his name and when he saw me, he ran. He looked like he had been beat up. His forehead was bleeding and he might have had a black eye. Also, he was really dressed up—a nice-looking suit, much newer than his normal clothes. He was sweating a lot. I don't know. That's all I remember."

"When he ran off," said Elder Toronto, "did you see anyone follow him?"

Elder Schwartz thought about this.

"No," he said. "We followed him a minute later, but I didn't see anyone else go after him."

"Fascinating," said Elder Toronto, his fingers tented at his mouth. "This is what we know, then. Thursday morning, an unusually well-dressed, sweaty, and beaten Marco Aurélio shows up at the street market. He sees us and he runs away. We can't find him at home that day, or the next, or the next. At church on Sunday, we learn that nobody else has seen him for days. Then, the meeting is interrupted by a stranger in a brown suit, one Ulisses Galvão, who—"

"Wait, he never told us his name, did he?"

"No," said Elder Toronto.

"Then how do you know that his name was—what was it?"

"Ulisses Galvão."

"Yeah. How do you know his name?"

"I'll get to that in a minute," said Elder Toronto. "So Ulisses Galvão makes an appointment with us for eight o'clock that evening at an out-of-the-way address near the river. He tells us he'd like to discuss Marco Aurélio. We arrive at the address soon after eight. We knock on the door. We wait. We look inside. We find the brutally murdered body of Mr. Galvão and we run away. After calling the police we wait, probably for several hours. When the police finally arrive, they take us to the scene of the crime, but not before examining it themselves and telling us they found nothing. Back inside the little shack, while looking for traces of blood, I see something under the table. I pretend to drop my pen and then I crawl under the table to find this—"

Elder Toronto reached into his pants pocket and with a flourish produced a small, black notebook.

"You found this at the crime scene and you didn't show it to the police?" said Elder Schwartz.

"Are you being serious?" said Elder Toronto.

"Well," said Elder Schwartz.

"No, I didn't show it to the police," said Elder Toronto. "Do you honestly think I should have?"

"No," said Elder Schwartz.

Elder Toronto opened the notebook and leafed through its pages. He said it belonged to the tall, thin man in the brown suit.

"Remember? The paper he gave us with the address came from a black notebook."

"Oh yeah," said Elder Schwartz.

"And look at this," said Elder Toronto flipping to the first page of the notebook.

In neat, slanted handwriting was the following bulleted list:

- Marco Aurélio Veríssimo de Camões, alias Aureliano Ribeiro, alias Marcos Mêlo
- Mormons—Rua Santos Dumont, #143. 9 am.
- R$55000
- the Argentine

"What—" began Elder Schwartz.

"Hang on," said Elder Toronto.

He flipped to the back of the notebook. He reached into the envelope attached to the inside cover and pulled out a folded photograph and a few business cards. The cards advertised the services of Ulisses Galvão, private detective.

"So that's the man in the brown suit," said Elder Schwartz.

"Right."

Elder Toronto unfolded the photograph. To the right of the crease was a young, smiling Marco Aurélio. He wore a tan suit and stood on a balcony overlooking a stunning ocean sunset. His hair was thick and his face was smooth. Next to him, on the left side of the crease, stood a man several years his senior, arms folded. He had a thick, pointed beard graying around the mouth. He was missing most of his left ear.

"Who is this with Marco Aurélio?" said Elder Schwartz, pointing to the bearded man in the photograph.

"Wait," said Elder Toronto. He refolded the photograph and put it and the notebook back into his pocket. "No questions yet. We still need to finish discussing what we know for sure. This all has to be done as systematically as possible."

"Fine," said Elder Schwartz.

The bus stopped again and the woman with the baby got off.

"About time," said the bearded old man in the fedora as she passed. She glared back at him.

"So," said Elder Toronto when the bus started moving again, "I slipped the notebook into my pocket without those two fine officers of the law noticing what I'd done. After some more bluster, they left us alone, and we walked home to our apartment without further incident. Is there anything you'd like to add?"

"No," said Elder Schwartz. "That was very thorough."

Elder Toronto nodded.

"Now," he said, "on to questions. Keep in mind, I won't be bringing up every single question that's occurred to me. That would take hours. But I will hit the most important ones, because I'd like you to be at least near to the same page that I'm on."

"Of course," said Elder Schwartz.

"Good. So first of all we need—Wait. No. let's do it this way instead. You tell me what you think the most important questions are. That could be interesting."

"Okay," said Elder Schwartz.

At the next stop, the old man got off. Elder Toronto waved and wished him a good morning. The old man ignored him. The bus started moving.

"So with the notebook," said Elder Schwartz, "I wonder—"

Elder Toronto held up his hand.

"Sorry," he said, "hang on. Let me clarify. We should start at the beginning. Start at the street market and we'll go from there."

"Okay," said Elder Schwartz.

He thought about what happened at the street market.

"Well," he said, "to start with, why did Marco Aurélio run when he saw us? That's the first question, I think."

"Good," said Elder Toronto. "And there are a few fundamental sub-questions I'd add to that: Did he run because we posed a threat to him? Or could it be that he, by association, posed a threat to us? There are more possibilities, but I won't get into them right now. Go on."

"Okay. The next thing is that detective—Galvão, right?"

"Right."

"So how did he know where to find us? And what information did he have about Marco Aurélio?"

"If he had any, right?" said Elder Toronto. "There's also the question of why he'd come to us, specifically. But go on."

"Then there's the big question. Who murdered Galvão?"

"Yes," said Elder Toronto, "that's a big one, but I think there are some smaller questions we'll have to answer before we can get to that one: Why would someone kill Galvão? In other words, what could be accomplished by killing Galvão and who stands to benefit? Also, as I brought up before, was it important to whoever killed Galvão that we were the ones who found the body?"

"Like, was it a message?"

"Exactly," said Elder Toronto. "This is also a good place to start connecting the dots. Somebody beat up Marco Aurélio and somebody was chasing him. Could that somebody, or either of those somebodies, be the same person who killed Galvão?"

"And if so," said Elder Schwartz, "then what's the connection?"

"Yes," said Elder Toronto. "Go on."

"So, now to the notebook, I think."

"Not quite," said Elder Toronto. "What about the police?"

"The police?" said Elder Schwartz. "I don't know."

"Think about it," said Elder Toronto.

He thought about it.

"Well," he said, "why was the body gone when we went back?"

"Good," said Elder Toronto. "And the timeline is very important on this one. Was the body already gone when the police first got there? If so, who moved it? If not, why did the police get rid of it?"

At the front of the bus, a woman spilled a cup of caldo de cana into the aisle and the cobrador yelled at her that there was no food or drink allowed.

"You saw me bring it on," she said, and the cobrador rolled his eyes. Everyone on the bus laughed.

"Okay," said Elder Schwartz. "Now the notebook."

"Sure," said Elder Toronto. "Let's talk about the notebook."

"Who's the guy in the picture?" said Elder Schwartz. "The guy who's missing part of his ear."

"Right," said Elder Toronto. "Any other questions with the notebook?"

"That's the biggest one I could think of."

"It is an important question. And it ties in, I think, to a question we haven't brought up yet—who hired Galvão? He's a detective, remember. And I suspect that whoever hired him either took this picture or is in it."

In spite of himself, Elder Schwartz felt drawn into the puzzle, beset by a growing desire to make sense of the increasingly strange situation. By daylight, all of the previous night's dangers seemed almost hypothetical.

"So we need to find the guy with the missing ear," he said.

"That would sure help," said Elder Toronto. "Look, we have to wrap this up—we're almost to our stop."

The missionaries got up from their seats and stood by the door.

Elder Toronto said, "I think it's a travesty we have to waste two hours at an inane district meeting, but I couldn't think of a good way out of it. If we didn't show up, it would set off alarm bells, and even if we called with an excuse, someone would come around to follow up on it. But as soon as it's over, we make a beeline back to Vila Barbosa, and we start knocking on some doors and asking some questions. Right?"

"Right," said Elder Schwartz.

"And we don't mention any of this to anyone at the meeting," said Elder Toronto.

"Right."

The bus's brakes screeched softly as it pulled up to the curb and the hydraulic doors hissed open. The two missionaries stepped off the bus and, still running late, started jogging toward their meeting. As they bounded along the broken sidewalk, Elder Schwartz realized that neither one of them had brought up one essential question: What did they really know about Marco Aurélio?

CHAPTER 7

Two months earlier, on the night of his baptismal interview, Marco Aurélio sat with Elder Toronto and Elder Schwartz in the foyer of the Parque Laranjeira ward house, waiting for Elder J. da Silva to arrive. Unlike the Vila Barbosa ward, the Mormons in Parque Laranjeira had a building of their own, a spacious, tiled monument to the steady growth of their congregation. In a room down the hall, a group of youths assembled hygiene kits for needy families. In the building's administrative offices, the bishop of Parque Laranjeira discussed with his counselors how the ward might raise its profile in the community. In the chapel, the women of the Relief Society listened attentively to a lecture on time management. The building crackled with optimistic energy.

Sitting in their metal folding chairs in the foyer, Marco Aurélio and the two missionaries commented quietly on the contrasts between Parque Laranjeira and Vila Barbosa.

"I mean, it boggles my mind that there are more people here on some random weeknight than have attended any one Sunday meeting in our ward for years," said Elder Toronto. "I've been in Vila Barbosa so long that I've forgotten what it's like anywhere else."

"How long have you been here?" said Marco Aurélio.

"Seven months and counting," said Elder Toronto.

"Is that a long time?" said Marco Aurélio.

"Yeah," said Elder Toronto. "Most missionaries don't spend more than four months in an area before they're transferred. I feel like I'm spinning my wheels here."

"This is not a very encouraging conversation for a prospective member, by the way," said Marco Aurélio. "Or your new partner." He nodded at Elder Schwartz.

"No, I mean, I hope the ward grows," said Elder Toronto, "but things have just been so stagnant for so long that it's hard to imagine things changing. But they are—you're getting baptized, for one, and

I think that will really revitalize things. It's a great opportunity for you, because you'll definitely get a chance to be really involved. They need you over there. In a lot of ways, it's a great place for you to be."

"I agree," said Marco Aurélio. "Assuming I pass my interview."

"You'll pass your interview," said Elder Toronto. "Don't worry about it."

"Thanks," said Marco Aurélio.

He turned to Elder Schwartz.

"Has Elder Toronto told you the story of how I decided to be baptized?" he said.

"No," said Elder Schwartz.

Marco Aurélio cleared his throat and scooted forward in his chair. One afternoon, he said, he was walking home from visiting a friend. On a whim, he decided to take a different route than he usually did. He had just diverged from his usual route when he saw two young men standing on the sidewalk consulting a map. He would later know them as Elder Toronto and Elder de Assis—Elder Schwartz's predecessor, a pudgy, bespectacled elder with dreams of becoming a dentist after the mission. But at the time, they were just two outsiders in graying white shirts and frayed ties. Marco Aurélio had heard of the Mormons, had probably even seen other missionaries before, but he had never given them much thought. Today, however, he felt an inexplicable urge to talk to the two young men, to find out what they were all about. Although Marco Aurélio generally kept to himself, the urge was so strong that he approached the two young men.

"Excuse me," he said, "are you the Mormons?"

Elder de Assis looked up from the map, adjusted his glasses, and said that they represented the Church of Jesus Christ of Latter-day Saints, also known as the Mormon church.

"You come to people's houses to teach them, right?" said Marco Aurélio.

"That's right," said Elder de Assis.

Unsure of what compelled him to do so, Marco Aurélio asked if they could come over to his house and teach him what they had to teach. The elders looked at each other and said they'd be happy to. They folded up their map and accompanied Marco Aurélio the rest of the way home.

Back at his house, the elders taught him the message of the restoration—the sweeping saga of God's true church coming and going from the earth, with Joseph Smith acting as God's agent in restoring the church in modern times, receiving visions, fighting mobs, translating golden plates. The elders explained that through this church, all people could come to know Jesus Christ, could receive the saving ordinances necessary to return to live with God the Father and His Son. As they spoke, Marco Aurélio felt that what they said was true. When the elders finished their lesson, they asked Marco Aurélio if he had any questions.

"How can I become a member of your church?" he said.

Elder Toronto explained that they would leave a copy of the Book of Mormon with him, that he could read the passages they had marked, and pray to know if the things he read and the things the elders had taught him were true.

"But I already know," he said.

The elders told him that joining the church was a big commitment, not something to be taken lightly. They said he should think it over, pray about it, and they could discuss it further when they came back. They made an appointment to return in a few days, shook his hand, thanked him for his time, and left.

They didn't come back for nearly a month. When they did, they were full of excuses—crises with other investigators, mission conferences, his address somehow misplaced. They asked him if he had read the passages they had marked and prayed about the things they had told him.

"I read the whole book," he said. "And I prayed about it all, and I would like to be baptized in your church."

Marco Aurélio explained his situation to the missionaries: He was unemployed, middle-aged, alone. He had done some reasonably fulfilling things in his younger days, but certainly nothing remarkable. Without realizing it, he had been looking for some kind of larger meaning to his life for years, and when he saw the missionaries that afternoon a month ago, something told him that they might have the answer.

So Elder Toronto laid out the process for becoming a member of the church—Marco Aurélio would need to continue praying and reading the Book of Mormon and other scriptures on a regular basis. He would need to attend the Sunday meetings for at least three consecutive weeks. He would need to receive the rest of the missionary lessons and uphold the various commitments: to pay tithing; to give up cigarettes, alcohol, coffee, and any drugs, if applicable; to abstain from sex outside of marriage; and so on. He would need to repent of past sins and transgressions. And finally, he would be interviewed to determine if he was ready for baptism.

So he continued praying and reading the Book of Mormon. He attended Sunday meetings, received the rest of the missionary lessons, and upheld the various commitments. Throughout all of this, he felt those same warm, fulfilling feelings that he had felt on the missionaries' first visit.

"And now here I am," said Marco Aurélio to Elder Schwartz, "getting baptized on Sunday. At least I hope so."

"That's great," said Elder Schwartz.

Elder Toronto said nothing, his face a round, studied blank.

Just then, Elder Christiansen and Elder J. da Silva arrived with apologies for being late, and whisked Marco Aurélio off to be interviewed.

He passed, and in a jubilant mood, the three of them rode the bus together back to Vila Barbosa. They parted ways at the bus stop, the missionaries congratulating Marco Aurélio once again as he headed off in the direction of his house.

"He has a great conversion story," said Elder Schwartz as the two elders waited to cross the street.

For a moment, Elder Toronto didn't respond.

"I mean, it's a nice story, and I'm glad he remembers it that way," he said finally, his round forehead creased. "But that's not how things happened."

He said that it happened like this:

He and Elder de Assis stood at an intersection one afternoon, map open, arguing over which street they should knock doors on next. Rua Jacaré was more densely packed with houses, Elder Toronto pointed out; Elder de Assis countered that they had worked sections of Rua Jacaré several times already in the past months; Rua Lorena, on the other hand, hadn't been touched in ages. Elder Toronto was about to contend that they had avoided Rua Lorena for good reason—the street contained three rival churches, a love motel, and a guy who bred Rottweilers that he wasn't too diligent about keeping chained up—when a voice from behind them said, "This is a pretty rough part of town for a couple of young foreigners, don't you think?"

The elders turned around to see a slight man with dark, thinning hair, the man they would later know as Marco Aurélio.

"He's a foreigner," said Elder de Assis, pointing to Elder Toronto. "I'm not."

"But you're not from Vila Barbosa," said Marco Aurélio.

Elder de Assis conceded the point with a shrug.

"So are you guys lost?" said Marco Aurélio.

"No," said Elder Toronto, "we work here all the time."

"Really?" said Marco Aurélio.

"Yeah," said Elder Toronto.

"You just walk around this part of town?"

"Yeah," said Elder Toronto.

"And you're not concerned you'll be kidnapped?" said Marco Aurélio.

"It doesn't worry me," said Elder Toronto.

Marco Aurélio looked around, and then leaned in closer to the two missionaries.

"I mean, everyone assumes you're foreign," he said, "and around here, foreign means rich, with rich relatives willing to pay a lot of money to see you safely returned should anything ever happen to you."

Elder de Assis pointed out for the second time that he was not a foreigner. Marco Aurélio ignored him. Elder Toronto acknowledged that he was an American, but not a wealthy one—far from it, in fact.

"Doesn't matter," said Marco Aurélio. "People around here assume all Americans have loads of money."

"You seem to have thought about this a lot," said Elder Toronto. "Are you going to kidnap us?"

Marco Aurélio smiled.

"In this neighborhood, I wouldn't joke about that if I were you," he said. "But I'm sorry if I alarmed you. I'm a worrier by nature. All I'm saying is that you should be careful. I had a friend—actually more of an associate—who was kidnapped once when he was a young man."

This associate, he said, because of his line of work, always appeared to be much wealthier than he actually was—he dressed well, ate at the best restaurants, the works. This guy was in another big city on business, staying there for a couple of months, putting on a show, and one morning on his way out of the padaria, coffee and pãozinho in hand, he was jumped by three armed men in ski masks who handcuffed him, blindfolded him, and loaded him into the trunk of their little Volkswagen. This was in broad daylight on a crowded street. They took him to a tiny, mildewed closet of a house, tied him to some pipes, and beat him up a little. Then they left.

Two of them came back a while later, still masked, one of them holding a knife. The one with the knife cut off the ear of this acquaintance of Marco Aurélio. The knife was not particularly sharp, and some amount of sawing was involved in the process. In fact, they didn't even get the whole ear. During the process, Marco Aurélio's acquaintance passed out. When he came to, the third ski-masked assailant had returned and was scolding the other two. He said that first they were supposed to contact the family, and *then* cut off the ear. If they gave a shriveled, old ear to this guy's family, they might get suspicious. It had to be fresh. He sent one of them off to find some ice and told the other one to stop the guy's head from bleeding—they didn't want to kill him yet.

To make a long story short, the kidnappers, who later admitted to Marco Aurélio's acquaintance that this was their first time, that they were still getting the hang of it, discovered that the man they had kidnapped had no family to speak of and that the man himself had only a few hundred reaís to his name. The kidnappers figured that a few hundred reaís was better than nothing, so they got his bank information, withdrew all his money from an ATM, beat him up a little more, and then sent him on his way.

Elder de Assis asked if they ever found the kidnappers.

"This acquaintance of mine," said Marco Aurélio, "has a longstanding distrust of the police. So he counted himself lucky to be alive, and went about his business."

"Wow," said Elder Toronto.

"But I interrupted you two earlier, looking over your map," said Marco Aurélio. "I'll let you get back to it."

He turned to go.

"Wait," said Elder Toronto. He introduced himself and explained that he and Elder de Assis were representatives of the

Church of Jesus Christ of Latter-day Saints, and asked Marco Aurélio if they could come by his house to share an important message.

"I'm on my way to another appointment right now," said Marco Aurélio, "but if you two came by my house later today and wanted to talk, I wouldn't stop you."

He gave the elders his address and went on his way.

In response to such a halfhearted invitation, the missionaries would not normally have followed up with a visit, but all of their other plans fell through that afternoon. And so they found themselves at the address Marco Aurélio had given them, clapping at the old, rusted gate. Marco Aurélio came out the door of the narrow cinderblock house and let them in.

"You're welcome to stay and talk as long as you want," said Marco Aurélio as the two elders sat down on his dusty couch, "but my one condition is that you don't give me some canned spiel about your church. In fact, I'd prefer it if we could avoid the subject of religion completely."

"You do know that we're missionaries, right?" said Elder de Assis. "By definition, what we do is talk about religion."

"That's fine," said Marco Aurélio. "But my house, my rules."

Elder de Assis stood up.

"Then we can't stay," he said.

"Are you sure about that?" said Marco Aurélio, addressing Elder Toronto.

"I have to say, my companion's correct," said Elder Toronto.

"I'm sorry to hear that," said Marco Aurélio.

"Let's go," said Elder de Assis, and Elder Toronto held up a hand to silence him.

He reached into his bag and pulled out a copy of the Book of Mormon.

"If I give this to you, will you read it?" he asked Marco Aurélio.

"Sure," said Marco Aurélio, and Elder Toronto handed him the book and stood up.

Marco Aurélio saw the elders to the door.

"Come back any time," he said to the missionaries as they left.

Any time turned out to be a month later. Neither elder had thought much of their visit with Marco Aurélio, and had no real intentions of returning. Then, one afternoon, their primary, secondary, and tertiary plans all fell through, and they found themselves at a dead end just a couple of blocks from Marco Aurélio's house. Elder Toronto suggested that they stop by and follow up on their last visit. Elder de Assis reluctantly agreed. When they clapped their hands at his gate, he emerged from his home with a smirk, opening the door and inviting them in.

Seated once again on Marco Aurélio's dusty couch, Elder Toronto asked him if he had had a chance to read the book that they had left with him.

"Yeah," said Marco Aurélio.

"Really?" said Elder de Assis, straightening his glasses. "Which parts did you read?"

"I read the whole thing," said Marco Aurélio.

"Really?" said Elder de Assis.

"Really," said Marco Aurélio.

"So what did you think of it?" said Elder Toronto.

"It's not exactly a page turner, but there's some interesting stuff in there," said Marco Aurélio.

"Tell us about one specific interesting part," said Elder de Assis, obviously still unconvinced.

Marco Aurélio ignored him.

"I do have some questions," he said to Elder Toronto.

"Great," said Elder Toronto. "We have a brief lesson we can share with you that explains where the Book of Mormon came from, and then we can go from there."

"No," said Marco Aurélio. "I'd like to just ask you my questions."

"We'd prefer to teach the lesson first," said Elder de Assis.

"I'll be right back," said Marco Aurélio, still ignoring Elder de Assis. He got up from his chair and left the room.

"I told you this was a mistake," said Elder de Assis. "He's just wasting our time."

Marco Aurélio came back into the room with the copy of the Book of Mormon that the elders had left with him. The spine was creased with wear and he had dog-eared several of the pages.

"Okay," he said, sitting down. He opened the front cover of the book, where he had apparently written a list of questions. "First off—what are the mysteries of God? Not, what are they specifically, but what does that mean?"

Elder Toronto nodded.

"The way I understand it," he said, "is that the mysteries of God are ideas that we can only understand through personal revelation from God. Does that make sense?"

"Sure," said Marco Aurélio. "And how do you get these revelations?"

"Study, prayer, meditation. Also God has to decide that you're ready."

"I see," said Marco Aurélio. "So only God can reveal these mysteries, and if one of them was given to you, you wouldn't be able to just explain it to me? I'd also have to be given it from God?"

"Right," said Elder Toronto.

"Then if I understand right, you could claim that God had revealed a mystery to you, but there's no way you could ever prove it," said Marco Aurélio.

Elder Toronto thought about this for a minute.

"Yeah, I think that's fair," he said.

"That's very convenient," said Marco Aurélio.

"It's just how it works," said Elder Toronto.

"I see," said Marco Aurélio.

Elder de Assis, silent through the whole exchange, finally jumped in.

"Listen," he said, "if we don't teach you about Joseph Smith and the restoration of the church, we have to go."

He stood up and swung his bag over his shoulder. Marco Aurélio looked to Elder Toronto.

"Is that true?" he said.

"Technically, yes," said Elder Toronto. "Although, personally, I'm happy to sit here and answer whatever questions you have."

"I see," said Marco Aurélio, a slight smirk on his lips. "Well, I wouldn't want you breaking rules on my account. Why don't we call it a day."

He saw the two missionaries out and told them, again, to come back any time.

To the missionaries' great surprise, they arrived at church the following Sunday to find Marco Aurélio there, dressed in a shirt and tie, chatting amiably with Bishop Claudemir. During the meetings, he paid polite attention to the talks and the lessons, and at the end of the three hours, he approached the missionaries.

"When can you two come over again?" Marco Aurélio said.

Using his sternest voice, Elder de Assis explained that this wasn't some kind of game. If they came over to his house, he would need to listen to the missionary lessons and uphold the various commitments that were extended to him: to give up cigarettes, alcohol, coffee, and any drugs, if applicable; to abstain from sex outside of marriage; to keep the Sabbath day holy; and so on. And ultimately, he would need to decide whether or not to be baptized in the Church of Jesus Christ of Latter-day Saints.

"Okay," said Marco Aurélio when Elder de Assis had finished.

"Okay what?" said Elder de Assis.

"Come on over after lunch, and we'll see how it goes," said Marco Aurélio.

And so they began their visits to Marco Aurélio, teaching him the principles of the gospel and inviting him to repentance. During this time, Marco Aurélio entered into a battle of wills with the two missionaries. He agreed, for example, to obey the Word of Wisdom by giving up coffee, alcohol, and cigarettes. In the same visit, however, he refused to promise to pay tithing after being baptized in the church.

"I don't even know if I want to be baptized," he said.

"But if you were to decide to be baptized," said Elder de Assis, "do you promise you would pay tithing?"

"That's too hypothetical," said Marco Aurélio. "I can't answer that question."

In another visit, he told the elders that he believed completely that God communicated with His children through a living prophet on the earth today. Then, later in the lesson, he said he thought that most of the Bible was completely bogus, and he couldn't accept it as scripture—no one could write the word of God.

"That doesn't even make sense," said Elder de Assis. "If you believe that a contemporary prophet can speak for God, then why can't the Bible?"

"I'm just telling you what I believe," said Marco Aurélio.

During many of these conversations, Elder Toronto remained silent, spectating. Marco Aurélio seemed to know just how far to push Elder de Assis before the bespectacled elder would jump up from the couch in frustration and head for the door. More than anything else, Marco Aurélio seemed to treat these conversations like a complex game, to which only he knew the rules.

At the end of every visit, Elder de Assis invited Marco Aurélio to be baptized, and each time, Marco Aurélio refused, explaining that once God sent him a revelation telling him to be baptized, he would be baptized, but until then he wouldn't do it.

Tim Wirkus

Due mainly to Elder Toronto's insistence—he felt deeply responsible for Marco Aurélio's spiritual well-being in a way that he couldn't fully explain—the elders continued their visits. After the tug of war between Marco Aurélio and Elder de Assis had been going on for weeks, however, even Elder Toronto began to doubt their investigator's sincerity. More and more, it seemed that Marco Aurélio was toying with them, but Elder Toronto couldn't fathom to what end.

Finally, one morning as they were evaluating the progress of the people they were teaching, Elder de Assis put his foot down—Marco Aurélio had ceased progressing. They were wasting their time with him and needed to move on. Reluctantly, Elder Toronto had to agree. Prepared to deliver their ultimatum, they arrived at Marco Aurélio's cinderblock home to find their investigator in an uncharacteristically cheerful mood.

"Have a seat," he said, ushering them onto his dusty couch. "I'll be right back."

He came back with two chilled glasses of lemonade.

"Here you go," he said with a smile. "I made lemonade."

"Listen," said Elder de Assis. "Before we get any further—"

"Wait," said Marco Aurélio, taking a seat in his armchair. "I've got something exciting I want to tell both of you."

He said that the night before he had dreamed that he was in a large building—someplace stately—standing in front of a heavy wooden door. While he had been standing there, his grandmother had appeared at his side. She had smiled at him and had pushed open the door. Taking his hand, she had led him into a great room, in the middle of which had been a marble pedestal. Resting on top of the pedestal had been a leather-bound book.

"Open it," his grandmother had said.

He had opened the book to find its pages filled with names. He had turned page after page after page before coming to one that had read *Vila Barbosa* along the top. Under the heading had been a list of the members of the Vila Barbosa ward—Claudemir, Fátima, Beatrice, all of them—and at the bottom had been his own name, written in his own handwriting.

"The book is good," his grandmother had said, and then he had woken up, feeling wonderful, feeling that pleasant burning in his chest that someone had described to him at church.

"What I'm saying," he said to the missionaries, "is that I'd like to be baptized."

CHAPTER 8

They ended up being only five minutes late to district meeting, slipping in through the front gate, crossing the courtyard, and entering the cool, tiled interior of the Parque Laranjeira ward house just after ten o'clock. They found the other missionaries gathered in the Relief Society room, Elder J. da Silva stationed at the chalkboard and the other missionaries—Elder Christiansen, Elder Reis, and Elder Fontura—sitting in a semicircle of metal folding chairs facing the front.

"Sorry we're late," said Elder Toronto. "We missed our normal bus."

In the presence of the other missionaries, Elder Schwartz realized how raggedy he and his companion must look. He glanced at Elder Toronto. With his hair uncombed, his skin oily, his face stubbled with a day's beard, he looked—as was the case—like he had been up all night. And Elder Schwartz could practically see the wavy cartoon stink lines radiating from their wrinkled, sweat-soaked clothes.

"Please," said Elder Toronto. "Go on. We didn't mean to interrupt."

He and Elder Schwartz set up a pair of chairs and joined the semicircle. The other missionaries stared at them.

"That's fine," said Elder J. da Silva. "We're just starting our weekly reports."

Elder J. da Silva, their district leader, was a few years older than the other missionaries, somewhere in his mid-twenties, and always wore a long-sleeved shirt to hide the tattoos that covered his arms. Before his mission, he had worked as a guard in one of the big prisons up north. It was there that he had first heard of the church, when an inmate's cousin had tried—absurdly—to smuggle a small knife into the prison inside a hollowed-out copy of the Book of Mormon. The cousin had been arrested and da

Silva had confiscated both the weapon and the book. During one of his breaks, da Silva had read through the first several pages of the book, which were still intact. What he read had piqued his interest, and he had asked his coworkers what they knew about the book. One of them had heard of the Mormons and had told da Silva to stay away from them, that they were a cult, not a group you wanted to get mixed up with. But da Silva had continued to read and reread the intact pages of his copy of the book during every break he had at work.

Then one day he had run into the inmate's cousin, now an inmate himself, who had brought the book into the prison in the first place. Da Silva had stopped him, had asked him what he knew about the Mormons. The cousin had shrugged and told J. da Silva that his family had belonged to the church for a while when he was younger, but they didn't anymore and he couldn't remember much about it. Da Silva had asked where the Mormons's church was, and the cousin had told him there was one he used to pass every day on the way to work that wasn't too far from the prison.

After that, everything had fallen into place for da Silva—he had gone to the church, met the missionaries, taken the lessons, and been baptized. A year later he had decided to serve a mission and now here he was. His background gave him a macho credibility among the other elders, a credibility that was only enhanced by his unrelenting geniality. He was, as they say, tough but fair.

"We'll start with our area," said Elder J. da Silva, standing at the chalkboard. "We had an interesting week in Parque Laranjeira."

He said that Bete, an older lady they had been teaching for several weeks now, had told them she didn't want any more of the lessons, that the elders could stop coming to her house. They had asked her why and she had been very vague about her reasons, but insistent. They wished they knew what the problem was, but it looked like they wouldn't have another chance to meet with her.

In better news, they had an appointment scheduled later today to follow up with a new couple they had started teaching, the husband a cobrador on the bus the elders sometimes rode home in the evenings.

Elder Toronto, who had been staring out the window during the entire report, turned and nudged Elder Schwartz. "This may have been a tactical error," he said under his breath. "We're wasting time."

"Come on," Elder Schwartz whispered back. "You have to pay attention. You're going to make everyone suspicious."

"But I never pay attention at district meeting," whispered Elder Toronto. "It would be suspicious if I did."

Although this was true, his disregard for the meeting was never quite as flagrant as it was today.

"You're going to blow it," whispered Elder Schwartz.

"What was that, Elder Schwartz, Elder Toronto?" said Elder J. da Silva.

"We didn't say anything," said Elder Toronto.

Elder J. da Silva looked concerned for a moment, and then moved on.

"Okay," he said. "Who wants to report next? Elder Fontura and Elder Reis?"

Elder Fontura nodded and stood up. He said that Carlos, one of their longtime investigators, was scheduled to be baptized this coming Sunday, and that everyone in the ward was really excited about it. Also, they had started teaching one of Carlos's cousins, João, a young man who was engaged to a Mormon girl from another ward and played the clarinet in a local band. Their other investigators were all doing well, more or less—Erika was still trying to quit smoking, Paulo had traded shifts with someone at work so he could come to church on Sundays, Chiquinho and Ana Paula were looking into what they needed to do to get married,

Guilherme was finally reading in the Book of Mormon, and Nina had prayed to know if this was the church of Jesus Christ and had told the elder she had received an answer that it was.

"So that's us," said Elder Fontura, sitting down.

Throughout Elder Fontura's report, Elder Toronto had been tapping his pen insistently against his leg. The other missionaries stared at him, but he didn't notice. They looked at Elder Schwartz, who only shrugged.

"Thank you, Elder Fontura," said Elder J. da Silva. "That leaves Vila Barbosa."

Elder Schwartz elbowed Elder Toronto, who stopped tapping his pen and looked around, eyes red-rimmed, at the other missionaries.

"Are we done, then?" he said.

"No," said Elder J. da Silva. "We're not. It's your turn tell us how things are going in your area."

"Oh," said Elder Toronto, "sure."

He tucked in his grimy, wrinkled shirt and straightened his tie. He said that he and Elder Schwartz had had better weeks in the past. They had lost every single one of their investigators, and Marco Aurélio, who had been baptized recently, had disappeared—hadn't come to church and they could never catch him at home. But they were doing everything they could to get back in touch with him. The other missionaries nodded.

"Any idea what the problem is?" said Elder J. da Silva.

"We're not sure," said Elder Toronto.

Elder J. da Silva said they should be sure to stay on top of this. President Madvig was very concerned with retention these days, and whatever was going on with Marco Aurélio—if someone at church offended him, or if he was doing something he was ashamed of, or if neighbors were giving him anti-Mormon propaganda—it was important to catch the problem early on and work with the bishop to help Marco Aurélio resolve it.

"We'll do everything we can," said Elder Toronto.

"Sounds good," said Elder J. da Silva. "Next up we have a treinamento from Elder Fontura.

Elder Toronto groaned, not quietly. "This was a mistake," he whispered to Elder Schwartz.

"Elder Toronto?" said Elder J. da Silva.

"It's fine," said Elder Toronto, waving a hand dismissively. "Go ahead."

For the next half hour, the missionaries, led by Elder Fontura, discussed the most effective ways to make a street contact, and practiced incorporating a miniature lesson into their approaches. Throughout the treinamento, Elder Toronto fidgeted with the knot in his tie, scratched impatiently at his earlobe, and tapped his pen against his knee. He clearly wasn't listening to a word his fellow missionaries said. Again, this was not unprecedented behavior from Elder Toronto, but it still made Elder Schwartz nervous. He didn't want to be found out.

Aside from the tension of keeping the previous night's events secret from the other missionaries, Elder Schwartz didn't enjoy the treinamento any more than his companion did. The role plays in which they practiced the skills they learned were yet another occasion for him to broadcast his shoddy Portuguese skills to the world. In casual conversation with other missionaries, he could do just fine. Sure, his American accent was as thick as ever. Sure, he still misconjugated verbs and stumbled over half-remembered vocabulary. But the other missionaries, even the native Portuguese speakers, all had enough experience with elders who struggled to learn the language that they could follow what he said. And knowing that helped Elder Schwartz to keep it together, to keep from collapsing into complete incomprehensibility.

Any time the speaking situation became even remotely formal, however, Elder Schwartz fell apart—street contacts, lessons, interactions with church members, conversations with store owners, even these ridiculous role plays in front of other missionaries. It wasn't that Elder Schwartz didn't work at learning the language. The problem was that in the line of fire, all his practiced skills left him, rendering him flummoxed and incomprehensible. When he saw the look of absolute confusion in the eyes of his listener, he might struggle through a few more words or phrases and then his mind would stop up and he would fall silent.

When his turn came to practice making a contact—in the scenario, he was waiting in line to pay his power bill, and decided to strike up a conversation with the man in front of him, played, in this case, by Elder Reis—he stumbled through the interaction as best he could. When it was over, he sat back down, tongue-tied and sweaty. Elder J. da Silva leaned in and told Elder Schwartz that his Portuguese was really improving.

They practiced a few more times with a few more staged scenarios—waiting for a bus, buying groceries, walking home for the night—and then wrapped up their meeting with a prayer from Elder Toronto which lasted all of seven seconds. Elder J. da Silva distributed the mail he had picked up from the mission office, and also gave new bank cards to Elder Schwartz and Elder Toronto to replace the ones that had been stolen from them.

"The secretary at the mission office said that he'll have to make an appointment for you two with the Polícia Federal to get some new papers, but until then, just carry these photocopies," said Elder J. da Silva, handing them both a folded piece of white paper. Elder Toronto thanked him and said they'd try not to get mugged again.

"Oh, and one more thing," said Elder J. da Silva.

"Yeah?" said Elder Toronto, already walking backward out the door, pulling Elder Schwartz along with him.

"President Madvig is going to spend a few days visiting your area this week. He'd like you to show him around Vila Barbosa."

"What?" said Elder Toronto, stopping in his tracks. Elder Schwartz stumbled into him. "No. Not this week."

"Why not?" said Elder J. da Silva. "Is something going on?"

"Why can't he come next week?" said Elder Toronto.

"Next week is transfers."

"So he's just dropping by for a surprise inspection, then?" said Elder Toronto, striking an indignant pose. "What is this, a police state? You know, I would really prefer it if my leaders—"

"Elder Toronto," said Elder J. da Silva. "You asked him to visit. He's coming on your request."

"What?" said Elder Toronto. "That's ridiculous. I never requested anything like that."

"You did," said Elder J. da Silva. "I was there. It was at the last mission conference. During lunch. We were all sitting at the same table and you told President Madvig that you knew he was thinking of shutting down missionary work in Vila Barbosa. And you laid out a whole big case explaining why he shouldn't. And then you told him that at the very least, he should come see the area for himself before he made any final decision. On the phone this morning, he told me you had convinced him, and he'd like you to show him around."

"I don't remember any of that," said Elder Toronto, eying Elder J. da Silva suspiciously.

"Elder Toronto," said Elder J. da Silva, lifting his hands in exasperation. He turned to Elder Schwartz. "You were there, Elder Schwartz. You remember."

"Well," said Elder Schwartz.

"Look," said Elder J. da Silva, shaking his head. "It doesn't matter. Wednesday morning, President Madvig is coming to see your area. Okay?"

Elder Toronto hitched up his pants and all but rolled his eyes.
"Wednesday morning, you say?" he said.
"That's right," said Elder J. da Silva.
"Fine," said Elder Toronto. "We'll plan on it."

CHAPTER 9

It took the elders over two hours to get from Parque Laranjeira back to Vila Barbosa. Normally the trip took only thirty minutes, but just after the missionaries boarded, their bus got a flat tire and the driver ordered everybody off. After radioing in to headquarters, he explained to his disgruntled passengers that another bus was on its way, and if they would just be patient, they'd get to wherever they needed to go in no time. The replacement bus didn't arrive for half an hour, and after they boarded it, it didn't take long for the passengers—including the now-apoplectic Elder Toronto—to notice that the bus was headed in the wrong direction.

Shouting to be heard over the angry din of her passengers, the new driver explained that the term "replacement bus" may have been misleading. There was a shortage of working buses, and this one was on its way to another assignment. It would drop the passengers off at a stop along the way, where a different bus would pick them all up—assuming there was enough room—and drop them off at another stop where yet another bus would pick them up, etc., etc. All this was in compliance with official policy.

"We would have been better off just waiting back there for the two-oh-five bus," yelled an elderly woman with a scarf around her hair.

There were general shouts of agreement from the other passengers.

"It was a mistake to go to district meeting," said Elder Toronto to Elder Schwartz. "Why did you let me go through with it?"

"We had to go," said Elder Schwartz. "It's like you said before. Plus, now we have a heads-up on President Madvig's visit."

"Maybe," said Elder Toronto.

He fidgeted with a loose piece of plastic on the seat in front of him.

"What are we going to do about that, by the way?" said Elder Schwartz. "President Madvig, I mean."

"There's nothing we can do," said Elder Toronto. "Now there's just more of a ticking clock. We have until Wednesday morning to figure all of this out."

"That's only two days," said Elder Schwartz.

"More like a day and a half," said Elder Toronto.

"So what do we do?" said Elder Schwartz.

"Why don't you sit there quietly and let me think," said Elder Toronto, waving a dismissive hand at his companion.

So that's what they did.

When they finally made it back to Vila Barbosa, it was already mid-afternoon.

"We shouldn't have gone to district meeting," said Elder Toronto again. "That was a stupid, stupid call."

"I'm sorry," said Elder Schwartz, apologizing by habit as they filed off the bus. "Where are we headed?"

"Just follow me."

They stepped off the bus into the business district of Vila Barbosa. A hodgepodge of open-front electronics stores, papelarias, locksmiths, sundries shops, and record stores lined either side of the street.

"Come on," snapped Elder Toronto, hurrying down the crowded sidewalk. "Don't slow us down."

They covered several blocks at this pace until they came to the lanchonete where Elder Schwartz had first met Marco Aurélio. Elder Toronto stopped and the two missionaries went inside.

The place was doing okay business for the middle of the afternoon. Three young Franciscans sat at the metal table in the corner sharing a single esfiha among them and having an urgent discussion in low, respectful voices. A well-scrubbed little man with the look of a recovering alcoholic about him sat at the counter nursing a caldo de mocotó. A fleshy woman holding a tiny dog in her arms stood at the cash register arguing with the owner—the same woman who had been there on the missionaries' previous visit.

"You have no right to kick me out of this establishment," said the woman with the dog. "I'm a paying customer."

"Thanks for stopping here," said Elder Schwartz to Elder Toronto. "I'm starving."

They hadn't eaten since lunch the day before.

"We're not here to eat," said Elder Toronto. "We're here to ask some questions."

"What?" said Elder Schwartz.

"Excuse me," said Elder Toronto, approaching the counter. The owner stood with her hands on her hips, her wiry arms angled, staring down the woman with the tiny dog. "We need to ask you some questions."

The owner turned and pointed an angry finger at Elder Toronto.

"You need to sit down and wait your turn," she growled, and returned her attention to the woman with the dog.

After a moment's hesitation, the missionaries sat down on two stools at the other end of the counter from the little man with the caldo de mocotó. At the cash register, the woman with the tiny dog declaimed in outraged tones that she had paid for her food, and she intended to eat it right here in the lanchonete.

"I don't allow animals in here," said the owner, "so either you put your little dog outside, or you take your food with you."

"You should have told me that before you accepted my money," said the woman.

"You should have read the sign on the wall. *No Pets Allowed!*" said the owner, pointing at the sign in question.

"I didn't see it," said the woman with the dog.

"Then why did you keep your dog hidden in your purse when you ordered?" said the owner.

The woman with the tiny dog launched into a noisy diatribe against the lanchonete, the food it served, and the people who staffed it.

"What are we doing here?" said Elder Schwartz.

"We're going to ask the owner how she knows Marco Aurélio."

"You think she knows Marco Aurélio?" said Elder Schwartz.

"Based on what we saw last time we were in here, yeah—I think it's a pretty safe bet."

At the cash register, the owner was countering the loud diatribe with a threat of her own to call the police if the woman with the tiny dog didn't get out.

Elder Toronto leaned over and dropped his voice. "I don't think Marco Aurélio killed Galvão."

"What?" said Elder Schwartz.

"The detective," said Elder Toronto. "I don't think Marco Aurélio killed him."

"Why would he?" said Elder Schwartz.

Elder Toronto looked around at the patrons of the diner. None of them seemed to be paying any attention to the missionaries. At the register, the tiny dog began yipping and its owner changed her strategy from belligerence to tears.

Elder Toronto said, "There are clearly plenty of things we don't know about Marco Aurélio. But you saw what happened to that guy's face. I suppose it's possible that Marco Aurélio's capable of killing a man, but I don't think he could kill someone that way."

"I would hope not," said Elder Schwartz.

"Right," said Elder Toronto.

The scene at the cash register seemed to be wrapping up.

"I hope you're proud of yourself," said the woman with the tiny dog. She picked up her food and stormed out of the lanchonete, dog in hand. The owner watched her leave with a slight smile. She made a note on a pad next to the cash register, and then walked over to where the missionaries sat.

"What'll it be?" she said. Her long, dark hair was pulled back in a ponytail. She wore a red apron, a simple gray polo shirt, and black slacks. The expression on her face suggested the missionaries better be quick about it.

"We actually just have a few questions," said Elder Toronto.

"Nope," said the woman. "You order something or you leave."

Elder Toronto looked up at the menu.

"All right," he said. "A limeade."

"And for you?" she said to Elder Schwartz.

"He's fine," said Elder Toronto.

"No," she said. "I don't have much patience for groups of people who come in and share some tiny order between them while they sit and talk for hours."

She said this loudly enough that the brown-robed Franciscans in the corner could hear. They looked up sheepishly and began to gather their things.

"I'd like a limeade and four coxinhas," said Elder Schwartz.

"Come again?" said the woman.

Elder Schwartz repeated his order.

"I still didn't understand that," said the woman.

Elder Schwartz repeated himself again, pointing at the menu on the wall and indicating quantities with his fingers.

"Got it," said the woman, writing it down on her notebook.

The Franciscans stood up to leave.

"Thank you," they said, as they exited the lanchonete. The owner didn't acknowledge them.

"I've got two limeades and four coxinhas," she said.

"Right," said Elder Toronto.

She gave him his total, and he paid for both orders. The woman pulled four coxinhas from under their heat lamp by the cash register and handed them on a plate to Elder Schwartz. He thanked her and began eating immediately. Then the owner grabbed a handful of limes from a plastic basket.

"You boys have been in here before," she said as she quartered the limes with a paring knife. "But last time you were here with a friend."

"That's right," said Elder Toronto. "He must have made an impression."

She shook her head.

"Nope. I just have a good memory for faces. Especially customers' faces. Like that one," she jerked her thumb in the direction of the entrance. "That lady with the dog? I won't be serving her again."

"But you do remember the man who was here with us before?" said Elder Toronto.

"Sure," said the owner, quartering another lime. "I could pick him out of a lineup, anyway. Like I said, I've got a good memory for faces."

"But you two know each other, right?" said Elder Toronto.

"What?" she said, dropping the quartered limes into a blender. "No."

"Then why did you ask about him?" said Elder Toronto.

She added a scoop of sugar to the blender from a jar under the counter.

"I didn't," she said. "I was just making conversation."

"Really?" said Elder Toronto.

The owner turned around with a glare.

"What's this about?" she said.

"Just tell me how you know Marco Aurélio," he said.

"Excuse me?" she said.

"Our friend," he said. "The man we came in with last time."

"No, I got that," she said, "I'm just not sure where you get off taking that tone with me in my own establishment."

"Look," said Elder Toronto, "I saw you two talking after my companion and I left. What did he say to you?"

She shook her head and turned around, adding water, ice, and a dollop of sweetened condensed milk to the blender as Elder Toronto repeated the question. She turned on the blender, silencing him with the noise. She let it run for a minute before turning it off and removing the pitcher.

"Here you go," she said, pouring the juice through a strainer into two chilled glasses. The missionaries drank their limeades in silence as the woman washed the blender in the sink behind the counter.

"Please," said Elder Toronto, "I really need to know what he said to you."

"I am this close to kicking you out," said the woman. "Maybe you'd like to join the lady with the dog?"

"Please," said Elder Toronto.

"Does your friend not understand Portuguese?" said the woman to Elder Schwartz, who had already eaten three of the four coxinhas and downed half the glass of limeade.

"It was obvious you two knew each other," said Elder Toronto.

"Do you have any idea where he's getting this?" she said, still addressing Elder Schwartz.

Elder Schwartz pointed to his full mouth.

"He said something to you and you got really upset," said Elder Toronto. "We saw it."

The woman turned to Elder Toronto.

"Really upset like I am right now?" said the woman. "Listen. I don't know what he said to me. Chances are, he was trying to pick me up and I wasn't interested. I'm not as young as I used to be, but it still happens, believe it or not."

"I don't think that's what it was," said Elder Toronto.

The woman slapped the countertop with her hand.

"We can talk about something else, or I can throw you out," she said.

Elder Toronto looked at her. He opened his mouth and she raised a threatening eyebrow. Elder Toronto closed his mouth and nodded.

"Okay," he said. "How about a tall, thin man in a brown suit? Scars under his eyes? Have you seen anyone like that?"

"What, do you think you're a cop or something?" she said. "What's with the questions?"

"I'm just asking," said Elder Toronto.

She shook her head.

"This conversation is over," said the owner. "Finish your food and get out of here."

THE ARGENTINE

They say the career change from criminal administrator to taxonomist revitalized the Argentine, imbuing him with the energy and enthusiasm of a much younger man. Not only did he find the process of collection and classification to be deeply satisfying in itself, he also thrilled at his role in pioneering a new field of study. As far as he could tell, this project of collecting, naming, and categorizing discrete acts of human cruelty had never been undertaken, especially with this level of rigor. Pen and notebook in hand, he quietly observed and recorded every specimen he could find—every beating, every public insult, every exploitation, every deliberate slight, every rape.

In undertaking his project, however, the Argentine faced three key challenges:

The first challenge was to observe these acts of cruelty without being observed himself. During the early days, his strategy resembled that of a bumbling lover's in a Shakespeare comedy. He hid behind curtains, eavesdropped through open windows, concealed himself—poorly— behind rows of bushes. Although none of the residents acknowledged his presence, the Argentine knew they could see him, and knew that they altered their behavior accordingly. The Argentine considered these specimens tainted by the effect his presence had on his subjects. He needed a better method of concealment during this delicate field work.

Around this time, the population of Vila Barbosa skyrocketed. Sensing an opportunity in this boom, the Argentine built a secret system of tunnels that ran throughout the neighborhood. As the area's architecture transitioned from flimsy wooden shacks to manmade hills of irregular brick boxes, the Argentine ordered strategically selected spaces to remain unfilled. Linked together, these spaces formed long, twisting tunnels, branching and converging throughout the neighborhood like a dusty network of veins and arteries. These tunnels connected houses to train stations to churches to bars, allowing the Argentine to pass unobserved throughout the neighborhood, to peer out through nearly imperceptible peepholes.

They say that observant residents could detect evidence of these tunnels—the sound of shuffling footsteps audible through an apparently solid wall, or a crack in the floor that occasionally emanated light, or the faintest hint of what could be a moving panel in the altarpiece of a church—but these residents understood that keeping one's mouth shut was the greatest civic virtue in this neighborhood. And so they kept the evidence to themselves and the whereabouts of the tunnels remained the Argentine's secret.

They say he rarely went above ground after that. The tunnels concealed him from view, allowing him intimate, undetected access—through the neighborhood's alleyways, storerooms, bars, police stations, bedrooms—to the lives of Vila Barbosa's residents. With time, he became expertly attuned to the patterns of cruelty throughout the neighborhood—its usual habitats, its aversions, its migratory patterns—and was overwhelmed with specimens.

The tunnels solved his problem so well, in fact, that the Argentine wasted dozens, possibly even hundreds, of opportunities for observation every day. He needed research assistants to help him collect these acts of cruelty that regularly went unobserved. Once he recognized this, the Argentine began collecting his infamous staff of underground minions.

In the early days, those who roamed the tunnels with the Argentine were not only few in number, but recruited against their will. They say the Argentine kidnapped the neighborhood's best and brightest, imprisoning them in his subterranean labyrinth. One moment, a *talented resident of Vila Barbosa might be working out a mathematical proof, or tinkering with a motorcycle, or delivering a sermon, and the next moment they'd be gone, no trace of them ever seen again. Nobody is quite sure how the Argentine compelled those early conscripts to stay below ground and assist him. All that can be known for certain is that none of them ever escaped.*

However, as the residents of Vila Barbosa gradually learned of the catalog's existence—through obscure gossip, and rumors of rumors—a strange thing began to happen; certain members of the neighborhood sought out the Argentine and begged him for the opportunity to work in his underground labyrinth. They say that the Argentine explained to those who approached him that once they descended into the space below his little general store, they could never emerge again, that their life's work would become the compilation of his universal catalog of human cruelty. Astonishingly, these volunteers agreed to his terms and entered the Argentine's service within his massive labyrinth. In the ensuing years, a small number of Vila Barbosa's residents volunteered each year to descend forever into the tunnels, entering the Argentine's subterranean community of observers. The tunnels became a kind of perverse monastery, housing an ever-increasing number of devotees culled from the neighborhood above. They say that Vila Barbosa's only true idealists lived below ground.

• • •

The second key challenge was to effectively organize the specimens that the Argentine, and later his minions, collected. This difficulty didn't manifest itself immediately. In the beginning, the only problem seemed to be finding enough space to store the ever-growing collection of cruelty-filled notebooks. For this purpose, the Argentine constructed a massive underground library just below the little general store.

While most people agree on the space's magnitude, vastly differing opinions exist as to the layout and design of the library. According to

one camp, the library resembled a magnified honeycomb, its walls
made up of interlocking hexagonal chambers large enough to contain
a person. A lamp hung in the peaked roof of each compartment,
illuminating the shelves of notebooks lining the chamber's inner walls.
Cushions filled in the valleyed floor so that each hexagon could serve
as both storage space and reading room. They say that the Argentine
or one of his minions might spend hours sitting on the floor of a
compartment, studying and annotating the notebooks it contained.

According to another camp, the Argentine followed a more
traditional layout for the library—a single oak desk stationed in
the middle of the chamber, surrounded by floor-to-ceiling, ladder-
accessible bookshelves.

Others envisioned the chamber as a labyrinth within a labyrinth,
a microcosm of the larger system of tunnels. Towering bookshelves
formed narrow, winding passages that only the Argentine and his
minions could navigate with ease.

Still others imagine that there was no chamber below the general
store, and instead, shelves of notebooks lined the walls of the entire
system of hidden tunnels that ran throughout Vila Barbosa.

Regardless of its layout, the creation of the library illuminated a
larger challenge than finding storage space for all the notebooks. The
existence of a formal archival space forced the Argentine to organize
the notebooks that he and his minions filled with specimens.

First, the Argentine opted for a chronological approach, simply placing
a notebook in the next available space on the next available shelf once it
was filled. However, the Argentine found this system too haphazard, and
so he reorganized the library geographically—a bookcase here devoted to
the neighborhood's business district, one there devoted to the train station,
another there devoted to a certain cul-de-sac.

This didn't work either, and so he reorganized by person, the cruel
actions of each resident of Vila Barbosa occupying their very own shelf
or shelves. Still, the Argentine was unsatisfied.

After careful consideration he decided to attempt a truly taxonomic approach—phyla, classes, orders, etc. But this approach raised more vexing questions than any other system: Could he truly justify even his most basic divisions? Didn't, for example, physical cruelty and emotional cruelty overlap in significant, unavoidable ways? And how certain could he be of his specimens' qualities? Didn't some actions require insight into the motivations of those performing them to determine if they were truly cruel? Couldn't the act of classification itself obscure fundamental characteristics necessary to understanding human cruelty?

• • •

And thus the third key challenge revealed itself to the Argentine. As he pored over the thousands of notebooks, he discovered redundancy after redundancy. He had intended this catalog to be universal, to chart the outer limits of the phenomenon of cruelty by recording a staggering breadth of specimens, but here he had instance after instance of the exact same species of cruelty, of actions so similar that at times, the only variations were the names of the participants. How could he have missed this? How could he not have noticed the fundamental similarities among the specimens he collected?

This discovery devastated the Argentine—he wept and wailed and gnashed his teeth. Years of work, and what did he have to show for it? This third challenge threatened to destroy everything he had worked for. He could feel the project closing in around him, that same sense of claustrophobic limitation that had prompted him decades earlier to abandon his criminal empire in favor of this dark, subterranean existence.

CHAPTER 10

After their impasse with the owner of the lanchonete, the two elders headed across the neighborhood toward Marco Aurélio's house. As they walked the winding streets that twisted their way through mountains of dusty brick houses, Elder Toronto presented his new strategy.

"I played that all wrong," he said, "back in the lanchonete. We've got to be craftier about asking questions."

"Okay," said Elder Schwartz.

"Seriously," said Elder Toronto. "I came in there like some kind of police officer. That was exactly the wrong approach. We need people to trust us, or at least not to suspect what we're up to."

A motorcycle shot out of an alleyway in front of them and the missionaries stopped to avoid being run over. It sped up the street and the missionaries kept walking.

"Here's how we'll do it instead, next time," said Elder Toronto.

"Where are we going, by the way?" said Elder Schwartz.

They stepped around an impressive pile of feces on the sidewalk, and then another one, and then they opted to walk in the street.

"We're going to talk to Marco Aurélio's neighbors. Someone on his street has to know something that can help us."

"Okay," said Elder Schwartz. In the light of day, he was, if not content, then at least willing to go along with Elder Toronto's plans. Searching for Marco Aurélio was, after all, more interesting than what they did on a typical day. And maybe Elder Toronto was right—maybe they actually were in a position to help Marco Aurélio.

"Here's how we're going to do it," said Elder Toronto. "Like I said, we need to be crafty. We can't let people know what we're up to, or they won't tell us anything. And do you know how we're going to do that?"

"No, I don't," said Elder Schwartz.

"The answer's so obvious, I don't know why I didn't think of it back at the lanchonete," said Elder Toronto. "Just think about what we do every day. We knock on doors and we ask intrusive questions. On top of that, no one thinks we've got much going on upstairs. I mean, to a lot of people we're practically cartoon characters. It's the perfect cover."

"Our cover is that we're missionaries?" said Elder Schwartz.

"Right. That's how we're going to play it," said Elder Toronto. "We're just a couple of dopey missionaries trying to figure out why our friend hasn't been at church."

"But isn't that true?" said Elder Schwartz.

"Just follow my lead," said Elder Toronto. "Okay?"

They turned a corner onto Marco Aurélio's street. It was a short, uncluttered stretch of houses, one of the oldest streets in the neighborhood. The road had been paved at one time and the houses were mostly cinderblock, a sign of relative permanence.

"Remember," said Elder Toronto. "We're going to act like these are normal door contacts. We'll give our normal pitch about the church, and then ease into questions about Marco Aurélio."

The first house they tried was a bust. A young woman in a garish polyester fast-food uniform came to the door and told them she was leaving right now and didn't have time to talk. As she closed the door behind her and stepped out of the house, she explained that she wasn't interested in their religious message and that she didn't know Marco Aurélio, that she didn't know any of her neighbors, in fact, because she worked two full-time jobs, plus a part-time job in the summer, and was hardly ever at home. When the elders thanked her for her time, she didn't pause, but barreled past them with a forced smile in the direction of the train station.

The next house had once been painted a cheery shade of yellow, but years of neglect had left it flaking and stained. A man with a parrot perched on his shoulder came to the door when the missionaries clapped. It was Elder Schwartz's turn to do the talking, so he introduced himself and asked the man's name.

"What did you say, kid?" said the man with the parrot.

"What's your name?" said Elder Schwartz.

"Leandro," said the man, after a brief pause.

The parrot on his shoulder squawked, ruffling its feathers. Elder Schwartz told him that it was a handsome bird. Leandro nodded.

"Is it just you and the parrot who live here?" said Elder Schwartz.

"What?" said Leandro.

"Do you live alone?" said Elder Schwartz, gesturing at the house.

Leandro squinted at him and pointed back into the house at a woman inside on her hands and knees, scrubbing at something on the floor.

"My wife," he said.

"That's great," said Elder Schwartz. "It's good to live as a family."

"Hello," said the parrot. "Hello."

"How long have you and your wife been married?" said Elder Schwartz.

"What?" said Leandro.

"How long have you been married?"

Leandro shook his head.

"That's great," said Elder Schwartz.

Leandro grunted. The parrot screamed in a sharp, feminine voice and both missionaries jumped back.

"Sorry," said Elder Schwartz. "Your parrot surprised me."

"What do you want?" said Leandro.

"As I was saying," said Elder Schwartz. "It's great that you live here with your wife, as a family."

"Help me," screamed the parrot, in a voice uncannily similar to a woman's. "Help me."

"And we actually have an important message to share about families, and how they can be together forever."

"Stop it," continued the parrot. "That hurts. That hurts, Leandro. Stop. Please. Stop, stop, stop, it hurts. Leandro. Stop. Please. You're hurting me. I'm sorry. Please. Stop. Please, please. I'm sorry."

The parrot ruffled its feathers.

"Hello," it said. "Hello."

Elder Schwartz looked from the bird to Leandro. He started talking again.

"And so we would like to share this important message with you and your wife."

"I didn't understand a word you just said," said Leandro.

"Okay," said Elder Schwartz.

Leandro turned to walk back inside.

"One last question, sir, if it's all right," said Elder Toronto, jumping in. "Do you know Marco Aurélio, who lives across the street?"

Leandro looked at the house Elder Toronto was pointing to.

"No," he said. "That guy doesn't talk to anybody."

"He's a friend of ours from church and we're just wondering if you've seen him in the past couple of weeks."

"I mind my own business," said Leandro, and shut the door.

The elders walked back to the curb. Elder Schwartz glanced back to the closed door of Leandro's house.

"Should we talk to someone about—" he began, pointing back at the house, but Elder Toronto was already striding quickly across the street. Elder Schwartz jogged to catch up.

Several yards away, a group of boys tussled over a fallen kite. At the payphone on the corner, a young man shouted into the receiver, sobbing. At the house in front of them, an elderly woman swept at the dirt of her quintal.

"Let's talk to her," said Elder Toronto, nodding in the direction of the old woman.

As they crossed the street, Elder Schwartz looked back again at Leandro's front door.

The two missionaries approached the old woman's gate.

"Excuse me, ma'am," said Elder Toronto.

The woman didn't look up from her sweeping. She wore cracked rubber sandals, a faded cotton skirt, and a sagging T-shirt that may have been blue once. Her gray hair was pulled back in a tight bun.

"Excuse me?" said Elder Toronto, louder this time. "Ma'am?"

The old woman didn't look up.

"My name is Meire," said the old woman, "I talked to you two once before."

"Terrific," said Elder Toronto. "I actually don't think we've met, so you must have talked to some colleagues of ours. Did you get a chance to talk with them about our church?"

"I'm very content with my religion," said Meire.

She overturned a rock with the bristles of her broom and a pair of cockroaches ran out from beneath it, bronze wings glinting in the sun. She swept them toward the missionaries. Elder Schwartz jumped back, but the cockroaches scurried past him to the safety of a rubbish pile at the side of the street.

"That's fine," said Elder Toronto. "In fact, your neighbor, Marco Aurélio—he just lives two doors down from here—he's a member of our church."

"I know that," said the old woman.

She flipped the broom bristle-side up and leaned on it like a staff. Shading her eyes with her free hand, she glared at Elder Toronto.

"You know him, then?" said Elder Toronto.

"I know who he is," said Meire.

"Has he talked to you about our church?" said Elder Toronto. "Maybe in the past couple of weeks?"

The old woman shook her head.

"What Marco Aurélio does is none of my business," she said.

"So have you known him for a long time?" said Elder Toronto.

The old woman pursed her lips and looked up the street in the direction of Marco Aurélio's house. She looked back at the missionaries.

"If you want to talk about Marco Aurélio, then you should talk to his brother," said Meire.

"His brother?" said Elder Toronto.

"That's what I said."

Elder Toronto looked at Elder Schwartz. Marco Aurélio had never mentioned a brother before.

"Do you know where we could find him?" said Elder Toronto.

Meire pointed her wrinkled thumb at the house next door to hers.

"Grillo lives right there with his wife, Lucinda," she said.

"Do you know if he's home?" said Elder Toronto.

The old woman nodded.

"Hey," she yelled, startling both elders, "Grillo!"

There was no answer from the house next door.

"Hey," she yelled again, "Grillo!"

No answer.

"Try clapping," she said to Elder Toronto. "I know they're both home right now. I talked to Grillo not more than an hour ago."

So the elders walked the few feet up the sidewalk and clapped at Grillo's front door. They heard the sound of furniture shifting inside. They waited. No one came to the door. The old woman had crossed her quintal and was leaning on her broom, watching them. Elder Toronto clapped again. They heard a sound like a chair falling over, and then a gasp.

"Something's happening in there," said Elder Toronto. "Did you hear that?"

Meire nodded.

"Well, should we do something about it?" said Elder Toronto. "What do you think is going on?"

Meire said, "I think I know exactly what's going on."

"What?" said Elder Toronto.

Meire gave an exasperated sigh.

"Grillo and Lucinda both work long hours and are hardly ever home together. Right now, they're home together, husband and wife. You tell me what's going on."

The elders didn't respond.

"They're having sex," said Meire.

"Right," said Elder Toronto. "I got it."

He and Elder Schwartz stepped back to the curb. Meire slung her broom over her shoulder and walked back toward her house.

"Thanks for your help, ma'am," said Elder Toronto, but the old woman didn't turn around.

"What now?" said Elder Schwartz, looking nervously at Grillo's front door. "Should we go someplace else?"

"No," said Elder Toronto, "this is our best lead right now. We should talk to Grillo as soon as possible."

"Okay," said Elder Schwartz. "So do we just wait here?"

Elder Toronto looked up and down the street. The little mob of boys had dispersed with their kite. The young man at the payphone was gone. Late afternoon, and the street was momentarily empty.

"Come on," said Elder Toronto. "No one's watching. I think we have a golden opportunity right here."

They walked down the sidewalk to Marco Aurélio's narrow, cinderblock house. They found the gate ajar and, Elder Toronto leading the way, they approached the front door. Elder Toronto tried the door handle.

"It's unlocked," he said.

He looked up and down the street, and then opened the door.

CHAPTER 11

If, on breaking and entering, the missionaries had hoped to find some revelatory key to Marco Aurélio's inner life—a hidden journal, maybe, or a bundle of letters from a secret lover, or even a photo album—they were foiled by the almost absurd austerity of the house and its contents. A cursory examination of its three rooms suggested a lifestyle that could most generously be described as Spartan. It wasn't the poverty of the house that was striking; in fact, the furnishings, and even the house itself, were nicer than many that the elders encountered in Vila Barbosa. What struck the missionaries was the complete lack of personal effects, of anything beyond what was absolutely necessary for day-to-day living. The front room, which they had visited many times, contained a couch and an armchair. The kitchen had a small table with three chairs, a half-sized refrigerator with a pitcher of water and a moldy pot of cooked rice inside, and a makeshift shelf that held two bags containing, respectively, dry rice and dry beans. The bedroom had a twin bed with a single pillow and a single sheet, and a guarda-roupa, inside of which were a few worn shirts and slacks on hangers, and several pairs of socks and briefs folded on the shelf. The bathroom, aside from the toilet, sink, and shower, contained a roll of toilet paper, a bar of soap, a bottle of shampoo, a stick of deodorant, a razor, and a comb.

And that was everything in the house.

Nowhere did the elders find anything that might further illuminate Marco Aurélio's personal interests, his past life, or his current whereabouts—no framed photographs, no books, no sporting equipment, no magazines, no posters on the walls, no music, no letters or postcards, no magnets on the refrigerator, no memorabilia from local soccer teams, no used day planners, no drawers filled with receipts, no medications, no souvenir mugs or T-shirts, no lists of phone numbers, no carefully recorded family recipes, no card games, no board games, no sentimental heirlooms.

"Did someone clean this place out?" said Elder Schwartz.

Elder Toronto stood in the middle of the living room, hands on his hips.

"Hard to say," he said. "His house has certainly never seemed cluttered, but it's weird we can't find anything."

"Yeah," said Elder Schwartz.

"There's got to be something in here," said Elder Toronto. "Somewhere."

So the missionaries looked harder. They searched for hidden compartments within the light fixtures, for hollowed-out chair legs, for secret pockets in the upholstery of the couch, for envelopes taped to the underside of the table, for plastic bags in the toilet tank. They found nothing.

The last place they thought to look was behind the guarda-roupa. They found nothing there, either, and were just pushing it back against the wall when they heard the front door open. Both elders froze. They heard the door close and then the heavy breathing of a man who had recently been exerting himself. Footsteps crossed the living room and paused momentarily. The missionaries looked at each other. Elder Toronto gestured at the window in the back wall of the bedroom, but before the elders could move, the footsteps resumed and an enormous shape filled the frame of the open bedroom door.

"What do you think you're doing?" said the man in the doorway. He was still breathing heavily and his skin shone with sweat. He wore boots, jeans, and a tank top, which revealed shoulders and arms so massive that any other type of shirt would have trouble containing them. His hair was dark, oiled, and parted in the middle, and his face was clean-shaven; if he were to grow a handlebar moustache, however, he would look exactly like the strongman in a circus poster.

At the moment, his teeth were bared, not in a toothy smile, but in a threatening sneer. "I said, what do you think you're doing?"

Back home, when he was a teenager, Elder Schwartz often attended the youth firesides that his stake put on every month. These firesides tended to focus less on church doctrine and more on sensationalist accounts of daring survival. Speakers included a woman whose head had been run over by a car when she was a toddler, a man who had been kidnapped and briefly imprisoned in a sweltering chicken coop during high school, and a couple who had spent three days lost at sea on a tiny sailboat.

One speaker who made a big impression on the then-fourteen-year-old Mike Schwartz was a man who had been attacked by a grizzly bear while trail running alone in Grand Teton National Park. The man had survived—obviously—and relatively unscathed at that. No lasting injuries except for an assortment of pink, shiny scars across his body and neck. He would have lost an eye, though, he told the rapt audience of teenagers, if it hadn't been for the high-quality sunglasses he had been wearing. He held up the glasses in question and the audience oohed. A claw-shaped protrusion curved inward from the still-intact right lens.

But what made the greatest impression on young Mike Schwartz was the man's account of first running into the bear. He said the massive animal, standing right in the middle of the trail, looked up at him, clearly startled. He looked the bear in the eye—a mistake—and knew it would attack. He said he watched the bear charging forward, watched its muscles moving beneath its fur, and even before it touched him, the man could sense the bear's power to, if it so chose, tear his body apart.

Looking at the giant man in the doorway, Elder Schwartz felt the same potential for violence. He imagined the man bounding across the room, picking him up, tearing off a limb, gouging out an eye, crushing his throat. The dangers of their investigation had just become very real again. The man took a step into the room and Elder Schwartz cringed.

Elder Toronto didn't budge.

"You must be Grillo," said Elder Toronto as the man walked forward.

The man paused a couple of feet from the missionaries.

"From next door," said Elder Toronto.

The man raised an eyebrow.

"That's right," he said, an odd smile emerging on his face. "That's right. I'm Grillo."

Elder Toronto stepped forward.

"I'm Elder Toronto," he said, extending his hand.

Still smiling, the man swatted Elder Toronto's hand aside, the force of it nearly knocking the lanky missionary to the ground. The man pointed to the guarda-roupa.

"What were you looking for in there?" he said.

"Oh, we weren't," said Elder Toronto, his tone cheery and vapid. "We just haven't seen Marco Aurélio at church lately, so we thought we'd swing by to see if he was home. The door was open, so we figured he'd be here, but I guess—"

Ignoring Elder Toronto, the man picked up the entire guarda-roupa with his giant arms, raised it above his head, and threw it to the cement floor, where it splintered into dozens of pieces. Elder Schwartz recoiled in fright. The man crouched down and began sifting through the splintered wood. If the man hadn't been blocking the path to the bedroom door, Elder Schwartz would have sprinted right out of the house.

"What are you looking for, if you don't mind my asking?" said Elder Toronto.

Still ignoring Elder Toronto, the man stood up and crossed the room, where he threw the mattress off the bed, picked up the frame and smashed it against the cinderblock wall. Once again, he crouched down, sifting through the pieces.

"Excuse me," said Elder Toronto. "What are you looking for?

The man turned his attention to the mattress, ignoring Elder Toronto as he tore it apart with his bare hands, throwing coils of wire and chunks of foam to the ground behind him. When he had finished with the mattress, he walked into the living room and began tearing apart the sofa. Elder Toronto followed, with Elder Schwartz several steps behind.

"If you tell us what you're looking for," said Elder Toronto, "maybe we can help."

The man paused. He stood up and turned around, towering over Elder Toronto.

"You're a pretty nervy kid, you know that?" he said, his massive arms beaded with sweat.

"We'd just like to help if we can," said Elder Toronto.

"I know who you are, buddy," said the man, tapping the name tag on Elder Toronto's chest, nearly knocking him over. "You want to tell me where Marquinho is?"

"Who?" said Elder Toronto.

"My brother," said the man. "Marquinho. Marco Aurélio."

"We were actually hoping you might know," said Elder Toronto.

The man put his hand on Elder Toronto's shoulder and began to squeeze.

"You know," said the man. "I hear a lot of rumors about your church. Most of them pretty bad. Now, I'm not the kind of guy who believes everything he hears, so when someone like Marquinho decides he wants to be baptized, I figure I should give your church the benefit of the doubt. Maybe it's not so bad, maybe it could even help out a guy like Marquinho. I'll reserve my judgment. And then what happens? Marquinho disappears. Gone. Gone, gone, gone. And now I find the lock on his front door broken and the two of you snooping around in his things. Now, if you've taken him off to live in some kind of commune or something, I guess that's his choice, but don't you think his brother has a right to know where he is?"

He removed his hand from Elder Toronto's shoulder and folded his enormous arms.

"Grillo, I'm sorry," said Elder Toronto, rubbing his shoulder. "We don't know where he is either."

Grillo stared down at him. A breeze from the window picked up a piece of stuffing from the demolished couch and blew it across the cement floor. Nobody moved.

"Now," said Grillo, breaking the silence, "I'd like you to both turn out your pockets."

As the man checked his pockets, Elder Toronto asked if Marco Aurélio had been acting strange at all lately.

"Do you know how much time I spend with my brother?" said the man, pulling the black notebook from Elder Toronto's pocket and then putting it back.

"I don't know," said Elder Toronto.

"I see Marquinho once a month," said the man, moving on to Elder Toronto's bag, checking its various compartments, "when he brings over his rent money, or, more likely, his excuse for why he can't pay. And you want to know something? That's the closest we've ever been. He left home when he was seventeen. I would have been about eleven at the time. He never wrote while he was gone, never called, never let anyone know where he was. Then, a few years back, he showed up here in Vila Barbosa looking for a place to stay, with no explanation of where he had been for the past twenty-five-odd years. That's just about everything I know about Marquinho, buddy. But you know what? He's still my brother and I still want to know where he is."

Not finding anything of interest in Elder Toronto's bag, he moved on to Elder Schwartz's.

"Maybe we could go talk to Lucinda, and see if she remembers anything you don't," said Elder Toronto.

"Lucinda?" said the man, rummaging through the meager contents of Elder Schwartz's bag. "I don't think she could tell you anything more than I just did. Anyway, she's sleeping right now. I wouldn't want to disturb her."

"Do you think your parents might have any idea where Marco Aurélio could be?"

"They're dead," he said, pulling a copy of the Book of Mormon from Elder Schwartz's bag and flipping through the pages.

"Oh," said Elder Toronto. "I'm sorry."

"A bus accident about ten years ago. Marquinho was long gone by that point. Obviously, he didn't make it to the funeral. Didn't even find out about it until he moved back here."

"I see," said Elder Toronto.

The man zipped up Elder Schwartz's bag and handed it back to him.

"All right," said the man. "Time to go."

Elder Toronto said, "Actually, I was thinking maybe we could—"

"Nope," said the man, and herded them toward the front door, a moving wall of muscle.

"Just one more question, then," said Elder Toronto as the man bounced them out the doorway.

He fished the black notebook from his pocket and pulled out the folded photograph.

"Do you know who the man with your brother is?" asked Elder Toronto.

"Nope," said the man, without looking at the picture.

"Well, thanks anyway," said Elder Toronto, putting the photograph and the notebook back in his pocket. "And thanks again for talking with us. We'll let you know if we find out anything new."

The man stepped forward, his giant body filling the door frame.

"Maybe we'll stop by tomorrow," said Elder Toronto.

The man nodded his massive head. "Oh, I'll be seeing you soon, buddy," he said, smiling.

"Okay," said Elder Toronto, as Elder Schwartz pulled him by the elbow, eager to leave.

When the missionaries looked back at Marco Aurélio's house from half a block away, they could still see the man standing in the doorway watching them go.

CHAPTER 12

By nine o'clock that evening, much to Elder Toronto's chagrin, they had learned nothing new. No one else on Marco Aurélio's street, or any nearby street, knew a thing about him. As a last-ditch effort, the two missionaries headed over to Abelardo and Beatrice's house.

"Remember on Sunday," said Elder Toronto, by way of explanation, "Beatrice said that Marco Aurélio had been coming over to their house every night to talk to Abelardo. Those two have nothing in common—I think we need to find out what they talked about."

When they got to their house—a narrow little shoebox of brick sandwiched between two slightly larger houses—darkness had fallen. Elder Toronto clapped at the gate. Nobody came to the door. The two missionaries waited. They clapped again. Nothing. Peering through the gate, the elders could see that the house was dark.

Elder Toronto ran a hand over his oily face.

"This whole day's been a waste," he said.

Elder Schwartz said that he thought walking away unscathed from their encounter with Grillo had been success enough.

"Well, I'm glad you can be so glib about it," said Elder Toronto. "A friend of ours is in serious trouble, and you're just glad we didn't get roughed up a little."

"I think he could have done more than just rough us up a little," said Elder Schwartz. The interaction had left him shaken.

Elder Toronto turned and clapped again in case Abelardo and Beatrice were sleeping inside.

Just then, Leila, the woman who lived in the house on the left, stuck her head out the front window. The elders had met her before, had even taught her a few of the missionary lessons before she decided she wasn't interested in their church.

"Evening, elders," said Leila.

"Evening, Leila," said Elder Toronto. "Have you seen Abelardo or Beatrice today?"

"You just missed them," said Leila. "They left about half an hour ago to visit Beatrice's sister."

"Which one?" said Elder Toronto.

"The one in Parque Laranjeira. The one that Abelardo doesn't like. The other sister is on vacation."

"I see," said Elder Toronto. "So they won't be back for a while?"

Leila shook her head.

"Not until tomorrow."

"Tomorrow?" said Elder Toronto.

"That's right," said Leila. "Is something wrong, elders?"

"No," said Elder Toronto. "Did you actually see them leave?"

"Sure," said Leila. "Beatrice knocked on my door as they were leaving and asked me to listen for robbers, just like she does every time they go out together. Not that they have much worth stealing."

"I see," said Elder Toronto.

"Do you want me to tell them you came by?"

"No, thank you. We'll just stop by again tomorrow."

Leila wished the elders a good evening and withdrew back inside her window.

"Okay," said Elder Toronto. "I think I know where her sister lives. We should get moving."

"But we wouldn't make it there until after ten."

"So?" said Elder Toronto.

"So, they both know we're not supposed to be out that late," said Elder Schwartz. "And you know Abelardo—he's a stickler for the rules. He would definitely call President Madvig if he caught us out past curfew."

Elder Toronto frowned.

"That's true," he said. "Unless we come up with a good cover story. Which we can do."

He started walking in the direction of the nearest bus stop.

"Let's go," he said over his shoulder to Elder Schwartz.

"No," said Elder Schwartz, who hadn't moved.

In a show of defiance, he sat down on the sidewalk in front of Beatrice and Abelardo's house.

"Seriously?" said Elder Toronto, stopping.

"We're done for the day," said Elder Schwartz. "We need to go home."

"Come on," said Elder Toronto with a jerk of his head. "We need to talk to Abelardo."

"No," said Elder Schwartz.

He picked up a pebble and threw it into the street, watching it kick up a tiny cloud of dust where it landed. He glanced, from the corner of his eye, at the other missionary. With a forced breeziness, Elder Toronto ambled up the sidewalk to his seated companion.

"Hey, man, what's the deal?" said Elder Toronto, crouching down next to Elder Schwartz.

"I'm done for the day," he said.

"You've been a real trooper today," said Elder Toronto. "But I need—"

"Don't talk to me like I'm a three-year-old."

"Okay," said Elder Toronto, "but we've just got to do one more thing today. It won't be dangerous. We just need to go talk to Abelardo."

The evening light cast a rusty glow over the street.

"It'll be easy," said Elder Toronto. "We talk to Abelardo all the time. What do you say?" He elbowed Elder Schwartz conspiratorially.

"Don't touch me," said Elder Schwartz.

Elder Toronto rose from his crouch and leaned against the dirty metal bars of Abelardo's front gate. He rubbed at his eyes.

"See," said Elder Schwartz, craning his head around, "you're exhausted. You need to go home and sleep."

Elder Toronto stifled a yawn.

"Why can't I just figure this out?" he said softly.

"We should head home," said Elder Schwartz.

"No," said Elder Toronto, pushing away from the gate. "We've accomplished nothing today. We can't just go home."

"Maybe we'll have better luck tomorrow."

"We don't have that kind of time. Plus, nothing's going to change between tonight and tomorrow," said Elder Toronto. "What do you think will be different?"

"I don't know," said Elder Schwartz. He stood up. "For one thing, you've been awake for nearly forty hours. You'll think better if you get some sleep. We both need sleep."

In an almost unheard-of development, Elder Toronto conceded the point by not responding.

"You just need some sleep," repeated Elder Schwartz, taking advantage of his rhetorical momentum.

"Maybe so," said Elder Toronto.

He squinted into the setting sun.

"There's one more place we need to go," he said.

"No," said Elder Schwartz. "I'm done for the day."

"It's on the way home."

"No."

"It'll be quick."

"Where?" said Elder Schwartz.

"The lanchonete," said Elder Toronto. "I want to talk to the owner again."

"No," said Elder Schwartz.

"Come on," said Elder Toronto. "It'll take five minutes. Please? As a favor to me?"

Elder Schwartz looked at their two shadows stretched out on the sidewalk, a doubling of their face-off.

"Fine," he said. "But we go straight home afterwards, no matter what we find out."

"Absolutely," said Elder Toronto.

"Do you promise?" said Elder Schwartz.

"I promise," said Elder Toronto.

Whether or not his companion's promise was sincere, Elder Schwartz knew how to get back to their apartment from the lanchonete.

"All right," said Elder Schwartz, and they started walking.

When they got there, though, the lanchonete's rolling metal gate had already been pulled shut over the entrance.

"It's closed," said Elder Schwartz.

"Clearly," said Elder Toronto. He hitched up his pants and yawned, his exhaustion no longer concealable. "Well." He yawned again. "I'm out of ideas for now." He rubbed his eyes. "Maybe I just need some rest."

And with that, to Elder Schwartz's pleasant surprise, they walked home to their apartment.

"I'm going straight to bed," he said as Elder Toronto unlocked their front gate.

The two missionaries walked down the tiled staircase, Elder Schwartz already loosening his tie and undoing the top button of his shirt. Elder Toronto unlocked the door of their dark downstairs apartment and they stepped inside.

"Don't turn on the light," said a voice from the darkness. "I have a gun. I want you to close the door behind you, and then lie on the ground, face-down, with your hands behind your heads. If you do what I say, you won't get hurt."

"Okay," said Elder Toronto, and the two missionaries lay down on the ground.

CHAPTER 13

The owner of the voice turned on the light and Elder Schwartz twisted his head to look up. The owner of the lanchonete stood over him aiming a Beretta 92 at his head. She wore a crisp, gray skirt and a sleeveless, black blouse. She had a large, red handbag slung over her shoulder.

"Keep your face down," she said when she saw him looking up at her. She leaned over and pressed the barrel of the gun against his skull. Elder Schwartz lost control of his bladder. The woman crouched down, gun still pressed to the trembling missionary's head, and frisked him. She found, apparently, nothing of interest, and moved her attentions, and her gun, to Elder Toronto. She reached into his pocket and removed Galvão's black notebook. She opened the book with her free hand, pausing to read the small, neat handwriting at the front of the book. She flipped to the back and pulled the photograph from its paper compartment with her thumb. She set the notebook on Elder Toronto's back and unfolded the photograph. She looked at it, and then slipped it back into its paper compartment.

"All right," said the owner of the lanchonete. "I want you boys to sit up. Slowly."

The two elders maneuvered their bodies into a sitting position. In an attempt to hide the dark stain at the front of his pants, Elder Schwartz pulled his knees up to his chest. A puddle remained on the floor where he had been lying, and the sharp smell of urine began to fill the room.

"Where did you get this notebook?" said the woman.

"I bought it from a stationery store," said Elder Toronto. "It's just something I keep track of addresses in."

"No," said the woman, stepping forward and leveling the gun at Elder Toronto's head. "It belonged to the man in the brown suit. Tell me how you got it."

"Who are you?" said Elder Toronto.

"You're really not in a position to ask questions," said the woman, smoothing her skirt with her free hand. She spoke in the same measured, professional tone that she had used in the lanchonete and, overall, seemed very comfortable holding a gun.

"Please," said Elder Schwartz, breaking into the conversation, "don't shoot us."

"What did he say?" said the woman to Elder Toronto.

"He asked you not to shoot us," said Elder Toronto, sounding almost bored.

"Then tell me where you got the notebook," she said.

"How do I know you won't just shoot us once we've told you what you want to know?" said Elder Toronto.

"That's not how I do business," said the woman. "But if you don't tell me, I will shoot you both. I can promise you that."

A whimper interrupted the conversation. Elder Schwartz had started crying and was attempting, unsuccessfully, to keep his sobs inaudible. When he saw the other two looking at him, he turned away, wiping at his tear-stained face. The woman took a step back, gun still aimed at Elder Toronto's head.

Elder Toronto said, "He's had a long day."

The woman looked back at Elder Toronto.

"I'm not sure why both of you aren't crying," she said. "Who, exactly, do you think you are?"

"I'd say I'm someone who wants to help Marco Aurélio," said Elder Toronto. "I'd also say that I'm someone who doesn't respond well to threats."

The woman rolled her eyes. She looked down at the puddle of urine and then at Elder Schwartz. She nodded at the gun and said, "If I put this down for a minute, can we talk like civilized people?"

Elder Toronto said that it seemed a little late for polite conversation. She shrugged.

"A woman has to take precautions," she said. "I'm not going to apologize for that."

"You can put the gun away if you want to," said Elder Toronto.

"I don't want to unless I have your word as missionaries that you're not going to try anything funny."

Elder Toronto looked at Elder Schwartz, who nodded.

"As long as things stay civilized, we're not going to cause you any trouble," said Elder Toronto.

"Good," said the woman.

She pulled the chair out from Elder Schwartz's desk and sat down in it. She set the Beretta on the desktop and rested her hand within grabbing distance of it.

"I'm not your enemy," said the owner of the lanchonete.

"Okay," said Elder Toronto. He scooted back and leaned against the wall. "Who are you then?"

"That's not important," said the woman, "I just want to know how you got that notebook."

Elder Toronto stretched out his legs.

"Why should we tell you anything?" he said.

"Because we both want to help Marco Aurélio," she said. "And because I still have a gun."

"How did you find our house?" said Elder Toronto.

"Don't change the subject," she said.

"I'm not," he said. "I'd really like to know."

"How did you get this notebook?"

"How did you find our house?"

"I'm the one asking questions," said the woman.

Elder Toronto shrugged and looked away. The woman smiled.

"You want to know how I found your house?" she said. "I asked, 'Where do the two American kids who dress like bus drivers live?' and everyone pointed me here."

Elder Toronto looked back at her.

"If you think you're well-hidden here, or safe from whoever Aurélio's mixed up with, you're wrong," she said. "You're a couple of sitting ducks."

Elder Toronto didn't respond. Instead, he picked at a loose thread in his tie, his face like a sulking turtle's. Elder Schwartz sniffled quietly.

"Listen," said the woman. "I'm not the bad guy in this situation. I want to help Aurélio, if I can. I just need to know what you two know."

Elder Toronto pulled the thread in his tie between his fingers until it snapped.

"What's your name?" he said, looking back up at her.

"Sílvia," she said.

"Is that true?" he said.

"Yes," she said.

"How do you know Marco Aurélio?" he said.

"I'll tell you that once you tell me what I want to know."

"Do you promise?"

"I promise," she said.

Elder Toronto looked at Elder Schwartz, who had managed to stop crying.

"You can tell her if you want," he said, wiping his nose with his handkerchief.

"Okay," said Elder Toronto, after a considered pause. "Here's what we know."

He told her about Elder Schwartz's sighting of Marco Aurélio at the street market, about Ulisses Galvão's visit to the church meeting, about their discovery of Galvão's murdered body, and their subsequent encounter with the police. He told her about what he had deciphered from the notebook, about their visit with Grillo and what they learned there.

"And that's about it," he said.

Sílvia said nothing.

"So?" said Elder Toronto.

"You're sure Galvão was dead?" she said.

"His face was smashed in," said Elder Toronto.

Sílvia nodded.

"Now, we need to figure out how to get to Marco Aurélio before he gets killed," said Elder Toronto. "Can you help us with that?"

"No," said Sílvia. "If what you say is true, then Aurélio is already dead."

Elder Toronto shook his head.

"I disagree," he said. "I can't get into all the reasons now, but I think there's still time to find him."

"It would be nice to think that was true," she said.

"No," he said. "He's still alive."

"Maybe," she said.

Sílvia crossed her legs. For a minute, nobody spoke. The smell of urine permeated the room.

"I told you what we know," said Elder Toronto. "It's your turn to tell us how you know Marco Aurélio."

She fingered the gun as she seemed to contemplate where to begin.

"We were married for a while," she said "when we were younger. Before either of us lived here. When he came into my lanchonete with you two, it was the first time I'd seen him since we'd split up."

CHAPTER 14

Her fascination with criminals began, she told the missionaries, long before she met Marco Aurélio. If any single event could be pinpointed as the catalyst for this fascination, it would be when her grandmother suffered a debilitating stroke on Sílvia's eighth birthday. Her grandmother wasn't present at the party, having phoned earlier to explain that she had a terrible migraine, that it would be better if she just stayed home. The headache, as it later came out, had actually been a symptom of her stroke, and as Sílvia was blowing out the candles on her multitiered, fondant-wrapped cake, her father received a phone call that his mother had been hospitalized. Apologizing profusely to the guests at Sílvia's party, he bustled his wife and daughter down to their armored town car and set out for the hospital.

The stroke left her grandmother unable to live alone, and so it was decided that she would move in with Sílvia and her parents in their two-story penthouse at the top of the city's most exclusive high rise, an arrangement that would have previously been unthinkable. Since being widowed in her early fifties, Grandma Eva had remained single, living alone and gaining a reputation throughout her social circle as a force to be reckoned with. She had served on the committees of countless charities, museums, and political causes. She had held a spot on the city council for twelve years running, and there had even been talk of a bid for the mayor's office.

Now, her own body had betrayed her. Where a kind of idealistic restlessness had defined her personality in the past, she was now—post-stroke—contentment personified, apparently happy with a life spent sitting in her son's second living room, and beaming indiscriminately at whoever happened to enter the room. Both the house staff and Sílvia's parents found this beatific grin so disconcerting that they took to stationing the old woman in front of the TV where she could direct her smiles to the people on the screen. And so she passed her days sitting in an overstuffed armchair watching telenovelas and true-crime programs.

For the most part, Sílvia avoided her grandmother. They had never been close, and the added dimension of the old woman's illness only rendered her more alien in Sílvia's eyes. One day, however, while sitting in her bedroom playing with her toy horses, Sílvia told her nanny Lilian—a stocky, longsuffering woman who had cared for Sílvia since she was a baby—that she had to go to the bathroom, that she'd be right back. But instead of going to the bathroom, she crept, on a whim, upstairs to the second living room where her grandmother sat beaming in front of the TV. Her grandmother turned and smiled at her. Sílvia smiled back, cautiously, and then sat down cross-legged on the porcelain tile floor next to her grandmother's chair.

To say that Sílvia had led an insular existence to this point in her life would be an understatement. She spent much of her time playing alone, supervised by Lilian, in one of the many rooms available to her in the apartment. When she grew tired of the solitude, she enlisted Lilian as a playmate or a punching bag. Occasionally, children from the lower floors of the building were invited over to amuse her. If these other children balked at any of Sílvia's demands, they were sent away.

When Sílvia went outside, it was to a gated park about half a block away, where she and a handful of playmates—the children of other penthouse dwellers from around the city—interacted under the careful supervision of a cadre of brawny bodyguards, many of whom had been hired away from stellar careers in military and law enforcement.

Her TV watching was similarly restricted to a narrow list of cartoons and children's programs. Lilian diligently monitored Sílvia's viewing habits, ensuring that she didn't stray from the programs on the list, and so, sitting here on the floor next to her grandmother, what she saw on the TV came as a revelation. The images on the screen alternated between a man in a studio yelling out the details of the city's most shocking crimes of the day, and footage of the crime scenes themselves, frantically narrated by the same man.

". . . TWO WOMEN BRUTALLY MURDERED AND A THIRD CRITICALLY WOUNDED IN A NAIL SALON IN ARAMBÚ," blared the man in the studio. The show cut to footage of the salon where the two dead women on the floor were being examined by men in uniform. There was blood everywhere. One of the men in uniform waved his hand at the camera, and when it didn't move, stood, and pushed the cameraman out of the salon.

". . . THE GUNMAN, APPARENTLY A FORMER BOYFRIEND OF ONE OF THE DEAD WOMEN, ENTERED THE SALON, GUN DRAWN, TO CONFRONT HER REGARDING HER NEW LOVER. THE WOMAN REFUSED TO LOOK AT THE GUNMAN AND HE OPENED FIRE, SHOOTING WILLY-NILLY UNTIL HIS GUN WAS EMPTY . . ."

Outside the salon, two police officers loaded a man, presumably the gunman, into the back of a squad car. He was a paunchy, middle-aged man dressed in shorts and a soccer jersey. The surrounding street was like nothing Sílvia had ever seen— dusty brick houses piled one on top of the other; cracked, potholed asphalt; dirty, sullen-looking children lurking at the edges of the police tape. The cameraman moved in close to the squad car, and the gunman looked out the window, directly at the camera.

". . . FIRED TEN SHOTS INTO THE BODY OF HIS EX-GIRLFRIEND, YELLING ALL THE WHILE . . ."

The man in the car didn't turn away from the gaze of the camera.

"Why did he do that?" said Sílvia.

Grandma Eva beamed down at her.

"He's a criminal," she said, "and criminals commit crimes."

Sílvia nodded and turned her attention back to the TV. The program transitioned from there to a rape/murder committed in

Parque das Palmas, another of the city's neighborhoods, then to a bank robbery gone wrong in the city's financial district, then to a car bombing in Vila Barbosa.

"Come here," said Grandma Eva when the program cut to a commercial break. She pointed to a spot on the floor just in front of her armchair.

Sílvia obliged, and stood in front of her grandmother. The old woman smiled invitingly.

"Here," said Grandma Eva, beckoning.

Sílvia took a step closer. Leaning forward, Grandma Eva reached out and held Sílvia's face in her papery hands. She drew her granddaughter closer. Her watery eyes stared into Sílvia's. Her perpetual smile disappeared. Dismay registered on her face. Sílvia would have stepped back if her head wasn't in her grandmother's grasp.

Still holding her granddaughter's face, Grandma Eva said, "Would you like to know something?"

Nervous but intrigued, Sílvia nodded.

"Those people on TV," said Grandma Eva in her wavering voice, "you're no better than they are. Let me be clear—I'm not telling you, Sílvia, that everyone in the world is good on the inside or that everyone is a little bit guilty. No. That's not what I mean. Some of us, such as myself, your father, your mother, are decent people. Good people. On the inside. These people on the TV? They're criminals. And I look at you—I truly look at you—and I can see that you're no better than they are. In your heart, is what I mean. You have a criminal heart, Sílvia."

Grandma Eva removed her hands from her granddaughter's face, eyes narrowed. Sílvia, unsure how to respond, nodded and sat back down. The TV program resumed, and with it, Grandma Eva's smile. After a minute, Sílvia heard footsteps coming up the stairs and spun around. Lilian emerged into the second living room and saw what was on the TV.

"This is not for young ladies," she said, leading Sílvia out of the room by the arm. "You're not to watch those programs."

In spite of her nanny's prohibitions, Sílvia slipped into the living room at every opportunity to watch the crime show with her grandmother. It wasn't that she enjoyed watching it, at least not in the same way she might enjoy eating a Popsicle or spending a day at the beach. In fact, the show usually left Sílvia's head slightly dizzy, her palms sweaty. Still, she felt compelled to watch, compelled to confront the expanded view of reality that she had encountered. She thought often about what her grandmother had told her, and was convinced that if she kept watching the crime TV shows, her grandmother's statement might someday make sense to her.

Lilian became increasingly exasperated with Sílvia's disobedience, never letting her young charge out of her sight. Somehow, Sílvia still found ways to catch fleeting segments of the program. Finally, at Lilian's request, both the grandmother and the television were permanently relocated to a previously unused room with a locking door, effectively barring Sílvia from the crime program. Her grandmother spent her days stationed alone in that room for another year, until her health deteriorated further and she passed away. The TV was given away to charity.

Sílvia's interest in crime, however, only increased. She took to waking up early in the morning before anyone else was out of bed, and bringing in the newspaper from the front doormat. She sat at the long, granite dining table skimming the thin, gray pages of the paper for its reports on crime in the city—a shootout with police in the Praça do Imperador, a series of carjackings in Aranté, a murder/ suicide in Vila Barbosa. She read the articles carefully, committing to memory which neighborhood the crime took place in, what methods were employed in its committing, what suspects were being questioned, which detectives were assigned to the case. Then when she was done reading, she carefully refolded the newspaper, returned it to the front mat, and went back to bed. Reading about these crimes in the newspaper left her feeling nervous and slightly ill. But the thought of not knowing about these things, of not trying to understand them, left her feeling even more uneasy. At the heart of her studies lay the initial question she had asked of the crime show—who were these people who committed these crimes? The question continued to trouble her, her grandmother's pronouncement gaining greater purchase in her young psyche.

Around this time, a wave of kidnappings hit her parents' social circle, and Sílvia no longer had to be so surreptitious in seeking out accounts of local crime. The kidnappings were all anybody ever talked about, and Sílvia followed the developments in each case with the same passion, the same attention to detail, with which the boys her age followed the exploits of their favorite soccer teams. She listened in whenever her parents discussed the most recent kidnapping, taking careful note of the details. For each case, she knew how much ransom money the kidnappers demanded. She knew which officer from the anti-kidnapping squad was taking point on the case. She knew the exact time the kidnapping took place. She knew when the kidnappers used heavy weaponry to penetrate the victim's armored car, or when they snatched the victim in one of the rare moments when he or she was not in a car, a helicopter, or a highly secure building. She knew how the kidnappers had shown the family they meant business—a severed finger, or, more probably, a severed ear. Back in the privacy of her own room, Sílvia pored over the details she had recorded. Noting the similarities and differences among the various cases, Sílvia speculated with reasonable confidence as to which kidnappings were carried out by the same gang, which families were likely to pay the ransom, which victims were likely to emerge relatively unscathed from the ordeal. Of course, she worried over the fates of those who had been kidnapped—feared being kidnapped herself, even—but what interested her more were the kidnappers themselves. She wondered with that familiar sweaty, dizzy feeling who these people were.

Then at dinner one evening, Sílvia's father, who rarely spoke at meals, said he had something important to discuss with them. Sílvia and her mother both lay down their silverware and gave him their full attention. Clearing his throat, he pulled a folded paper from the pocket of his suit jacket:

"As you are probably aware," he began, "kidnapping is becoming a greater and greater concern for the wealthy residents of our city. Up until this morning, my feelings were that we ought to stick things out, count on the police to take care of the problem, and not let those bandits scare us into leaving our home. But this morning, my longtime friend and business partner, António Lamy, was killed while trying to evade a gang of kidnappers on his way to work. For me, this death represents a tipping point—the city is no longer safe, and I have decided to move our family to a small town several hundred miles to the south of here called Santa Branca. This town is very small, very safe, and populated mainly by wealthy refugees from the city such as ourselves. Crime in Santa Branca is practically nonexistent. Our new home will be near the beach, and it's my opinion that we'll all like living there very much.

"I don't want to risk any more time than we have to here in the city, and so after dinner, I would like the two of you to pack your most important things and be ready to go. I've ordered a helicopter to pick us up; we can have the rest of our things sent down to us later."

He thanked them for their attention and returned the paper to his jacket pocket. After dinner, they each packed a suitcase and took the stairs up to the roof where a helicopter waited to take them away from the city and all of its crime.

• • •

It was in Santa Branca several years later—at a fundraiser for the incumbent mayor's reelection campaign—where she first met Marco Aurélio. The event was held at the Santa Branca Ballroom, an art deco-inspired historic space where all the town's most magnificent parties took place. The night of the fundraiser, the room bustled with women in flowing evening gowns and men in black-tie formalwear. On the ballroom's stage, a swing band played decades-old samba hits while a handful of couples danced with elegant abandon. The rest of the crowd mostly ignored the music, talking over the sound of it, applauding distractedly at the end of each number.

Sílvia normally didn't attend these black-tie events that her parents thrived on, but when her mother asked her to come, Sílvia couldn't summon even a flimsy excuse not to. She was home from university on summer break and, three days in, already wishing she was back at school. Having just changed her major for the third time in as many years—this time from pre-law to forensic archaeology— she was eager to dive into the new courses she would be taking.

Here she was instead, though, mingling with high school acquaintances and friends of her parents, answering the same set of questions again and again. No, she didn't have a boyfriend. Yes, she had changed majors several times. Yes, she had considered becoming a lawyer. No, she really didn't have a boyfriend right now.

After a long, circuitous conversation with a doggedly persistent friend of her mother's, Sílvia grabbed the elbow of a young man she vaguely recognized as having been in her year in school.

"Hey, grab me another drink, will you?" she said.

With an obliging smile, he took her empty champagne flute and told her he'd be right back. As soon as he walked away, Sílvia realized she had actually never seen the young man before in her life. When he returned, glass in hand, she apologized and said that normally she wasn't that forward, that she had thought they had gone to school together.

"I've just got one of those faces," he said.

Sílvia nodded, but as she looked at him, she still couldn't shake that deep feeling of familiarity. It wasn't that he resembled any one boy she had gone to school with. Rather, he resembled them categorically; he seemed, implicitly, to belong to their exclusive caste. He was dressed the part—tuxedo exquisitely tailored; the quality of his various accessories—watch, shoes, cufflinks—even greater than that of his suit; hair expertly cut, and equally carefully tousled to convey that certain boyish nonchalance. His face, neither handsome nor ugly, held an expression of relaxed confidence that suggested a deeply ingrained and fully justified assumption that his wants and needs, whether physical, social, or emotional, would be met as soon as he felt them. In a way, he looked more like the young men that Sílvia had grown up with than the young men themselves.

Sílvia realized that she was staring and apologized again, introducing herself.

"Felipe," the young man replied by way of introduction, and then without any further pleasantries, spent nearly an hour regaling her with anecdotes reflecting his extravagant life as a wealthy young playboy whose chief skills lay in spending his father's money as irresponsibly as possible—exotic restaurants, rare luxury cars, expensive women. After a few more drinks, he told her he was in the area on business for his father, Cândido Costa, a powerful oil magnate—maybe she had heard of him?—who had received a tip about some nearby land that might prove profitable, oil-wise.

There was something not quite right about the way the young man spoke. He used the bored, affected tone of the young men Sílvia had grown up with, the fluid, lilting accent of the wealthy, but as he drank more champagne, something else leaked through in the way he spoke, something she couldn't put her finger on.

There was also the conspicuous display of shallowness that didn't quite ring true—most of her male contemporaries spent inordinate amounts of effort trying to convince people of their substance, that they were more than just flighty playboys skilled at spending their parents' money. They made a show of reading massive philosophical tomes, or enlisting in scientific expeditions to exotic locales around the globe, or punctuating accounts of their prodigal exploits with damp-eyed speeches about the deplorable plight of the poor in this country. But this young man seemed to revel in his shallowness.

"I'm sure I'm boring you," he said. "I shouldn't monopolize you like this."

"It's fine," said Sílvia. "I want to figure out what your game is."

"Excuse me?" he said.

"I don't think you are who you say you are."

He giggled at this, assuming a drunken expression of bafflement.

"I'm still not sure what you mean."

"First of all, you're not as drunk as you're pretending to be," she said, "and second of all, you're not a wealthy playboy."

He slapped her shoulder in amusement. He told her she was very funny. His words slurred together perfectly, a spot-on mimicry of wealthy drunkenness. It could be the real thing if it weren't for the over-perfectness of it.

"Who am I then?" he asked with a smirk.

"You tell me," she said.

This inspired another fit of laughter.

"Really," she said, "who are you?"

He looked around and then leaned in close to her, their cheeks brushing against each other.

"Do you want to get out of here?" he said.

"I want you to tell me who you are."

He took a step closer to her, their bodies touching.

"My father could buy and sell anyone in this room," he said. "Do you find that exciting?"

He kissed her cheek. She pushed him away.

"No," she said, "that's not going to work. The only thing I'm interested in is finding out who you really are."

Felipe frowned thoughtfully.

"I don't plan to leave this party alone tonight," he said. "I was hoping I might leave with you, but if that's not going to happen, I'd better be moving on."

"You haven't fooled me," she said.

He smiled in a way that could pass for genuine. "It was very nice to meet you."

He kissed her hand with a smirk and walked away. As soon as he had gone, Sílvia's mother sidled up next to her.

"So you've met Felipe," she said to her daughter. "What did you think?"

She watched him introduce himself to a cluster of women across the room. Observing him from a distance, he still gave her the distinct impression of someone playing a part—just a little too deliberate in his gestures, his body language, his dress.

"What do you know about him?" said Sílvia. "He strikes me as odd."

"I imagine he should," said Sílvia's mother. "Coming from that much money must have some effect on a boy."

Although the citizens of Santa Branca were, to a person, absurdly wealthy, Cândido Costa, the man Felipe claimed as his father, possessed such astronomical riches that he inhabited a rarified level all his own. Though not well known to the general populace, the Costa name was whispered among the nation's most affluent citizens with the kind of awe-filled reverence normally reserved for pagan deities. Felipe's presence in the town brought its residents that much closer to the man's greatness, and the vicarious proximity thrilled them.

Sílvia's mother's voice dropped to a whisper. She told Sílvia that this wasn't common knowledge, but Felipe's father was interested in some land in the area.

"You don't say," said Sílvia.

"Yes," said her mother, "but he told me I'm to keep it an absolute secret."

"I see."

Felipe looked in their direction and smiled boozily. Sílvia didn't smile back, and just a few minutes later watched him leave the party arm-in-arm with Sandy Nascimento, a young woman Sílvia's age whose primary goal in life was to land a husband even wealthier than her father.

"We should have Felipe over for dinner," said Sílvia. "I'd like to get to know him better."

This proved impossible. Over the following weeks, Sílvia watched Felipe become the darling of Santa Branca, his every minute booked with social engagements. His visit presented the transplanted urbanites with the rare opportunity of trying to impress someone much, much wealthier than themselves. The townspeople rose to the occasion with enthusiasm. The men took him shark fishing on their sonar-equipped boats; flew him over the region's rolling countryside in their private planes; served him the finest cuts from the finest Japanese cattle at their beachside barbecues. They told him that their homes were his homes, their cigars his cigars, their imported alcohol his imported alcohol. The women of Santa Branca matched their husbands' efforts with élan. They bombarded Felipe with invitations to brunches, lunches, teas, dinners, auctions, cotillions, fundraisers, cocktail parties. Any time he dined with their families, the women sent their cooks out with instructions to discover what he had been served the night before, and then to do whatever necessary to eclipse that meal.

Sílvia watched all of this with alternating feelings of amusement and disgust. She had never seen her parents and their friends—normally so careful not to seem impressed by anyone or anything—so starstruck. And what none of them seemed to notice was the thorough unremarkability of the young man they fawned over so gratuitously. After those initial few days spent dropping unsubtle hints regarding his ultra-wealthy father, Felipe had gradually clammed up and now rarely said a word. He had subtly transformed himself into a nondescript vessel for the loving attentions of the town.

During this time, for lack of anything better to do, Sílvia devoted herself to discovering Felipe's true identity. She became a fixture at the town library, digging through stacks of yellowing newspapers and skimming ghostly microfiche to cull every bit of information she could find concerning Felipe's supposed father. To her great chagrin, she could find nothing to either confirm or debunk any of the young man's claims. From what she could ascertain, Cândido Costa did indeed have a son named Felipe who would be about the age of this young man. The younger Costa was known for his womanizing and his profligate spending habits, for circling the globe in his leisurely, city-hopping escapades. In spite of his high profile—or more likely because of the silence his father's money could buy—few concrete news stories about the young man existed. He was mentioned only in passing in articles about his father, the reporters alluding to a reputation that readers were clearly assumed to already know. The only picture of Felipe Costa that she managed to unearth was five years old and taken from behind; the adolescent in the picture had the same hair color and the same general body type of the young man masquerading as Felipe. This imposter had clearly done his homework. If Sílvia had been hoping to find some damning tidbit that would contradict the counterfeit Felipe's story, she was foiled by the dearth of any kind of substantiating information about the young heir's life. This lack of evidence did not dissuade her, however, from her belief that their Felipe was a fraud. If she kept at it, she was bound to discover who this young man really was and what he wanted from the citizens of Santa Branca.

The answer to the latter question became clear soon enough. She came home from the library one evening to find her father in his office, huddled over a calculator and surrounded by stacks of financial statements. Sílvia leaned against the doorframe. He didn't seem to notice her there.

"What's going on?" said Sílvia.

Her father punched the keys of the calculator and wrote something down on one of his ledgers before looking up and replying.

"I'm figuring out how much money we could potentially afford to invest in a new enterprise," he said.

"What kind of enterprise?" said Sílvia.

Her father removed his half-moon reading glasses and gave her a pleased smile. He said that the night before, at a bull session with the men of the town, Felipe had let slip that if the land he was checking out for his father proved promising, there might be opportunities for investment. And if there were opportunities, he had told the other men, he wanted to let them in on the ground floor as an expression of gratitude for the hospitality they had shown him. Of course, he had made it clear that none of that information could leave the room.

"You're not seriously thinking of giving him money, are you?" said Sílvia.

Her father gave a short bark of incredulity.

"And why shouldn't I be?" he said. "Cândido Costa is the greatest business mind of our generation. It would be foolish not to."

Sílvia crossed the room and sat in the chair across the desk from her father.

"This guy isn't really Cândido Costa's son," she said.

"Of course he is," said her father.

"How do you know?" she said, leaning her elbows on the desk.

"I've looked into it," said her father.

"Really?" said Sílvia. "So you can prove that this guy is Felipe Costa?"

"Can you prove that he's not?" said her father. "And anyway, who else would he be?"

"He's a con man," said Sílvia.

"And you have concrete evidence to support this claim?"

"Not exactly," said Sílvia, "but—"

"Trust me," said her father. "I've looked into it. You can rest assured that this young man is exactly who he claims to be."

"I don't think so," said Sílvia.

"If I understand correctly, then," said her father, "you're saying that I should trust your hunch over the proof I've seen that this young man is Cândido Costa's son?"

"I'd like to see the proof you're talking about," said Sílvia.

Her father shook his head.

"I don't have time for this now," he said, replacing his half-moon glasses.

He stared at her with stern expectancy until she got up from the chair.

"Okay," said Sílvia, "good luck," and left her father with his calculator and his books.

Felipe's revelation had set off a town-wide evaluation of financial assets. The men pored over their books, talking with their wives to decide just how much they could afford to invest. They eagerly awaited any new word from Felipe, any further indication of what move his uncannily wealthy father might make next. There was constant dinner-table talk of what they could do with all of the new money they'd soon be making— vacation homes in Europe, newer and bigger yachts, daring plastic surgeries. Collective enthusiasm rose with each passing day.

The spell was soon broken, however, at a seaside cookout. While the women sat at picnic tables chatting, and the children played at the edge of the water, the men stood around the smoking grills, bantering cheerily as they supervised the cooking meat—the picanhas, the linguiças, the costelinhas. During a lull in the conversation, Felipe cleared his throat and said that he was afraid he had some disappointing news. He had just received a letter from his father—apparently, the geologists he had hired had concluded that the land in question, while promising at first glance, did not hold great potential for oil drilling. The whole venture was off. Felipe told the men that he appreciated all of their enthusiasm and support, that they would be remembered by him and by his father, and that he hoped sometime in the future he would find a way to show his gratitude for their kindness and hospitality. The men nodded gravely, a solemn air descending over the event. As the sun went down, the men, women, and children of Santa Branca ate their barbecued meat, their potato salad, and their rice with a funereal air, glancing sadly from time to time at Felipe. Sílvia, for her part, found the town's reaction baffling. She watched Felipe smiling bravely at the melancholy faces of the citizens of Santa Branca with that over-perfect earnestness of his, and wondered how no one else could see through him like she did.

The next morning, Sílvia was jogging along the same beach, the sun just coming up over the water, when she came across Felipe sitting in a squat folding chair, staring out to sea. She stopped running. It was her first chance to talk with Felipe one-on-one since their conversation at the fundraiser three weeks earlier.

"Hey," she said.

"Morning," he said, not looking up at her.

She stood there, sweating, until she caught her breath.

"You chickened out," she said.

He looked up at her.

"Excuse me?"

"It was a scam," she said, "the whole oil thing."

He frowned. She sat down in the sand next to his chair.

"I don't necessarily mind that it was," she said.

He scratched at the stubble on his face. A seagull landed a few feet away and began picking at the carcass of a dead crab.

"I'm not going to tell anyone," she said. "I'd just like to know who you really are."

"Listen," he said, "I'm very hung over and the things you're saying to me right now aren't making a whole lot of sense."

The seagull, apparently dissatisfied with the crab's remains, squawked indignantly and flew away.

"You're not hung over," said Sílvia.

Felipe said, "Believe me, I wish I wasn't."

Sílvia slipped off her shoes and dug her toes into the sand. The two of them watched the waves creeping closer and closer to where they sat. A little cluster of sandpipers scurried by, digging occasionally into the wet sand, careful to avoid the water as it rushed toward their twiggy feet. Out at sea, a yacht raised its flags.

"Well," she said finally, "I just wanted to let you know that I thought it was an impressive performance."

She stood up and brushed the sand off of her running shorts as he watched her with what could have been a look of genuine bafflement. She slung her shoes over her shoulder and told Felipe she'd see him around.

• • •

Three days later, she found the evidence she needed. Concealed from view behind a magazine rack in a roadside convenience store in Verópolis, a dumpy, mid-sized city about a hundred kilometers north of Santa Branca, she watched Felipe emerge from the restrooms and walk toward the front of the store. Felipe had left Santa Branca in the small hours of the morning, having been sent off by the town with a lavish party the night before. Unbeknownst to him, as he had set out on the highway heading north, a taxi—Sílvia tense and alert in the back seat—had followed his car from a distance. Before leaving, Sílvia had written a note to her parents explaining that she and Felipe had been seeing each other in secret—which wasn't true—and that she had decided to travel the country with him; she would check in when possible. Among the necessities of travel she had loaded into her backpack, Sílvia had included the Beretta 92 that her father always kept in his nightstand drawer. Her backpack in her lap, Sílvia had given the cabbie constant instructions in a low voice—as if her quarry might hear her from several cars ahead—until Felipe had finally pulled off the highway and parked his car in front of a rental agency and then crossed the street on foot to the convenience store. Sílvia had paid the cabbie, tipping him generously, before sending him on his way.

Now, from behind the magazine rack, Sílvia watched Felipe pick up a pack of gum, and approach the register, smiling.

"Good morning," he said, and handed the gum to the young woman behind the counter.

She rang it up, eyes still on her magazine, and he handed her a fifty. She looked up from the magazine.

"A fifty?" she said. "Really?"

Felipe gave her an apologetic smile.

"Sorry," he said, "it's the smallest bill I have."

As the young woman began counting out his change from the till, Felipe leaned against the register.

"Listen," he said, and she looked up at him while she counted out the bills, "this isn't a line, I'm genuinely trying to figure this out—I've seen you somewhere before, but I can't quite place where it was. Were you—" He prolonged the final vowel as if searching for a word, his face quizzical, his thumb pointing vaguely in the direction of what could have been anything from a childhood apartment building, a nearby grocery store, a dance club. From her vantage point behind the magazine rack, Sílvia watched on, fascinated. This flustered, bumbling persona was a far cry from the suave, indifferent Felipe of Santa Branca.

"On TV," said the cashier. "I was in some commercials."

"Yeah," said Felipe, flushing. "Of course. The TV. I mean, I thought it was the TV, I just couldn't remember the place you were advertising."

"Florentino Optical," she said.

"That's right. It wasn't that the commercial wasn't memorable or anything—" he said, and without breaking eye contact or pausing in his speech, he slipped the stack of bills she had counted out into his pocket "—it's just that it slipped my mind briefly, you know? You're an actress then?"

"I'm working on it," she said.

"I think you're very talented," he said.

She leaned back.

"Listen," she said. "I have a boyfriend. I'm flattered and everything, but—"

"No, no," said Felipe, flushing more deeply. "I'm really not trying to pick you up, it's just—"

"Don't worry about it," she said. "Like I said I'm flattered."

"But you look upset," said Felipe. "I've made you uncomfortable. I feel really bad about this. I really shouldn't have—"

"Really," she said. "Forget about it."

"No, no, I'm just so embarrassed. I don't usually—"

"Really," she said. "It's fine."

Felipe stuck his hands in his pockets.

"I feel very silly," he said.

She smiled politely.

"Really, I do. I don't normally do this kind of thing," he said. "I'm usually very considerate of boundaries and things like that."

"It's really okay."

"That's good of you to say but—oh."

He pulled some coins from his pocket and counted them out in his hand.

"Now I feel even sillier—I had exact change this whole time."

He handed the coins to the girl who dropped them in the open till.

"Once again, I apologize. I shouldn't have—"

As she began to close the till, he stopped her.

"My fifty?" he said.

"Right," she said, and handed him the bill. He kept talking as he slipped it into his pocket with the change she had given him earlier.

"And again, I'm sorry," he said. "You must get tired of dealing with blockheads like me all the time, trying to get your number—"

"It's fine," she said, trying to stop him.

"—and here I am, and you have a boyfriend, and I feel very silly, and I'm sorry."

"Really, it's fine," she said with an edge to her voice now.

"And now I'm over-apologizing. I'm sorry. Sorry," he said, red-faced, backing out of the store. When the door closed behind him, the young woman shook her head and went back to her magazine.

From the convenience store, Sílvia followed Felipe for several blocks. Along the way, he stepped into a padaria and emerged a few minutes later having abandoned his linen suit and tailored shirt in favor of heavy boots, thick cotton pants, and a worn work shirt. Sílvia almost didn't recognize him; he looked like a different person. He crossed the street to the Verópolis bus terminal where Sílvia watched him buy tickets at one of the booths and then disappear into one of the covered waiting areas.

After hanging back for a few minutes as a precaution, Sílvia approached the booth where Felipe had bought his tickets, and asked the clerk if her boyfriend had just bought one ticket or two.

"I don't know who your boyfriend is," said the clerk, a middle-aged woman who looked like she hadn't slept in days.

Sílvia described Felipe.

"And we've been fighting all morning," she said. "I found out he's been meeting his ex-girlfriend for lunch, and he doesn't see the problem with that. Obviously I do, and we're supposed to be at his sister's wedding tomorrow morning, and—"

"That's none of my business," said the clerk, "and I don't really care. He only bought one ticket. Would you like another one?"

Sílvia nodded and the clerk rang her up. She took her ticket and noted which bus she would be riding.

Staying out of Felipe's line of sight, Sílvia waited to board until the last call before departure. She found Felipe sitting near the back of the mostly empty travel bus, seat leaned back, eyes closed. She took the seat next to his. He didn't open his eyes. She remained silent for several minutes as the bus made its way across town and onto the freeway where it picked up speed and commenced on its journey up the country's coast.

"Wake up," she said after a while.

He opened his eyes. There was a half second of panicked disorientation before he assumed his bored playboy face and asked why she had followed him all the way up here—if she was looking for some sort of steamy fling, that moment had passed.

"I know what you are," she said.

"A tired person trying to sleep?" he said. "Yes, I am. And also confused as to what you're doing on this bus."

"I've been following you all morning," she said.

"That's very disturbing," he said, yawning.

"I saw you with that girl at the convenience store," she said.

"You can't win them all," he said, folding his arms and shifting away from Sílvia. He leaned against the window and closed his eyes.

"You did very well," she said. "When she realizes you walked off with nearly fifty reaís from her till, she might even think it was an honest mistake."

"I'm not sure what you mean," he said, not opening his eyes.

"Come on," she said.

His breathing slowed in a convincing imitation of sleep.

"You know, I could call the police," she said.

He didn't stir. For a brief moment she doubted herself—he was so convincing in his denials, and anyway, even if he wasn't who he claimed to be, why was she here on this bus, following him up the coast? But for reasons she couldn't articulate, she knew she couldn't leave this alone. She needed to find out who this young man was in the same way she had needed to catalog and dissect the details of each kidnapping case all those years ago, the same way she had needed to sit cross-legged on the floor next to her grandmother's chair watching shaky footage of violent crime scenes. She felt that familiar dizziness in her head, that sweating in her palms, and she doubled down in her interrogation of Felipe.

"I'm going to keep following you," she said. "I don't plan on leaving this alone."

She saw what could have been a shadow of a grimace on his face.

"I'm going to keep following you, and if you aren't more cooperative, next time you try to con some cashier out of a fifty, I might make sure she notices," said Sílvia.

He opened his eyes and sat up.

He looked around, and when he saw that no one else on the bus was paying attention, leaned in close to her, dropping his voice to a low murmur.

"You know how it is to grow up in a wealthy family," he said. "You get everything you want your entire life, and before too long, it gets dull. You try touring the world, try a million different hobbies, try anything you can think of to take the edge off that monotony."

He leaned in a little closer.

"So, yeah," he said. "You got me. I get a thrill out of conning people sometimes. It's just a hobby. It's what I do to keep the edge off."

She said that was fine, but it didn't explain why a wealthy heir would dress up like a regular, working-class guy to ride on a rickety travel bus for hundreds of miles. She said that he had to admit that it all seemed a little strange.

"I don't know what to tell you," he said.

"Tell me the truth," she said. "Tell me who you really are."

"You're delusional," he said.

"And as curious as I am about who you are, I'm nearly as curious as to why you didn't seal the deal in Santa Branca," she said. "First of all, it must have cost you a fortune to get set up down there—the clothes, the car, the beach house. And second of all, you had them eating out of your hand. You could have made a killing. Did you lose your nerve, or what?"

He didn't respond.

"I know you're not the son of an oil tycoon," she said.

They sat there for a minute, neither of them talking, cityscapes blurring by in the window of the bus.

"Are you done?" he asked finally.

"That depends," she said.

"Let's say, just for the sake of argument, that everything you said is true," he said. "If I'm not who I say I am, then you're putting yourself in a pretty dangerous position. If I'm not some wealthy playboy, then you have no idea who I am or what I'm capable of."

He had dropped his upper-crust accent and now spoke with the clipped delivery of the urban tough guys in the city where Sílvia had grown up. It was an accent that made the fine hairs on her arms stand on end, an accent so familiar from her grandmother's crime show.

"How do you know I'm not going to kill you the first chance I get?" he said.

"You're not going to hurt me," she said.

"You don't sound as sure of yourself as you did a minute ago."

She looked around at the other passengers on the bus, all of them asleep.

"You're not the violent type," she said. "If you could stand the violence, you'd be committing violent crimes. I figure you commit the kinds of crimes that you do for a reason."

"That seems like pretty shaky logic to stake your personal safety on."

She slipped her hand into her backpack.

"Also," she said, "I have a gun."

She pulled her hand far enough out of the backpack that he could see the butt of the handgun.

He shook his head.

Sílvia waited for his next move, her hand still gripping the gun. After a minute, he pulled a duffel bag out from under the seat in front of him. She shifted her backpack so the gun barrel pointed directly at Felipe's torso. Inside his duffel was a brown paper bag from the padaria he had visited earlier that day. He pulled out a loaf of bread, tore off a chunk, and handed it to Sílvia.

"You're probably hungry," he said.

She looked at his face and, after considering for a moment, took the bread with her free hand. They ate in silence as the bus jostled over a pothole-ridden section of freeway, Sílvia's grip on the gun gradually relaxing.

• • •

In front of a desolate restaurant in a northeastern beach town, Sílvia and Marco Aurélio—he had told her his real name but little else after two weeks of working together—sat at a table nursing a pair of caipirinhas. Sílvia swirled the ice in her glass and took a drink, the husk of the lime bumping against her upper lip.

"A good thing about you," said Aurélio when she put down her drink, "and don't take this the wrong way, is that you're not too pretty. Junior Cabral says that there's an ideal range of human beauty if you're in the business. Too ugly, and people dislike you. Too attractive and they instinctively know that whatever you're pitching is too good to be true. But with you, if you start chatting up some mark, he's flattered because you're certainly not bad looking, but you're not attractive enough that he starts to wonder, you know?"

"I hadn't really thought about that," said Sílvia.

The waiter/bartender/owner of the restaurant stepped out onto the patio and asked if he could get them anything else.

"We're fine, thanks," said Aurélio.

The man bowed facetiously and went back inside. Rather than appearing grateful for the presence of actual paying customers, the owner seemed to resent Sílvia and Aurélio for their part in witnessing the slow-burning failure that was his restaurant. On the other end of town, all of the restaurants, lanchonetes, and juice bars, with their postcard-worthy views of the bay, constantly teemed with tourists. The steady influx of money from the tourists allowed for regular remodeling, repainting, and refitting, lending the buildings overlooking the coast a cheery, bustling, welcoming air.

On this end of town the buildings had a grimy, abandoned quality to them, their lack of an ocean view rendering them valueless to the hordes of vista-hungry tourists that infested the northeastern seaside town almost year-round. It was a wonder that any business stayed afloat in this landlocked neighborhood. For Sílvia and Aurélio, however, the privacy these floundering businesses offered suited their needs perfectly.

The ice in Sílvia's glass shifted with a faint clatter. Years later, after they were married, Aurélio would admit to her that his plan that first afternoon on the bus had been to play the reluctant friend, stringing her along for a few hours, or days if necessary, until she let down her guard and he could lose her in a crowd, disappearing from her life completely. Instead, Sílvia had proven to be an adept con artist in her own right, insisting on being included in one job, and then another, acquitting herself admirably in both instances. Aurélio had begrudgingly admitted that having a partner could come in handy, that he could vastly expand his repertoire if he had someone else to work with. He had agreed to a trial partnership—six weeks of working together, and then he would make a decision. Now, two weeks in, the initial hesitancy with which he had approached the venture was fading quickly.

Sílvia ran her finger along the rim of her chilled, sweating glass.

"How much longer do you think we can work this town?" she said.

Aurélio raised his glass and took a drink.

"I don't know," he said. "Another two days. Maybe three."

He set down his glass.

"And then what?" she said.

"And then we keep following the coast," he said. "Wherever there's a beach, there are tourists."

Although he favored working tourist towns, Aurélio rarely conned the tourists themselves. He had explained his theory to Sílvia like this:

"Wherever there are tourists, there's a lot of money changing hands, which represents, of course, a great opportunity. To a novice in the business, the tourists seem like ideal marks—they've got disposable income that they're excited to spend; they travel in big, dumb herds; and they're usually not from the area. But the money's not in the tourists. Sure, you can earn some pocket change with an occasional Upstairs Dry Cleaner or a Fumbled Baby, but these routines are crude, and more importantly, they're unprofitable. What's more, tourists are much warier than you'd think. They read the safety tips in their guidebooks, and most of them are at least somewhat aware of how conspicuously foreign they are. So they compensate by being suspicious of any sort of financial proposition that seems out of the ordinary, which makes them terrible marks.

"Most importantly, though, tourists aren't bored. They're on vacation, they're having a good time. And I'm more and more convinced that boredom in a mark is at least as important as greed."

"Then tourist towns are a wash?" Sílvia had said.

Aurélio had shaken his head.

"Don't forget about all that money. Where there are tourists, there's money. This is true. So if we're not getting the tourists' money directly from the tourists, then we have to take it from the people who take it from the tourists. The restaurant owners, the tour guides, the souvenir vendors—these are the ideal marks, and I'll tell you why.

"First, they overcharge for everything. Really overcharge. Because they can. And that shows us that they're greedy. But more important than that, they're bored. Their jobs are just like any job in that they're doing the same repetitive thing every single day of the tourist season, but it's worse because they spend their working hours watching people on vacation, people having a good time, which reminds them that they're *not* having a good time, that they're tired of selling the same snow globes, or giving the same tour, or whatever it is, every single day. Most cons bring some novelty to their routine, and even if there's a risk involved, it's an escape from the grind of their boring, repetitive jobs.

"So basically, they have all this money from tourists, they're greedy, and they're bored. They're the ideal marks. Also, most of them like to consider themselves savvy businessmen, so even when they do realize they've been conned, they're unlikely to tell their friends about it. You can work one tourist town pretty securely for five days, maybe a week."

Sílvia had listened carefully, taking note of not only what he had said, but what his face, his body, his voice had been doing while he said it. In that conversation and in others like it, as Aurélio explained some personal theory or trick of the trade, Sílvia couldn't help but feel that she was being given temporary, unfiltered access to Aurélio's mind. Having seen him adopt so many other personas so convincingly, however, she suspected that this apparent openness could just as easily be yet another pose for yet another willing mark.

Aurélio ran his thumb over the moisture condensing on the outside of his glass.

"So how do you think that last one went?" he said.

"I don't know," said Sílvia. "I thought it went fine."

Aurélio nodded.

"Specifically, I guess, I pulled off the 'I'm in a hurry' attitude more naturally than I have before—that seemed to work well."

"I agree," said Aurélio.

"I also didn't worry as much about what to do with my hands while I was talking."

"Good."

"I did feel like I pushed a little too hard after you called him on the payphone. I could see him hesitating and I got nervous."

"Yeah," said Aurélio. "It's a natural mistake. That's why Junior Cabral's first rule is 'Be a good listener.' Let the mark make the proposition himself. You've just got to drill that into your head."

Despite the youthfulness that his name suggested, Junior Cabral was a bearded, middle-aged legend of a con artist. During his prime, he had sold a nonexistent copper mine to a former vice president; convinced a small neighboring country that he was a double agent willing to give up his country's secrets, if the price was right; and conned an elite coalition of leading businessmen out of half of their fortunes by claiming to be a descendent of Sir Francis Drake in possession of information that would lead them directly to the legendary privateer's as-yet-undiscovered personal store of Spanish gold. He had also mentored the promising young Marco Aurélio. Any time Aurélio brought up Junior Cabral, it was to invoke the man's sacrosanct authority, an authority that carried the same weight as scripture.

"Right," said Sílvia.

"But overall, you're really getting the hang of it," said Aurélio.

He looked at his watch.

"We should get back to work."

"Okay," she said, but he didn't stand up.

"Just to be clear on something—" he began, and paused.

"What?" she said.

He said, "I don't think you're unattractive."

She shrugged.

"I don't care if you do or you don't," she said.

"I'm just saying, that's not what I meant earlier."

"Fine," she said.

Aurélio nodded. He pulled a few bills from his pocket and left them on the table next to his half-empty glass. Sílvia got up from the table and the two of them headed off to their next job.

• • •

Almost by accident, six weeks became six years. During the initial month and a half of their then-tentative partnership, Sílvia mastered the Fisherman's Widow, the Cairo Bait-and-Switch, the Vasco da Gama, and the Embassy Turnaround. She revised and updated several old cons—the Pigeon Drop, the Old Violin, the Bootlegger's Gambit—to great success. Together, she and Aurélio even developed a few scams that, as far as they could tell, were entirely original. Without ever explicitly discussing it, Aurélio took Sílvia on as a full partner in his business, and their life together fell into a regular pattern.

They would spend a month working a series of coastal tourist cities, spending five or six days in each one before moving on to the next. Once they made enough money, they would hole up for a few months in some small, inland town, developing new scams, polishing old ones, and consulting maps and tourist guides to decide where they would work next. To help them maintain their focus, the towns where they stayed during this downtime boasted nothing that might be of interest to even the most curious vacationer—no colonial-era churches, no ocean views, no remarkable restaurants, no museums of any kind. Finding towns like this was no easy feat, but with time, the two partners had accumulated a respectable list, a kind of anti-tourist guide of places that suited their particular needs. Distraction free, they found it easier to stay confined in their rented rooms, dedicating themselves to their craft.

During this time, they reassured one another that their relationship was strictly professional, that neither of them had any intention of complicating a perfectly functional business partnership with any kind of romance. Never mind that the two of them were inseparable, even when they weren't working. Never mind that Aurélio got upset—"You don't want to overdo it," he'd say—every time that Sílvia's flirting with a mark seemed too sincere. Never mind that they shared a bed everywhere they stayed; it was more cost-effective, they reasoned, and any activities that might be construed as romantic could be justified as an effective means of unwinding from the stresses of their chosen line of work.

This carefully maintained illusion was shattered after six years of working together, when, one morning, Aurélio suggested that they get married. They were on the bus, which had become not only their physical means of transport from the tourist cities to the small towns where they holed up, but also an important liminal space, a chance to decompress between identities. As usual, they sat next to each other, Sílvia with her eyes closed, sleeping or trying to sleep, and Aurélio paging through a magazine he had picked up at the bus terminal.

"Hey," said Aurélio, nudging Sílvia awake.

"Hm?" said Sílvia, opening her eyes and looking around in an almost-concealed panic.

"No," said Aurélio, "nothing's wrong."

She looked at him.

"Then why did you wake me up?"

"We should get married," he said.

She pulled the jacket she was wearing more tightly around her body.

"What?"

"We should get married."

"Like, for a new scam?" said Sílvia.

"No," he said, "because I love you."

She said that certainly complicated things. He said he knew that. She told him she'd need some time to process this. He said that he'd expected she would, that he hoped she'd take some time to think it over before giving him an answer.

For nearly a month after that, neither of them mentioned Aurélio's proposal. If waiting for Sílvia's answer bothered Aurélio, if it was any kind of strain on his psyche, he, not surprisingly, didn't let on. Sílvia tried her best to match Aurélio's poker face, but she worried that her unease was beginning to show.

When Aurélio had asked her to marry him, she had felt not shocked, but pleased—relieved almost. Her reflexive, unspoken answer to his question had been an unqualified yes, a reaction that, when she had recognized it, had startled her. She thought back to the first job that she and Aurélio had worked on together. Beforehand, he had explained the bare bones of the routine to her:

"Accomplice One—in this case, you—comes out of the restaurant of an upscale tourist bar holding what looks like an expensive diamond bracelet, but is actually just a piece of costume jewelry. It's important, by the way, to start the routine soon after, but not during, a busy time at the bar. Also, Accomplice One should look like a solidly middle-class tourist. That way they trust you, but still believe that you wouldn't turn down some money if it was coming your way. So Accomplice One approaches the bartender and explains her dilemma—she found this bracelet on a sink in the ladies' room. She would like to try to return it to its owner—it looks valuable—but she's not sure how to go about it, and she has to be to the airport to catch her flight home in just a few minutes. Accomplice One and the bartender puzzle over the dilemma.

"About this time, Accomplice Two—in this case, me—calls the bar, and in his most convincing imitation of a middle-aged rich man, explains that his wife has lost her bracelet somewhere, that she has no idea where it could be, that it means a lot to her, and he's offering a reward of a thousand reaís to anyone who can find it. The bartender tells him he's in luck. Someone at the bar has found the bracelet on a sink in the ladies' room. Accomplice Two tells the bartender that he'll be there in half an hour with the reward money.

"At this point, the bartender hangs up the phone and explains the situation to Accomplice One who, although relieved that the owner has been found, reminds the bartender that she can't wait around for half an hour, that she has a flight to catch. Now, this point in the routine is key. It's best if Accomplice One waits for the bartender to make the suggestion, and given time, he usually will. If he's like most marks, the bartender will usually give Accomplice One a song and dance about how he'd be happy to stick around and return the bracelet himself, but his shift is ending and he has someplace to be. If there were some incentive, though, maybe—

"It's tempting for Accomplice One to jump in at this point and make the proposal, but it's better to hold out and let the mark do all the work. So Accomplice One plays dumb and asks if he has anything specific in mind. And then the bartender makes the following proposition: what if they split the reward money? He'll give Accomplice One five hundred reaís from the till right now, and when the guy comes with the reward money, the bartender will replace the cash from the till and keep the other five hundred for himself. It's a fifty-fifty split. Now Accomplice One agrees, with just a hint of reluctance. She might even propose a lesser share for the bartender, but in the end, she agrees to his terms, takes the money, leaves the bracelet, and gets out of there to catch her flight. The wealthy guy never shows up, of course, and the bartender is stuck with what he discovers to be nothing more than a convincing piece of costume jewelry."

When Aurélio had finished explaining the routine to her, Sílvia had refused to believe that it would work.

"It's so obvious," she had said.

"No," he had said. "It works. It's like a magic trick. If you don't know what's going on, it seems impossible—how did he find my card? Where did those doves come from? How did he catch that bullet in his teeth? But once you know how it works, you're not sure how you were ever fooled to begin with. It all seems so obvious. It's the same with cons. When something's happening in the moment, most people don't question it, and if they do, they ask the wrong questions. And if you run a con quickly enough, and with enough nonchalance, your mark won't even have a chance to question it."

And sure enough, their first job together had gone exactly as Aurélio had described it.

Now, six years later, Sílvia felt like the victim of a grand misdirection. It wasn't that she thought Aurélio had conned her into loving him, but that she had somehow conned herself out of realizing how she felt about him, keeping her own attentions carefully focused elsewhere as she secretly fell in love with her business partner. She had never intended for her current lifestyle to become permanent. She had assumed, on following Aurélio to Verópolis all those years ago, that her then-burning interest in Aurélio's line of work would, after a few months of firsthand experience, be extinguished, just as her interest in being a lawyer or a detective or a coroner had. Satisfied with what she had learned from the partnership, she would slip away one night while Aurélio slept and return to her university just in time for classes to start, just in time to change her major yet again. But she hadn't lost interest and she hadn't left. Over the years she had gradually severed ties with her school friends, her university professors, even her parents. And now here she was.

Sílvia finally broke her silence on the subject of Aurélio's proposal as the two of them pored over a map of the nation's coastline, looking for cities they hadn't worked over yet, or that they had worked over so long ago that they could now safely return. They were in bed at the time because that's where Aurélio preferred to work. He would often spend hours a day propped up with pillows like an ailing king, his maps, almanacs, and notebooks spread out on the rumpled sheets before him. Although Sílvia preferred the stable austerity of a desk or a kitchen table, when the two of them collaborated she would generally concede to Aurélio's preference and join him in bed. He would sweep aside his unruly spread of papers and she would sit next to him, cross-legged and upright in contrast to his sprawling slouch. As far as she could tell, working in bed was one of the few, if not the only indulgence that Aurélio allowed himself. Moving from town to town, the only possessions he carried with him were the ones absolutely necessary for the work—he owned no clothes that weren't part of his working wardrobe, no books that didn't relate in some way to the business. If he had a hobby, Sílvia didn't know about it.

The closest thing he did have was his plan for the Ultimate Con. From time to time, Sílvia found him scribbling away in a battered composition notebook that contained—he had explained to her— his developing ideas for the greatest con imaginable. Sílvia had looked inside once and found the pages filled with indecipherable notations that looked almost mathematical. Aurélio had told her the project was more a thought experiment than anything else—it was what he did to unwind. Even in his recreation, then, Aurélio behaved with disciplined, priestly dedication to his craft.

Given this asceticism in all other facets of Aurélio's life, Sílvia found his habit of working from bed deeply endearing.

"Look," he said, pointing to a city on the map. "We haven't been here yet."

"Are you sure?" said Sílvia, leaning in closer for a better look.

"If we have, I don't remember it," he said.

He reached back and fluffed one of his pillows.

"Hand me that book, will you?" he said.

She handed him the book that lay next to her foot, a tourist's guide to the country's best beaches.

"Thanks."

As he flipped through the book, she pulled the bed's soft, woolen blanket over her feet.

"Are you cold?" he said, looking up from the book.

She shook her head.

"There's another blanket in the closet, I think."

"I'm really not cold," she said.

"Okay," he said, and handed her the book he was holding. He picked up the atlas that lay between them and flipped to a map near the middle. He ran a finger down the page, and then stopped at a tiny dot of a city.

"Here," he said, "Praia Negra. We stopped there a few years ago, but it was so small that we didn't bother staying. I saw an article in a magazine that said it's a new hotspot—they just built a bunch of luxury condos and a big, new mall."

"Great," she said, the travel book still clutched in her hand.

"Is everything okay?" he said.

She set down the book.

"I'd like to marry you," she said.

"Are you sure?" he said.

She nodded. Smiling, he set aside the atlas and kissed her on the cheek.

• • •

Since it would only be the two of them, no guests, they decided on a simple wedding. Sílvia bought a lavender sundress from a shop in town, and talked Aurélio into buying a blue seersucker suit, a proposition he resisted until Sílvia convinced him he could also use it for work. On Saturday, they went to the cartório where, after a clerk determined that their papers were in order and they paid the necessary fee, they were ushered into the cramped offices of the corpulent registrar, who said he'd prefer to conduct the ceremony from the convenience of his desk, if that was okay with them. The two requisite witnesses—in this case, the clerk from the front desk and the woman who had sold Sílvia her dress—squeezed into the office, shutting the door behind them. Sílvia and Aurélio stood before the desk.

"Have you prepared any vows?" said the registrar.

"No," said Aurélio, "we hadn't thought to."

"That's not a problem," said the registrar. "Do you both want to marry each other?"

"Yes," said Aurélio.

"Yes," said Sílvia.

"Okay then," said the registrar. He signed the marriage certificate and handed it to Aurélio. "You two are married."

The two witnesses applauded politely and Sílvia pulled Aurélio close for a kiss.

"Well," said the registrar, "you might be expecting me to give you some advice, but I've been married a couple of times and it's never gone well for me. I live alone now, and that's the way I prefer it. So I wish you two the best of luck."

He shook their hands without standing up and Aurélio thanked him for performing the ceremony. Then he and Sílvia exited the building to another round of polite applause from the shopkeeper and the clerk.

And so they were married.

• • •

Three years later, Junior Cabral appeared and everything fell apart. They ran into him at an ice cream shop in Vale do Ouro, a town where they frequently stayed when they weren't working. One evening, beset by a rare case of cabin fever, they set aside their notebooks, their travel guides, their maps, and took a stroll through town. After passing by the open front of an ice cream shop, Aurélio stopped.

"Hang on," he said.

"What is it?" she said.

They walked back to the shop and stepped inside. They found the place empty except for its proprietor, the twenty-four flavors of ice cream he had to offer, and a middle-aged man sitting at a round table in the corner with a banana split in front of him.

"Can I help you?" said the proprietor, picking up his scoop and standing at the ready behind the freezer full of tubs.

"Sure," said Aurélio. "I'll have two scoops of brigadeiro."

The man at the table didn't look up at them.

"Two scoops of floresta negra for me," said Sílvia.

"Sure thing," said the proprietor, and set to work with his scoop.

From the corner of her eye, Sílvia watched the man at the table, whose gaze didn't wander from the banana split in front of him. He had the full, pointed beard of a satyr, and the thick, compact body of a dangerous man who was used to living comfortably. The spreading gray in his hair and his beard softened his appearance somewhat, rendering him, not grandfatherly—he was still too young for that—but just the slightest bit merry. On the whole, his appearance balanced on a fulcrum between jocular and threatening.

When the proprietor handed him their ice cream, Aurélio made a beeline for the table in the corner where the bearded man sat. Sílvia followed a few steps behind.

"Cabral?" said Aurélio in a hushed voice.

The man looked up at him from his ice cream, his expression noncommittal.

"Hello, Aurélio," replied the man, just as softly. "Are you working right now?"

"No," said Aurélio, "are you?"

"No," said Cabral with a laugh, no longer talking softly, "we can speak freely."

He got up from the table and extended his hand to Sílvia, who stood just to Aurélio's side.

"Junior Cabral," he said. "I'm an old friend of Aurélio's."

"Sílvia," she said. "I'm Aurélio's business partner." She paused. "And his wife."

"Very good," said Cabral. "Please, have a seat."

They joined him at his table. The three of them talked shop for a while, comparing notes on what kind of routines they were using, where they were using them, what kind of success they were having. Cabral admitted that he was semi-retired, running only the occasional minor scam, and spending the rest of his time living off the small fortune he had conned a bank manager out of a few years earlier. He seemed genuinely interested, though, in the routines that Aurélio and Sílvia had developed in their time together.

"That's brilliant," he said after Sílvia had explained one of their routines to him. "Almost makes me want to get back into the business full time."

He directed most of his questions to Sílvia, apparently captivated by her thoughts on their profession, by her anecdotes of working with Aurélio, by her general perspective on life. He practically ignored Aurélio, who sat between them taking the whole conversation in with an unreadable expression on his face. Before Sílvia knew it, it was dark outside, and the proprietor, who had stood diligently behind the counter the whole time they were there, was now closing up his shop.

"I should be going," said Cabral. "All the hotels here in town are booked, so I'm going to try my luck over in Porto Grande."

"Porto Grande is two hours away," said Sílvia. "You should just stay with us. The place we're renting has a fold-out bed in the couch."

"I couldn't impose," said Cabral.

"It would be no trouble at all," said Sílvia.

He pulled at one of his tiny, pointed ears as he contemplating the offer.

"Please," said Sílvia. "Don't be silly."

"Only if you're sure I wouldn't be imposing," said Cabral.

"Of course not," she said.

"All right, then," he said, with an odd smile.

Within seconds of his reply, Sílvia realized she had just been conned; he had been waiting for her to invite him to stay since the conversation began. She hoped that he was just a freeloader, trying to get a few days of room and board out of an old friend, but she suspected that some murkier designs were being set into motion.

It took only a few days of hosting the legendary criminal for Sílvia's suspicions to be confirmed. Where his behavior toward Sílvia in the ice cream shop had been warm and deferential, it became increasingly chilly and dismissive once he set up camp in the small apartment they were renting. Subtly at first, he began to exclude her from conversation, to pretend not to have heard her when she spoke, to position his body so that she was always out of his line of sight. And it all happened so gradually that she didn't notice what he was doing until she found herself alone in the kitchen one evening washing an imposing mound of dirty dishes while Cabral and Aurélio sat on the living room couch drinking beers and reminiscing about the old days. The whole tableau was so trite. How had she ended up here? How had she not caught on to what he was doing before now?

Even more upsetting was Aurélio's attitude toward Cabral. In the presence of his former mentor, Aurélio assumed a puppy-dog eagerness. He followed Cabral around the apartment, lapping up his anecdotes of recent cons, scurrying to attend to his increasingly demanding requests, nearly wetting himself with laughter at every joke or witticism that sprang forth from the man's mouth. For Sílvia, who had grown accustomed to her husband's hermetic self-containedness, this shift in personality came as an unpleasant jolt. Part of Aurélio's appeal had always been his island-like individualism, and this current fawning, this apparent emotional neediness, represented a complete reversal in what she thought was her husband's personality. Did he sincerely crave Cabral's approval as much as it seemed? Or was he playing the older man?

Sílvia put down the plate she was washing and walked into the living room.

"I'm not going to be cooped up in the kitchen washing dishes while you two sit around shooting the breeze," she said.

The conversation between the two men came to an abrupt stop and they both looked at her in surprise.

"You don't have to wash the dishes," said Aurélio. "Why don't you sit down and join us."

She sat down in the rocking chair across from the couch. Cabral looked at his watch.

He said, "Time for me to shower off and get to bed," and got up from the couch.

Once Cabral was inside the bathroom and she could hear the shower running, Sílvia pulled Aurélio to the corner of the living room.

"This needs to stop," she said. "Your friend has to go."

Aurélio slipped his hands into his pockets and bowed his head. "I'm sorry," he said. "I really am, but we're in kind of a tight spot here."

"What do you mean?" said Sílvia, hands on her hips.

"I can't just ask him to go."

"Why not?" she said. "Because he helped you out when you were younger? Because you learned a lot from him? I know you respect him, and maybe you do owe him something, but this has gone on long enough."

Aurélio shook his bowed head.

"No," he said, "that's not it."

He explained that Junior Cabral was a very dangerous man— brilliant, but volatile. Most people in the business didn't like violence, but Cabral was a notable exception. He and Aurélio had parted ways all those years ago because Cabral had killed a mark when one of their scams had gone awry. And if rumors were to be believed, that wasn't the first, or last, person he'd murdered.

"I'd love to get rid of him," said Aurélio, "but Junior Cabral comes and goes on his own terms. We'll just have to wait to see what he wants."

The conversation was brought to a halt as the water shut off and Cabral emerged from the bathroom, towel around his waist, whistling the national anthem.

The following morning, Cabral made his next move. The three of them sat quietly in the living room after breakfast, conversation having died out minutes earlier.

"I have a confession to make," said Cabral, breaking the silence.

"What's that?" said Aurélio.

Cabral pulled at one of his tiny, pointed ears. He said that it was no coincidence that he had run into Aurélio here. Sílvia looked up from the newspaper she was reading. Cabral explained that he was getting older—not old, he emphasized, just older than he used to be—and thought he should quit the business while he was still ahead. But before he did, he wanted to pull the proverbial last big con, a con whose memory would keep him warm in the long twilight of his retirement years. In planning the job, he had decided that there was nobody he'd rather work with than Marco Aurélio. Cabral paused, allowing Aurélio to take this in.

"You can count on me," said Aurélio after a moment.

Cabral smiled, the whiskers of his beard bristling with the movement of his face.

"Then we should get started," he said.

Cabral looked at Sílvia.

"I'd like to borrow your husband for a few hours," he said. "I think we have some business to discuss."

She laid down the newspaper in her lap.

"Anything you can discuss with Aurélio, you can discuss with me," she said.

"I don't mean to offend you," said Cabral, pulling at one of his tiny ears. "It's not that I don't trust you. It's just that I've learned over the years that too many cooks in the kitchen will ruin the dish. We may need your specific talents at some point, I'm sure, but for now, the less you know, the better."

Before Sílvia could respond, Cabral took Aurélio by the arm and the two of them left the apartment. She considered following them, considered causing a scene at whatever quiet nook of the town they had chosen for their little powwow. Instead, she decided to stay behind and clean the apartment. If Aurélio wanted to play the neglectful husband, then she could match him in playing the sullen, neglected housewife. After mopping the tile floors, scrubbing the toilet and shower, washing the curtains and bedclothes, Cabral and Aurélio still hadn't returned, so she picked up a book that a previous tenant had left behind—a yellowing paperback collection of crummy science fiction stories by Eduard

Salgado-MacKenzie. She hated every page of it. When she finished, it was well past midnight and they still hadn't returned. She tossed the book in the garbage, went to her room, undressed, and got into bed where she lay awake for another few hours.

Her vigil ended when Aurélio came stumbling into the room, kicking off his shoes and collapsing onto the bed in a drunken heap. He put his arm over Sílvia and tried to pull her close. She pushed him away, told him not to touch her. He told her she had to understand, they only started drinking a little while ago. Most of the day they had been talking business.

"My hands are tied," he said, and tried to pull her close to him again.

She pushed him away, harder this time. She said that tonight it would be best if he slept on the floor, and that she wanted Cabral out of their house by the end of the week.

Sílvia slept late into the next morning and woke to find her bedroom empty. She put on a robe and walked out into the living room. Cabral was not on the couch, and all of his things were gone. She found Aurélio sitting at the kitchen table with a cup of coffee and a bag of rolls from the padaria.

"Hey," he said when he saw her walk in. "I'm really sorry about yesterday."

She pulled out a chair and sat down. She picked up a roll, still warm from the oven of the padaria, and tore it in half. She took a bite and chewed slowly.

"I told Cabral he should leave," said Aurélio.

Sílvia swallowed and said that that was a step in the right direction. She asked Aurélio how he was feeling. He said his head hurt like crazy. She told him it served him right. She took a drink of his coffee.

They spent a quiet morning together in the apartment. They ate leftovers for lunch, and were sprawled out on the couch when Aurélio looked at his watch and said that he'd better be going.

"Going where?" said Sílvia.

"Meeting with Cabral," he said.

Sílvia sat up.

"I thought you said he left."

"He left our apartment. He's staying in a hotel across town."

"You lied to me," she said.

"No," he said, "I'm sorry you got that impression."

He leaned over and kissed her on the cheek.

"I'll be back in time for dinner, okay?"

"No," she said. "This isn't okay with me."

He asked her what about it she wasn't okay with. She asked if he was serious. She said she didn't trust Cabral and she didn't like being left out of things like this. Aurélio said he was sorry. He said that he couldn't explain now, but this was the way he needed to play things. He asked her to please trust him. He said he would explain everything later, and that when he did, she'd understand.

"So you're conning him?" she said.

"I really can't tell you anything," he said.

"If this is a con," she said, "just tell me, and I'll stop asking questions. I don't even need to know the details."

He shook his head.

"You need to tell me what's going on," said Sílvia.

"Please," said Aurélio, "trust me," and then he left.

Their relationship had seemed so stable to her up to this point that Aurélio's behavior stunned Sílvia. But when she stopped to consider it, what grounds did she have for surprise? How well did she really know Aurélio? And how stable had their relationship really been? As she thought back on it, their married life seemed muddled and vague, as fast-moving and empty as one of their best cons. After nine years, Aurélio remained as much an enigma to her as he had when they first met.

For the next week, Aurélio left the apartment every day after lunch, returned home just in time for dinner, and said little to nothing about his meetings with Cabral.

"What's going on?" Sílvia would ask. "Who's conning whom?"

Aurélio would only shake his head sadly and say he couldn't explain just yet. After a few days of this, she stopped asking any questions, stopped giving Aurélio the satisfaction of withholding information from her. She began to keep silent in the evenings, matching her husband's imposed reticence with a reticence of her own. They ate dinner with little to no conversation before retiring to the couch where they read their respective magazines. And then they went to bed, where Sílvia slept with her back immovably turned toward Aurélio.

Sílvia knew that the current situation was unacceptable, that she needed to do something, but none of the options before her seemed appealing.

On the eighth day of this, Aurélio came home an hour later than usual with Cabral in tow, both of them already tipsy. Cabral set a bag of three marmitas down on the table and opened a bottle of cachaça. Aurélio got three plates and glasses down from the cupboard and set them on the table.

"We've got it all worked out," said Aurélio, pouring a glass of cachaça. "We start next week."

He handed the glass to Sílvia who shook her head. So he handed it to Cabral, who drained it in one go.

"I'd ask what the plan is, if I thought you'd tell me," she said.

Aurélio poured a glass for himself and sat down.

"We can let you in on the broad outline," said Cabral, tearing into his marmita.

"I picked up one for you," said Aurélio, opening the lid of his own meal.

"I already ate," said Sílvia. "So what's the plan, broadly."

Cabral brushed away a clump of rice that had stuck in his beard.

"First," he said, "a low-risk, moderate-yield venture up north. We need to raise funds for our big scheme. That should take two to three months. When we have enough money, the prep for our main venture should take another month or two. Then the big con itself will last about a month and a half."

"That's only a timeline," she said. "You told me next to nothing."

Cabral reached out and lay his thick hand on top of Sílvia's. She pulled her hand away.

"Unfortunately," said Cabral, "the details of our venture are limited to a need-to-know basis and I can say no more."

"I'm sure you can't," said Sílvia.

Cabral smiled and shrugged. Sílvia looked at Aurélio, stuffing his face, most of the way to drunk. She looked back at Cabral. He scratched at one of his pointy little ears.

"If you want to be so exclusive with your big con, I understand," she said. "But I don't see why I can't help out with the fundraising. If I'm going to be there anyway, it seems like a waste of manpower to have me just hanging around some apartment in a no-name town up north."

Cabral looked at Aurélio, who set down his fork and looked at Sílvia.

"What is it?" she said.

He looked down and straightened the fork.

"Actually," said Aurélio, "we were thinking it might be best if you stayed here."

He kept his eyes down, his fingers fidgeting with his fork.

"Are you serious?" said Sílvia.

Aurélio didn't respond.

"What am I supposed to do in this town for three months by myself?"

"It'll be closer to six months, actually," said Cabral, refilling his glass with cachaça.

"Look at me," she said to Aurélio.

He looked up at her.

"Leaving me behind isn't an option," she said. "I don't care what you're up to, you're not leaving me alone. We're going to talk this over in the morning when you've sobered up."

Cabral smiled and sipped from his glass.

"I'm sorry," said Aurélio. "But it'll be better if you stay. When it's over, we can—"

Sílvia got up from her chair and hit him across the face with the back of her hand. He gave a short, surprised yelp and hid his face from her. She turned around and left the kitchen.

She walked into the bedroom, closed the door, and got into bed without undressing. The apartment was silent for several minutes. Before long, though, Aurélio and Cabral were talking quietly, and then not so quietly, and then laughing and singing. Sílvia curled under the sheets and closed her eyes.

She woke up to a thick, rough hand pressed over her mouth. She opened her eyes. Junior Cabral loomed over her, and as she tried to squirm away, he grabbed her by the throat. He squeezed and said that if she put up a fight, he'd crush her larynx like it was an ice cream cone. He removed one hand from her mouth, maintaining a firm, steady pressure on her throat with the other. He moved in and kissed her face, the whiskers of his beard chafing against her skin. With his free hand he began unbuttoning her pants. She twisted away and he squeezed her throat until she couldn't breathe. She stopped struggling and he released the pressure enough for her to draw a breath. His thick fingers ran over her skin. She didn't move. He breathed heavily against her face.

"I'm not doing this because I want you," said Cabral, "I'm doing this because I can."

She listened to Aurélio snoring in the other room. Cabral held her closer. She raised her head and kissed Cabral. He froze for a moment. She kissed him again.

"That's right," he said.

She kept kissing him and he relaxed his grip on her throat. She kissed his lips, his neck, his ear. He let go of her throat, his hand moving down her body. She licked his tiny, pointed ear, and he laughed. He pulled her close to him. She wrapped her mouth around his ear and then bit down as hard as she could, the adrenaline clenching her jaw, jerking her neck back, the skin and cartilage giving way between her teeth, tearing away from his head. He yelled and jumped off the bed, his hand clutching the side of his head where a ragged flap of skin was all that remained of his ear. Sílvia spit the rest of his ear onto her pillow and wiped the blood from her face, gagging, but managing not to vomit. Cabral looked at the bloody chunk of ear on the pillow and pulled his hand away from the side of his face. He saw the blood on his hand, his eyes rolled back in his head, and he passed out, falling to the floor.

Sílvia didn't waste any time. She found Aurélio still asleep on the couch, undisturbed by the screaming in his deep, drunken slumber. She briefly considered leaving him a note, but then decided against it. She threw on a jacket, stuffed her pockets with some cash from their emergency drawer, and walked out of the apartment.

• • •

She worked on her own for a few years—avoiding the beach towns that Aurélio had always favored—until a big scam gone wrong forced her to move someplace where the police wouldn't come looking for her. She remembered Vila Barbosa from her grandmother's crime show, and so she settled down there, recognizing the neighborhood as a place so crowded and dangerous that a small-time crook like her could become invisible. She worked an assortment of odd jobs, most of them legal, although if an opportunity for a small con proved irresistible, she took it. Over time, she saved enough money to open the lanchonete that she currently owned.

She heard through the grapevine that Cabral had been arrested in the middle of a big con, had done a little hard time, but had been released early for helping the federal police track down and catch a few of his most notorious associates. He now operated a highly successful consulting firm here in the city, helping large corporations to protect themselves against fraud.

She heard nothing about Aurélio.

Sometimes on Sundays, Sílvia took the train downtown to the wealthy neighborhood where she had grown up. Walking down the sidewalk, she caught brief glimpses of the businessmen in their immaculate suits getting into and out of their armored town cars, always accompanied by musclebound bodyguards who looked at Sílvia with no small degree of mistrust. When she heard the once-familiar chop of rotors from above, she stopped walking and, shading her eyes, looked up at the helicopters taking off from the roofs of luxury apartment buildings, ferrying their human cargo to Sunday dinners across town with other members of the city's airborne elite. And when she got tired of walking, she bought a hot dog or a coxinha from a stand and ate it on a bench across from the gated park she had played in as a girl. Then when she finished eating, she got on the train and rode back home to Vila Barbosa.

CHAPTER 15

Elder Schwartz stood in their bathroom under the clunky electric showerhead, letting the spray of lukewarm water rinse away the outermost layer of sweat, grime, and urine that had accumulated on his body over the previous two days. As the dirty water pooled on the tiled floor below him, he tried to process everything that had happened that evening.

Sílvia had left only a few minutes earlier.

After explaining her history with Marco Aurélio, she had told the elders that she was getting as far away from Vila Barbosa as possible and suggested that they do the same. Whoever had killed Galvão wouldn't hesitate to deal similarly with a couple of nosy missionaries or a curious ex-wife.

"I don't plan on going anywhere until I find Marco Aurélio," Elder Toronto had said.

"Then you're being incredibly stupid," she had said.

And with that she had gathered up her purse and her gun and walked out their door.

Now, alone and safe in the bathroom, all Elder Schwartz had to worry about was getting clean and then getting some sleep. As he reached for his bar of soap, however, he caught a whiff of plastic melting above his head. With a whimpering yelp, he jumped out from under the stream of water just as the electric showerhead began to pop and spark. He leaned over and shut off the water, and with it, the heater inside the showerhead. The now-useless appliance emitted two thin lines of smoke, its plastic casing melted and charred.

Elder Schwartz stood there dripping, only slightly less dirty than he had been a few minutes before. He toweled off and, in what felt like an act of futility, put on some clean underwear. Head aching from the anxieties of the day, he sat down on the edge of his bed. He was too tired and overwhelmed to think, so he didn't. From the front room he could hear the sounds of Elder

Toronto rummaging through one of the desk drawers. He figured he should go see what Elder Toronto was up to, but first he would close his eyes for just a few seconds.

When Elder Toronto walked into the bedroom and asked where they kept the tape, Elder Schwartz sat up and realized he had fallen asleep, curled in a ball at the foot of his bed. He looked at his clock. He had been asleep for nearly three hours.

"What?" he said.

"The tape," said Elder Toronto. "Where do we keep it?"

"I've got some in the bottom drawer of my desk," said Elder Schwartz.

"Great," said Elder Toronto. "Why don't you get dressed and come help me out."

Still sleepily disoriented, Elder Schwartz put on a T-shirt and a pair of gym shorts. In the front room, he found that Elder Toronto had taken their map of the neighborhood down from the wall and was currently taping an assortment of three-by-five cards up in its place.

"Aren't you tired?" said Elder Schwartz.

"Couldn't sleep," said Elder Toronto, tearing off another piece of tape. "Here," he said and handed the roll to Elder Schwartz.

Elder Schwartz looked at the cards on the wall. Each one had a name written on it in heavy black marker and below that, in pen, a brief description of who that person was, how they were connected to Marco Aurélio, and what they had told the missionaries about his disappearance. They were arranged in a careful grid, alphabetically by name.

"Tape, please," said Elder Toronto.

Elder Schwartz obliged, tearing off a strip and handing it to his companion. Elder Toronto stuck another card to the wall.

"You made a card for Sister Beatrice?" said Elder Schwartz.

Elder Toronto held his hand out for another strip of tape, which Elder Schwartz handed to him.

"We have to consider everyone we're aware of who knew Marco Aurélio," said Elder Schwartz, "everyone who might be connected to him or his disappearance in any way."

He attached the last card and stepped back from the wall.

"There," he said.

There was a card for Grillo and a card for Lucinda. A card for Sílvia. A card for Bishop Claudemir and a card for Fátima and a card for each of their children. A card for Abelardo, a card for Beatrice. A card for Elder J. da Silva and for Elder Christiansen. A card for Ulisses Galvão, for each of the two police officers, for Junior Cabral. A card for Wanderley the cab driver, a card for Meire.

"I'm going to get some sleep," said Elder Schwartz. "You should, too."

Elder Toronto nodded and didn't move. Elder Schwartz walked back to the bedroom.

For the next few hours he slept fitfully, plagued by a looping dream in which a gun-toting stranger pursued him between teetering stacks of index cards that cataloged every person Elder Schwartz had ever met in his life.

THE ARGENTINE

They say that the redundancies in his collection deeply dismayed the Argentine. His catalog was meant, after all, to be a universal one, encompassing the full breadth of human experience. To accomplish this, he needed specimens of every conceivable iteration of cruelty. These bland repetitions that filled the notebooks of his library simply wouldn't do.

One day, while observing an act of domestic violence that was, for all taxonomic purposes, identical to countless acts before it, the Argentine came to a realization. If the conditions underlying life in Vila Barbosa contributed to the production of cruelty, then altering those conditions might result in new and different specimens for his collection. Although he had initially approached the project with a strict scientific integrity, doing everything he could to remain as unobtrusive as possible, the power available to him proved irresistible. With both his above-ground deputies and his subterranean minions willing to carry out his every command, the Argentine began engineering the conditions necessary to produce novel instances of human cruelty, to reduce the innumerable redundancies in his collection. Before long, he had come to involve himself, whether personally or vicariously, in every aspect of life in the neighborhood, ensuring that its residents produced every type of cruelty that he could possibly conceive of.

Just as a farmer understands the purpose of proper soil conditions to the success of his crops, the Argentine came to understand that some *varieties of human cruelty required a special blend of chaos and misery in which to flourish and bear fruit. To create the desired conditions, he might flood one household with more money than they'd ever seen in their lives, introduce slightly toxic chemicals into the water supply of another, deploy an undercover deputy spouting new and dangerous religious ideas to a popular church, murder the neighborhood's most popular samba group, and then harvest the new varieties of cruelty that these controlled conditions produced.*

This comparison of the Argentine to a farmer, however, breaks down if extended much further. Farmers—for all their hard work fertilizing, plowing, planting, irrigating—ultimately remain at the mercy of forces beyond their control. A late frost. A hailstorm. Drought. Adverse market conditions. Any number of things that ultimately frustrate the farmer's best efforts. The Argentine, on the other hand, left nothing to chance. Where a farmer can only control so many variables, the Argentine, for a time, controlled them all. He was not only the farmer, but also the soil, the seed, the rain and the hail, the frost, the sun, the chemicals in the ground, the competing farmers nearby and abroad, the pollen, the bee, the shade of the clouds, the worms, the rocks, the pestilent swarm of insects.

One morning, while shelving a notebook filled with observations of novel forms of cruelty, the Argentine realized a disturbing implication of his project. In taking this approach in his quest to comprehend human cruelty, he had transformed the neighborhood into no more and no less than the perfect embodiment of his elaborate imagination, rendering either Vila Barbosa, or perhaps the Argentine himself, superfluous to the compilation of the catalog. With the shock of this realization, he dropped the notebook from his hand, staggering backward, steadying himself against a bookshelf. When he had regained his balance he immediately called an unprecedented joint meeting of his closest above-ground deputies and his most trusted subterranean minions.

CHAPTER 16

Stepping into the air-conditioned waiting room, Elder Schwartz could feel the sweat evaporating from his skin. He looked around at the patterned granite flooring, the leather club chairs, the cherrywood reception desk, and tried to remember if he had ever been in a room so richly furnished. If so, it had been a while. The glass door eased shut behind the two missionaries.

"Can I help you?" said the receptionist, in a way that suggested she didn't think she could.

Their shower was still broken, so although the two missionaries had both put on a fresh set of clothes that morning, they still looked—and smelled—a bit the worse for wear. In spite of their unwashed state, they boldly crossed the granite floor and approached the desk.

"We're here to see Mr. Cabral," said Elder Toronto.

"Do you have an appointment, young man?" said the secretary, opening the leather-bound appointment book on her desk.

"I don't think I need one," said Elder Toronto. "I'm Ulisses Galvão."

"You're Ulisses Galvão," said the receptionist.

"That's right," he said.

The receptionist looked at the black nametag on Elder Toronto's front pocket.

"Let me clarify," said Elder Toronto. "I am not Ulisses Galvão. But I have an important message from Mr. Galvão to deliver to Mr. Cabral."

The receptionist closed the appointment book.

"A message about salvation, right?" she said.

"No," said Elder Toronto, "we're here on different business."

The receptionist looked the two missionaries over.

"I'm going to have to run this by Mr. Cabral," she said. "You can wait over there."

She pointed at the leather sofa in the waiting area and picked up the phone. The missionaries took a seat. After Sílvia had left their apartment the night before, Elder Toronto had found a business card on the floor under the chair where she had been sitting. Printed in an elegant font on the card were the address and telephone number of Junior Cabral's consulting firm. Now, the identity of the earless man in the photograph discovered, here they were.

On the street outside the office building where the elders currently sat, Wanderley—the driver of the unlicensed cab that had taken them to their original appointment with Galvão— waited in his car with explicit instructions to call the police if the missionaries weren't back outside within forty-five minutes. At least he was supposed to be waiting. Elder Toronto had promised the driver eighty reaís if he stuck around, but at the mention of the police, the man's assurances to the missionaries that he'd be there when they came out had held much less conviction.

The receptionist hung up the phone and stepped out from behind the desk. Her heels clacked against the stone floor as she crossed the room to the missionaries.

"Come with me, please," she said.

The missionaries stood up from the leather sofa and followed. She led them down a narrow hallway to an expensive-looking wood door, which she opened, gesturing for them to enter. They stepped into the office and she shut the door behind them.

An older version of the man from the photograph sat behind a massive battleship of a hardwood desk reading through a document, his once-graying hair and beard now completely white. Elder Schwartz noticed that his most distinguishing feature, or lack thereof, had been repaired in the years since the photograph was taken: He now had a complete left ear. Looking up at the missionaries, he removed his wire-rimmed glasses.

He said, "John, Mike, have a seat." He gestured at two leather chairs in front of his desk.

Elder Schwartz, disconcerted, wondered how he knew their names.

"Actually, we prefer to be called 'Elder,'" said Elder Toronto.

"And I prefer not to use silly titles," said Junior Cabral. "Have a seat, boys."

The missionaries sat down in the two leather chairs.

"The surgeons did a nice job with your ear," said Elder Toronto.

"Thank you," said Cabral. "I think so, too."

His hand reached up and stroked the new ear.

"That particular deformity," he said, "was a souvenir from my father. I grew up in the South, in a tiny armpit of a city. My father couldn't hold down a job. He was bad at taking orders and good at drinking, which never endeared him to his employers. On weekends, for fun, he would beat up my mother. One Friday night—I was eleven—I tried to stop him. He hit me, knocked me to the ground, and then held me down and cut off my ear with a kitchen knife. He said that that should remind me who was the father and who was the son in our house. I left the next morning, struck out on my own, and never went back."

"Impressive," said Elder Toronto.

"I certainly think so," said Junior Cabral. "I was an eleven-year-old kid, newly arrived in one of the largest cities in the world. For a couple of weeks I survived by stealing fruit and bread from stalls in the street markets when the vendors weren't looking. It was enough to get by, but just barely.

"One day I was sitting on a curb near a church. It must have been a Sunday because bells were ringing and people were coming out of the church in their best clothes. I got an idea. I stood up. I watched the people walking by me until I spotted a sentimental-looking middle-aged woman. I started crying, pretty loudly, and she looked over at me. I kept crying and she approached me. I told her the name of the little town I came from. I told her my family was very poor, that my father was drunk and unemployed, that sometimes he beat my mother. All of this was true.

"Then I started to embellish. I told her my mother was sick, that we had saved up all of our money to get her to a doctor, but when the doctor examined her, he told us the only cure was a very expensive medicine that we could only find here in the city. I told the woman I hadn't been able to get any money since I'd been here, and that my mother was going to die. What I told her wasn't that clever or original, just basic panhandling stuff, and it didn't hurt that I was a kid, but the story worked. The woman opened her purse and gave me a handful of bills. She stopped a bunch of her churchy friends and they gave me money as well, and told me I'd be in their prayers. What I learned that morning was that the best lies are the ones that are mostly true. That lesson served me well in my previous line of work."

He scratched at his well-groomed beard.

"That's a nice story," said Elder Toronto. "You say your family lived in the South?"

Cabral nodded, a gleam in his eye.

"And poor?"

"That's right," said Cabral.

"That's funny," said Elder Toronto.

"And why's that funny," said Junior Cabral, leaning forward.

"What I mean is, it's interesting," said Elder Toronto. "See, I hear your father was a big downtown banker right here in the city. A really important guy. In fact, I hear his name still holds enough sway that it got you out of prison early, helped you land this nice consulting gig."

"Is that right?" said Cabral with a soft chuckle.

"That's what I hear."

"And where did you hear this?"

"From a mutual acquaintance," said Elder Toronto.

"I see," said Cabral, leaning back in his chair, a satisfied smile on his face. "Very good. Very good."

He stood up from his desk and slid open one of the burnished metal wall panels to reveal a small fridge and three shelves of glasses. He asked the missionaries if they were thirsty.

"Sure," said Elder Toronto. Elder Schwartz just nodded.

He took down three tumblers from a shelf and set them on the desk.

"What about you, Mike?" said Cabral, opening the fridge and removing two bottled waters and two cans of guaraná. He set them on the desk. "Do you speak Portuguese?"

"Yes," said Elder Schwartz.

Cabral pulled a bottle of whiskey from a shelf above the glasses and sat down.

"Please," he said, "drink. The waters and sodas are for you."

Elder Toronto opened a can of guaraná and poured some of the amber liquid into his glass. Elder Schwartz didn't touch the drinks.

"So you do speak Portuguese, then," said Cabral.

"That's right," said Elder Schwartz.

"Excuse me?" said Cabral.

"I said, yes I do," said Elder Schwartz.

Cabral gave a slight shrug. He pointed to the drinks in front of Elder Schwartz.

"The drinks," said Cabral, still addressing Elder Schwartz. He spoke slowly and loudly. "They are for you. You can drink them." He mimed drinking.

"No thanks," said Elder Schwartz.

Cabral turned to Elder Toronto.

"Can he understand what I'm saying?"

"He understands fine," said Elder Toronto.

"Hmm," said Cabral. "You should tell him to speak more clearly."

"You can tell him yourself," said Elder Toronto, taking a drink of guaraná.

Instead, Cabral opened the bottle of whiskey.

"Do you mind?" he said.

"It's your office," said Elder Toronto.

Cabral filled the glass a quarter of the way full and closed the bottle. He took a sip.

"This probably won't come as any kind of surprise to you, but I'm not a religious man. I may not even be a very moral man. Who knows. But do you want to know why I was so successful in my former career?"

"Sure," said Elder Toronto.

"Because most people aren't too hard to figure out. Most people do the things they do because they want something. And the something that they want is rarely very noble. Even if they're religious. Why should you be meek? Because blessed are the meek. Why should you be a peacemaker? Because blessed are the peacemakers. What does it mean to be blessed? It means God gives you one of his heavenly mansions; you get rewarded."

Cabral ran a hand over his thick beard.

"A couple of you guys came to visit me not long after I got out of prison. They gave their little lesson about Joseph Smith, and then asked me if I wanted to be baptized. I asked what was in it for them if I got baptized. They said nothing was in it for them. I said I doubted that. They said they worked on a strictly volunteer basis. I told them I wasn't talking about money. I asked them who their boss was, and told them I didn't mean God. They said they had a mission president. I asked if their mission president would know if I got baptized. They said he would. I asked if he would give them any sort of praise for baptizing me. They said he probably would.

I asked them how they thought God would feel about them if they baptized me. They said they wouldn't presume to guess. I asked them if they thought God might bless them. They said they imagined he might.

"'Then don't tell me there's nothing in it for you,' I said to them. 'If I get baptized, you improve your reputation with your boss, and God adds another brick to your heavenly mansion.'"

Cabral chuckled and took a sip of whisky.

"There's something satisfying about watching someone's face as you perfectly articulate—better than they could, even—exactly what they want. I told your friends that if they were looking for rewards, they should find a sales job that pays a more immediate commission. They left my apartment with their tails between their legs."

Cabral smiled at the two missionaries.

"I don't think everyone's that predictable," said Elder Toronto.

"Neither do I," said Cabral. "That's why I said *most* people are easy to figure out. There are notable exceptions. Marco, for example—he's always been a cipher to me. I can't figure him out. Back when we worked together, I'd ask him all the time why he was in the business. I told him I needed to know—it's good practice to know what drives your partner. But he would just shrug and say he needed the money.

"But that wasn't it. Granted, he was always very smart about getting the most money possible out of our various business ventures. A truly canny young man. Once he got the money, though, he didn't spend it on anything. I mean, he bought basic necessities—food, clothes, and whatnot—but that was it. So with Marco, I know it's not the money.

"Now, with most guys in the business, if it's not the money, it's the sense of superiority that comes with duping people. It's a smartest-guy-in-the-room kind of thing. Makes them feel big about themselves. If I'm being totally honest with you, that's what drives me, or drove me, when I was still in the business. I got a thrill just thinking of some rich mark putting the pieces together after I've made off with his money, realizing how gullible he'd been, how trusting. I lived for that.

"But for Marco, that wasn't it either. When we worked together—and I'm not even sure how to describe this to you—there was almost a gentleness, a kindness, even, in how he conned people. Sure, he was still tricking them, still taking their money, but it wasn't like he got a thrill out of humiliating people. It was almost like he was helping them, but that's not quite it. Like I said, I can't describe it."

Elder Toronto poured some more guaraná into his glass.

"Speaking of Marco," said Elder Toronto. "When's the last time you saw him?"

Cabral smiled. "We can talk about that in a minute," he said. "I'm not finished yet."

"Fine," said Elder Toronto. "Go ahead."

Elder Schwartz could see his senior companion's patience wearing thin, the breeziness becoming more and more forced by the minute. Cabral polished away a smudge on the gleaming surface of his desk and returned his attention to the missionaries.

"Maybe the closest Marco ever came to revealing what made him tick was during this one summer—we had been working together four or five years by then, and if Marco had started out as my apprentice, by this point he had the skills to be my partner. We were on our way south to meet up with some colleagues for a job, but we stopped en route in a little beach town to try and earn some of the money we'd need to buy our way into the venture. It was in this little beach town that we met a small-time—and I mean small-time—grifter by the name of Fat Tiago. The guy wasn't even that fat.

"Anyway, Fat Tiago's racket was a shell game he ran down on the boardwalk. You know what a shell game is? It's where the operator has three shells, or little cups, or thimbles, or whatever, and he shuffles around a coin or a nut or a pea, and when he's done shuffling, the mark lays down a bet on which cup the pea is under. And the mark is always wrong because the operator's using sleight of hand. Like I said, this is small-time stuff. If you run a shell game, you're living hand-to-mouth, and that's only if you're very good at it. In the business, guys like Marco and me didn't run around with guys who did shell games. Different worlds.

"But this Fat Tiago had a gimmick. He used clear cups. Shot glasses, actually. And instead of a pea, he used a red rubber ball, which, if you've ever run a shell game before, you know is a terrible idea. I actually did a little shell work as a kid—it's good training—and you want everything to be small so it's harder for the mark to see and easier to hide in your hand.

"So we're walking along the boardwalk, Marco and I, and I see Fat Tiago's rig. I say to Marco that this guy's either an idiot or some kind of two-bit savant. I'm intrigued, so we stop to watch. There's one other variation to the act. Next to the cups there's one of those bells they have at customer service counters—you know, the kind you tap to ring? So Fat Tiago tells his marks that as soon as he's done shuffling the shot glasses around, he's going to reach over and ring this bell, and once the bell rings, the mark—except he doesn't call him the mark, he calls him the player—has to have his hand on the cup of his choice. This is only fair, says Fat Tiago, since the cups are clear.

"Now, by this point—hats off to Fat Tiago—I was hooked. Even with the bell gimmick it seemed much too easy for the marks to choose the right cup. I'll tell you, though, we watched a dozen of them play the game and not a single one put their finger on the right cup. They'd watch him shuffling the shot glasses and you could see the ball moving around, a red blur shooting back and forth. Then he'd stop shuffling, his hand darting for the bell, and the mark—thinking they'd followed the path of the red rubber ball pretty well—would put their finger down on the cup of their choice. Of course, all of this happened nearly simultaneously, but the bell would ring, and the mark would look down and see an empty cup under their finger, the red ball always sitting under a different shot glass, and Fat Tiago's hands nowhere near the playing surface. It was, I'll admit, an impressive little act. We probably watched him for over an hour, until it got dark and he closed down for the night.

"As he was packing his supplies into a little duffel bag, I said, 'That's a nice shell game you've got going.'

"And Marco said, 'Really impressive.'

"'Thank you,' said Fat Tiago. 'I noticed you two watching. You don't look like cops, so can I assume you're fellow members of the guild?'

"I told him, 'You can assume what you want,' and we both shook his hand.

"He said, 'If you enjoyed the performance, why don't you two buy me a drink,' so the three of us set off for a bar to do just that.

"Like I said, I was impressed by Fat Tiago's game, but Marco was captivated. After a few drinks, he convinced the guy to pull out the shot glasses and the ball and give an encore performance.

"Marco said, 'You've got to tell me how to do that.'

"'Sorry,' said Fat Tiago. 'Trade secret.'

"I have to admit, the guy was good. Even watching him up close, I couldn't figure out how he did it. Anyway, after another drink or two, we parted ways, and that was the last we saw of Fat Tiago.

"Well, about a year later, Marco and I were sitting in another bar having just successfully finished a pretty tough job. We were talking broadly about our future plans, when the topic of the

Ultimate Con came up. Now, everyone I know in the business has their own Ultimate Con, and it's different for everybody. For some guys, it's the amount of money at stake, for other guys, it's the complexity—how many layers, how many operators, that kind of thing. It really varies. So Marco and I were chatting and, as part of my ongoing efforts to figure out what makes him tick, I asked him what his Ultimate Con would be. And he surprised me by answering right away—he'd obviously given it some thought.

"'Fat Tiago,' he said.

"It took me a minute to remember who that was. When I did, I said, 'A shell game?'

"'No,' said Marco. 'Not literally. What I mean is, a long con where everything's transparent for the mark.'

"I said, 'So the mark knows he's being conned?"

"'Right,' said Marco.

"I said, 'That's just a Shuffle.'

"He said, 'No, this would be different. For one thing, you need at least three people working a Shuffle. Mine would be a one-man job. Other people might be involved, but they wouldn't know they were involved. Or they'd be involved, but not in the way they thought they were, if that makes sense. Also, with a Shuffle, you make the mark feel like they're smarter than they actually are—that's the hook. You only let them know obliquely that you're conning them. In mine, I'd be completely straightforward with the mark.'

"'So what,' I said, 'you just walk up to the mark and say, *Hello, I'm going to con you?*'

"Marco said, 'I know you're joking, but yeah, that's basically what I have in mind. I would approach the mark and say something like, *Hello, my name is Marco Aurélio, I'm a con artist, and I'm very good at what I do. Over the next few weeks, I'm going to con you into giving me a million reais.* Or whatever it is I want from them. It wouldn't have to be money.'

"'Fine,' I said, 'But you're telling me it's not a misdirection, right? You won't tell them, for instance, that you'll con them out of their prize racehorse, and then while they're focused on the horse, you get the deed to their mansion on the beach or something?'

"'That's right,' said Marco. 'If I tell them I'm conning them out of their racehorse, I'll walk away with their racehorse and not something else.'

"I said, 'It's all completely straightforward, then. You tell them who you are, you tell them what you're after, and then they give it to you?'

"'Yeah,' said Marco.

"I said, 'But this has to be a con, remember. You can't tell someone that they're going to hand over their prize racehorse and then, I don't know, you kidnap their daughter and trade her for the horse.'

"'Right,' said Marco."

"'Because that's extortion,' I said, 'not a con. You have to trick them, not pressure them.'

"'I know,' said Marco.

"'Also,' I said, 'you couldn't sneak in and steal it. It can't be a heist, either.'

"'I know,' said Marco. 'I know the rules.'

"I said, 'So let me get this straight. You approach the mark, you introduce yourself, and you tell him you will con him out of his prize racehorse. And then with the mark fully aware of what you're up to, you somehow trick him—not force him, extort him, bribe him, or blackmail him, but trick him—into giving you his racehorse.'

"Marco said, 'That's right.'

"I said, 'Assuming the mark is an even marginally intelligent human being, how does that work?'

"'Marco said, 'I don't know. I haven't worked out the details yet.'

"I said, 'But even broadly, can you explain to me what that might look like?'

"Marco said, 'Not yet—that's why it's my Ultimate Con.'

"At that point, I gave up on the conversation. I'm too much of a pragmatist to waste my time with stuff like that. Like I said, you have to know what drives the people you work with. I do, at least. Marco and I went our separate ways a year or two later—philosophical differences, I suppose. Still, you're not going to find someone in the business more talented than Marco."

Cabral picked up his tumbler and took a swallow of whiskey.

"You seem awfully nostalgic," said Elder Toronto. "Like maybe you know you're never going to see Marco Aurélio again."

"You're persistent," said Cabral. "I'll give you that."

"I intend to find Marco Aurélio," said Elder Toronto. "What can you tell us that would help me do that?"

With one of his thick, stubby fingers, Cabral tapped himself on the chest.

"Contrary to popular belief," he said, "I do have a heart inside here. That's why I hired Galvão, and that's why I'm talking to you. I care about Marco, and I want to find out what happened to him as much as you do."

"Great," said Elder Toronto. "Let's talk, then."

Cabral folded his hands and rested them on the gleaming surface of his desk.

"I have a heart," he said, "but I'm not stupid. Information has power, and I'm not going to give it to you for free."

"We're willing to tell you everything we know," said Elder Toronto. "We can exchange."

Cabral chuckled and shook his head.

"I already know everything that you know," he said. "I know that Galvão is dead, I know that the police don't care, I know that you've spoken with Sílvia. I know all of it."

"Are you sure about that?" said Elder Toronto.

"Yes," said Cabral with a broad smile. "I am. You can't bluff someone who was in the business as long as I was. However, I am willing to set up an exchange. I have some information that I'm sure would be of interest to you."

"What do you want for it?" said Elder Toronto.

"I hired Ulisses Galvão," said Cabral, "to find something out for me. He failed to do so."

"What was he looking for?" said Elder Toronto.

"Not so fast," said Cabral. "Here's my proposal: If the two of you can find out what Galvão couldn't, I will tell you what I know. However, I'd like a handshake agreement on that before I tell you what he was looking for."

Elder Toronto looked at his junior companion. Elder Schwartz wanted nothing more to do with Junior Cabral, but he figured that the sooner they made this deal with him, the sooner they could leave. So he nodded. Elder Toronto reached across the desk and shook Cabral's thick hand.

"You've got a deal," he said.

"Good," said Cabral. "Now. You've heard of the Argentine?"

"Of course," said Elder Toronto.

"The general store, the tunnels, the secret library?"

"Yeah," said Elder Toronto. "I said I'd heard of him."

"Good," said Cabral. "As you can probably guess, most of that is nonsense. Nearly all of it, in fact. But the Argentine does exist. That much is true. And he is a very powerful man, even to this day. If you assume otherwise, you do so at your own peril. Are you with me so far?"

"Sure," said Elder Toronto.

"About two weeks ago, I ran into an old business associate at a restaurant a few blocks from here. He told me that he heard from a friend that Marco's trying to set up a meeting with the Argentine.

This is no easy feat —the man is both powerful and reclusive, so, according to this friend, Marco was asking around, trying to find someone who knew someone who knew the Argentine."

"Why would Marco Aurélio want to meet with the Argentine?" said Elder Toronto.

"If someone wants a meeting with the Argentine," said Cabral, "it's for one of two reasons—either money or protection. Now, like I said, you shouldn't believe those stories you hear about the Argentine—the underground chambers of gold and whatnot. But the man does have very deep pockets, and he's not averse to investing in local business ventures. Most people over in Vila Barbosa could never get a bank loan, but if the Argentine likes the sound of their plans, he might give them enough money to get started in exchange for a percentage of the profits."

"You're saying Marco Aurélio wanted to start a business?" said Elder Toronto.

"If you'll let me finish," said Cabral. "The other reason people meet with the Argentine is for protection. If a resident of Vila Barbosa is being bothered or threatened, especially by somebody from outside the neighborhood, the Argentine might be persuaded to use his considerable local muscle to make the problem go away."

"And what does the Argentine get in return?" said Elder Toronto.

"Loyalty," said Junior Cabral. "A chronically underrated commodity."

"So did Marco Aurélio need money or protection?" said Elder Toronto.

"That's what I hired Ulisses Galvão to find out," said Cabral. "It could be that something or someone spooked Marco, that he ran into trouble with an old mark and needed a little extra muscle. Or he could be looking to start a business or a con or something that would require more seed money than he could rustle up on his own. Or it could be neither of the above. The thing is, though, you don't make an appointment with the Argentine if everything in your life is hunky-dory. Marco's an old friend and if he's in trouble, I'd like to help him."

Cabral lay his hands palms up on the surface of the desk.

"Really, I think we all want the same thing here," he said.

"Maybe," said Elder Toronto.

Cabral smiled back at him, hands raised beatifically.

"All right," said Elder Toronto. "So you want us to find out if Marco Aurélio met with the Argentine?"

"Correct," said Cabral. "And if so, what they discussed."

Elder Toronto tented his hands and held them to his mouth. After a moment's thought, he nodded.

"Sure," he said. "We'll see what we can do."

They all shook hands again and the missionaries left Junior Cabral standing at his vast office window, where he'd opened the blinds to gaze out at a sweeping view of the city's irregular skyline—skyscrapers scattered pell-mell among sprawling shopping malls, single-story restaurants, bustling plazas, mid-sized apartment buildings, and somewhere beyond all that, at the tobacco-colored skyline, the city's tired, dusty slums.

CHAPTER 17

Inside the battered, unlicensed cab, no one spoke. Wanderley, the driver, held tightly to the steering wheel, shaking his head from time to time in barely contained fury. The missionaries had found him waiting for them when they had emerged from Cabral's building, but, by his own report, he had nearly left them there, going so far as to drive a few blocks away before changing his mind and turning back.

"You should have told me when you first called me that the police might be involved," he said when the missionaries had entered his car. "That's something I need to know about."

"It's fine," Elder Toronto said, "We didn't have to involve the police. And anyway," he continued with a shrug, "you could have left if you were uncomfortable with our arrangement."

Wanderley responded in a soft, measured tone, clearly holding back his anger.

"I had already told you that I would stay," he said. "Plus, I've got a family to support."

Elder Toronto looked at him, not responding for a moment, a brief hiccup in his usual social fluency.

"I'm sorry," Elder Toronto finally replied, and Wanderley only shook his head.

Now, Elder Toronto stared out the window, his body motionless, his breathing regular. Elder Schwartz, observing from the back seat, would have guessed that Elder Toronto was sleeping if it weren't for the regular blink of his eyelids, a movement Elder Schwartz could just make out from his vantage point behind the driver's seat. What he hoped would happen next was that Elder Toronto would ask Wanderley to turn right at the upcoming intersection, and then the battered cab would carry them home to their apartment where they could sleep for the rest of the day, and for the night, not venturing out again until the following morning. Elder Schwartz needed the sleep—his head was fuzzy, his eyes hurt, and he was inexplicably chilly in the heat of the day. He wondered how Elder Toronto was managing to remain, by all appearances, fully functional; if he had slept at all the past two nights, it couldn't have been for more than a few minutes.

The cab approached the intersection.

"Left here," said Elder Toronto, and then gave him directions to the street where Marco Aurélio lived. Then he twisted around to face Elder Schwartz, sitting alone in the back seat.

"Can I bounce an idea off you?" said Elder Toronto.

"Sure," said Elder Schwartz.

Elder Toronto pushed the shoulder strap of his seatbelt out of the way, allowing him the full use of his arms as he spoke to his companion in the back seat.

"Okay," said Elder Toronto. "It's just that something feels off about all of this—I have this weird feeling I can't shake."

"It's because you haven't slept in days," said Elder Schwartz. "We should be going home right now."

"No, that's not it," said Elder Toronto. "And I have slept a little. No, this is something else. It's like—have I ever told you about this? I don't think I have. This was back in the CTM."

He paused.

"Go ahead," said Elder Schwartz.

"Okay," said Elder Toronto. "Well, this happened in the CTM, and you know how everyone gets a little stir crazy in there after about a month? You know, you've got the same routine every day and you rarely leave the building and it just gets a little edgy— cabin fever–type stuff."

He paused again, an unprecedented hesitancy manifesting itself.

Elder Schwartz thought back to his own time in the CTM, the training center where every English-speaking elder who came to this country spent the first eight weeks of their mission. He nodded in encouragement.

"Well," said Elder Toronto, "I was ready to get out of there. Couldn't stand being there anymore, you know? Classes were boring, food was boring, other missionaries were boring, at least after spending a month with them in close quarters. You can only have the same conversation so many times. So I decided I needed to do something to keep my mind occupied, or at least amuse myself.

"For the record, I'm not a big fan of pranks. I don't think they're funny. Usually they're just stupid. But after being cooped up in the CTM for five weeks, I could start to see the appeal—they disrupt the routine, if nothing else. So anyway, I knew an elder who helped clean the copy room during his district's service hour. His district and my district ate at adjoining tables during mealtimes, and we were both from Idaho, so we chatted from time to time. Come to find out, this elder was getting stir crazy as well, so he and I put together this plan in the cafeteria one morning of how we would forge a letter from the First Presidency and slip a copy into each district's mailbox. This other elder handled the first part—he found an actual letter from the First Presidency and made a blank letterhead out of it, complete with signatures, in the copy room. It looked great, completely authentic. My part of the bargain was to come up with some content. We hadn't actually figured out what we wanted the letter to say; it just seemed like a funny idea conceptually. So my job was to write the actual letter, print it out, and then get it back to this other elder so he could make copies for distribution. He gave me four or five of these letterhead templates in case I made a mistake or the printer ate one or something.

"I spent a good chunk of the next p-day drafting the letter by hand in a notebook. I don't even remember what it said, exactly. Something patently ridiculous, like all missionaries would now ride horses from appointment to appointment, or would be required to tattoo Joseph Smith's face on their neck, or something very silly like that. From there, the plan was that on the next p-day, I'd type up the bogus letter and print it off on the forged letterhead during our assigned e-mail time.

"Anyway, there I am. I have this notebook filled with drafts of fake letters from the Prophet, along with some suspicious, blank First Presidency letterhead, and I leave it just sitting in a manila folder on my desk when we all go down to the cafeteria for dinner that evening. Which was stupid of me, because when I get back from our evening class at nine-thirty, or whenever, the manila folder is gone.

"I ask the other guys in the room if they've seen it, playing it cool when I do, but none of them know what I'm talking about. So I start looking around, but I'm trying not to look like I'm looking for something, because I don't want my roommates asking too many questions.

"The point is, I don't find it, and I start to worry a little. I mean, this forged letter I'm working on is obviously a joke, but there are so many rules, and I'm sure it breaks plenty of them. Of course, I knew all that going into the project, but the whole plan was that we'd do it sneakily enough that we wouldn't get caught. Clearly, though, I've blown it. At this point I'm pretty concerned.

"The next morning we're all sitting in class learning how to teach about the Word of Wisdom when this elder I've never seen before pokes his head into the room and says that President DeWitt needs to see Elder Toronto, and it's urgent. Was DeWitt still president when you were in the CTM?"

"Yeah," said Elder Schwartz. "I was terrified of him."

"Right," said Elder Toronto. "Ex-military, I think."

"Yeah," said Elder Schwartz.

"Anyway," said Elder Toronto. "I follow this elder to President DeWitt's office and he tells me to go right in, the president is waiting for me. I knock anyway, and President DeWitt opens the door and invites me in. Thing is, he won't look me in the eye, which worries me. He's the kind of man who looks people in the eye, you know? So I'm pretty scared at this point. I figure someone found the folder on my desk, brought it to him, and now it's going to be my head.

"But then he's just standing there, with his crew cut and his perfect posture, not looking me in the eye. Finally, he shakes my hand, and opens his mouth to say something, but before he can get anything out, he starts crying. Which really freaks me out. At this point, I'm assuming that I'll be on the next plane back to the States, dishonorably discharged. Then things get weirder. He hugs me. He hugs me, and he's still crying, and he just holds me like that for a minute. Then he lets go of me and points to a chair and I sit down. He pulls over a chair so he's sitting right across from me, no desk between us, and he kind of pulls himself together. He says, 'Elder Toronto,' and starts tearing up, so he tries again. He says, 'Elder Toronto, I'm afraid that I have,' and then he just loses it. I mean, maybe not audible sobs, but close. Now I *really* don't know what's going on—there's this sixty-year-old man who wants to talk to me, but he's too emotionally devastated to get a word out.

"All told, he's probably crying like that for less than a minute, but it feels much longer. Then he pulls himself together and he apologizes. He says he's received some very upsetting news from Idaho. He tells me there's been a car accident, and my family's been killed. All of them—my mom, my dad, my two younger sisters. And I'll be honest with you here. My first reaction—and it only lasted a second or two—was relief that this wasn't about that prank. I actually thought, *Oh good, I'm not in trouble.* My next reaction was that this must be a joke—you know, is this to teach me a lesson not to do pranks? And obviously it wasn't. It was all true, and President DeWitt just kept talking to me and asking how I was feeling and telling me how sorry he was."

Elder Toronto paused, his eyes down, his chin in his hands. The morning sunlight flickered against his face through the window of the moving car. He went on:

"The point is, I guess, I walked into that meeting asking the wrong questions. That's why I bring all this up. I was so sure that President DeWitt was going to ask about that forged letter prank that I couldn't process anything else he said. I feel like we might be making the same mistake here, like we're asking the wrong questions. There was something off in that meeting with Cabral that I can't quite put my finger on—it felt a little bit like that meeting I had with DeWitt. Do you know what I mean?"

The whole account had left Elder Schwartz feeling even more exhausted and fuzzy-headed than before. He strained for a coherent response.

"Do you think Cabral might be playing us?" said Elder Schwartz.

"What?" said Elder Toronto. He waved a hand dismissively. "Yes. Cabral is definitely playing us. That is eminently clear, Elder Schwartz. But there's something else, don't you think?"

He looked expectantly at Elder Schwartz.

"I don't know," he said.

Elder Toronto waited, seeming hopeful that his junior companion was winding up to something bigger.

"I really don't know," said Elder Schwartz, disconcerted that, for once, his companion seemed to be asking a genuine question of him, a question he couldn't answer for himself.

Elder Toronto waited a moment longer, mouth slightly open, before his face sagged with disappointment.

"Well, forget it then," said Elder Toronto, and turned back around.

The three of them sat in discontented silence until the cab came to a stop between Grillo's house and Marco Aurélio's. The missionaries got out of the car. Elder Toronto pulled a roll of cash from his pants pocket and held it out to Wanderley. The cab driver looked at the roll of money for a moment before he took it.

"Don't call me again," he said.

Wanderley pulled the passenger door shut and drove away.

CHAPTER 18

Before they went looking for the Argentine—which, Elder Toronto said, was the next vital step—they needed to talk to Grillo again. Unfortunately, Grillo was dead.

After Wanderley dropped them off, the two elders clapped at Grillo's gate and waited for a response. Next door, the old woman—Meire—stood sweeping her quintal as usual. They clapped again and Meire looked up at them. Elder Toronto smiled and lifted his hand in greeting. The woman went back to her sweeping. Grillo didn't come to answer the door. Elder Toronto clapped again. They waited. Nothing.

"Maybe he's at work," said Elder Schwartz.

Elder Toronto called Grillo's name and waited. Still nothing.

They walked down the cracked, upheaving sidewalk to the gate next door.

"Excuse me," said Elder Toronto to the old woman.

"Yes?" said Meire, still sweeping, head down.

"Have you seen Grillo today?" he said.

She stopped sweeping and looked up.

"You're looking for Grillo again?" she said.

The missionaries nodded. She leaned her broom against the cinderblock wall that separated her house from Grillo's and approached the gate. She squinted at them from between the metal bars.

"I should have told the police that you boys were here yesterday," she said, "but I didn't."

"Police?" said Elder Toronto.

The old woman pulled a flowery handkerchief from the pocket of her apron and dabbed at the sweat that was beading on her wrinkled face.

"Grillo got killed yesterday," she said.

She folded the handkerchief and returned it to her pocket. Elder Toronto asked her what happened. She told the missionaries that the previous afternoon somebody had called the police to report a murder. The caller had given Grillo's address but had refused to identify himself. The police had found Grillo and Lucinda tied together in the kitchen, beaten to death.

"This was yesterday afternoon?" said Elder Toronto.

The old woman nodded.

"And did anyone on the street see anything unusual?"

Meire shrugged her shoulders beneath her thin, cotton dress.

"Just the two of you," she said.

"And he was beaten to death?" said Elder Toronto.

"That's right," she said.

Elder Toronto shook his head.

"I'm not sure how that happened with no one seeing it," he said. "One person wouldn't be able to beat Grillo to death."

"Grillo?" she said. "Why not?"

"The guy was enormous," said Elder Toronto.

The old woman squinted at him. She jerked her thumb at the house next door.

"The Grillo I knew was a little guy," she said. "Short and mousy. Maybe you're thinking of someone else."

Elder Toronto described the man they had met the day before, the man they had assumed was Grillo. Meire shook her head. She said it certainly wasn't Grillo, and that as far as she knew, nobody matching that description lived in any of the nearby houses. Elder Toronto thanked Meire for her help and she went back to her sweeping. The two missionaries started walking toward the neighborhood's business center.

"What's going on?" said Elder Schwartz.

"It's just what I suspected," said Elder Toronto.

"What?" said Elder Schwartz.

"The man we met was Grillo's killer. He either got all that information about Marco Aurélio from the real Grillo before he killed him, or he made it all up."

They sidestepped a bloated dead dog on the sidewalk and turned left onto a cross street.

"Just as you suspected?" said Elder Schwartz, his voice rising. "But if you suspected all that, then why didn't we do anything about it? And why were we coming back to talk to Grillo if you knew he was dead?"

"What could we have done about it yesterday?" said Elder Toronto. "The only reason we came back today was because I wanted to confirm my hunch."

"No," said Elder Schwartz. "You had no idea that man wasn't Grillo."

"I'm sorry you think that," said Elder Toronto.

"You had no idea," said Elder Schwartz again. "You just can't stand to be wrong about something."

"Look," said Elder Toronto, "I told you yesterday I'd be playing the naïve missionary. It was a tactical performance, and I think it defused a potentially volatile situation. I pretended that I thought that man was Grillo so he wouldn't kill us. I think it's just a testament to my skill that you're so convinced I didn't know what was going on."

"Shut up," said Elder Schwartz.

It took Elder Schwartz several paces to notice that his companion was no longer keeping up. He stopped and turned around. Elder Toronto stood several paces behind him, hands in his pockets, shaking his head. Elder Schwartz walked back to where his senior companion stood.

"What?" he said.

Elder Toronto pulled a hand from his pocket and wagged his finger at Elder Schwartz.

"We can't afford to fall apart at this point," he said.

"Come on," said Elder Schwartz, "just cut it out."

"No," said Elder Toronto. "Listen to me. I know I can be a little condescending at times and I know that I like to be right.

But now is not the time for you to quibble about the flaws in my personality. This is important, and I need you to be bigger than that. Marco Aurélio needs you to be bigger than that. Are you on board with this or not?"

Elder Schwartz had so many problems with this speech that he didn't know where to start. So instead, he did what he was best at and let the matter drop.

"Fine," he said. "I'm sorry."

"You're on board, then?" said Elder Toronto.

"I'm on board," said Elder Schwartz. "Lead the way."

"Trust me on this," said Elder Toronto, and they set out to find the Argentine.

CHAPTER 19

The two elders often asked impertinent questions—Are you religious? Can we come visit you at your house? Are you willing to obey the law of chastity and not have sexual relations outside of marriage?—and were used to the frequently dismayed reactions of the strangers or near-strangers to whom they posed these questions. However, as Elder Toronto and Elder Schwartz walked up the main street of Vila Barbosa, stopping people at random to ask them where they could find the Argentine, it quickly became evident that this question was exponentially more audacious than any of the other ones they often asked.

Although specific reactions varied, almost every one involved a gut-punched look of surprise before the questionee recovered and could respond more deliberately. An evangelical woman in a long skirt furrowed her brow and told them they obviously weren't from around here or otherwise they wouldn't be asking that question. A vendor of caldo de cana fed a long stalk of sugarcane into the turning metal press of his many-geared machine and said that he hadn't heard the question they'd just asked, and they'd better not ask it again. A small group of teenagers, still dressed in their school uniforms, looked nervously at one another and studiously ignored the two missionaries until they walked away. A mustachioed old man in a leather apron handing out business cards in front of a shoe repair shop told them there was no such person and then hurried back inside his shop.

The elders then tried their luck at a series of bars, bartenders being, in Elder Toronto's experience, a class of people rich in cartographical knowledge of the neighborhood and generally willing to share it. Today, however, the bartenders, one after the other, told the missionaries they couldn't help them, that the elders needed to leave unless they planned on buying something. One of the bartenders, an avuncular, one-armed northerner who, on especially hot days, was known to offer chilly glasses of free guaraná to tired missionaries, told the two elders that they didn't know what they were asking. He said that if they knew what was good for them, they'd drop it immediately. Elder Toronto explained that this was important and they were trying to help a friend.

"Listen," said the one-armed bartender, "I don't know if you think you're exempt because you're young or religious or from the States, or whatever, but the two of you can be killed—or worse— just as easily as anyone else in Vila Barbosa."

Elder Toronto thanked the man for his concern and they left the bar, continuing their search.

They clapped at an assortment of houses where they were received no more warmly. The residents peered out of their doors and windows as Elder Toronto asked as innocently as possible where they might find the Argentine. At most of the homes, the only response the elders received was a slammed door. The more communicative people said that they couldn't help, or that there was no such person, or that they couldn't understand what Elder Toronto was saying.

"Do you think this is a good idea?" said Elder Schwartz as they walked to the next row of houses.

"It's the next move," said Elder Toronto. "You heard Cabral."

"Yeah," said Elder Schwartz, "but was he telling the truth?"

"It's a good question," said Elder Toronto, "and I'm glad you're asking it. It shows you're thinking. Here's my take on the situation. If everything Junior Cabral told us about Marco Aurélio and the Argentine is true—which I doubt—then it's important for us to find out what they talked about. Then we can take what we know, find out what Cabral knows, and hopefully be that much closer to finding Marco Aurélio. If what Cabral told us is partly true and partly a lie—which I think is the more likely case—I'm guessing it's still important for us to find out if Marco Aurélio met with the Argentine. If I were a betting man, I'd bet Cabral is truly interested in some connection with the Argentine, even if the rest is lies.

"And then there's the possibility that this is a red herring, and Cabral wants us distracted from more important questions. It's possible, I suppose, but like I said, Cabral seemed like he really wanted us to talk to the Argentine. If that was an act, though, I figure the Argentine is an influential enough person in the neighborhood that he's bound to know something about what happened to Marco Aurélio."

Elder Schwartz said, "But what I meant was, is it safe to go looking for the Argentine? I'm not sure it's a very good idea."

"Don't worry," said Elder Toronto. "We'll find him."

"That's not what I'm asking," said Elder Schwartz.

Elder Toronto ignored this, stepping up to the gate of a house and clapping to get the attention of the occupants inside.

The day wore on with increasingly unpromising results. Elder Toronto attempted a wide range of approaches with the strangers they questioned—flattery, affected naïveté, mild belligerence, wheedling, bribery—all to no avail. He grew more and more despondent with each claim of ignorance as to the Argentine's whereabouts.

"Who's talked to us about the Argentine in the past?" said Elder Toronto. "There has to be somebody."

Elder Schwartz knew he had heard stories of the Argentine, and as he thought about it, he could recall dozens of anecdotes involving the man's memorable acts of violence, his arrival in Vila Barbosa and subsequent rise to power, his shaping of the neighborhood, his secret libraries, his hidden labyrinths of tunnels, his deputies and minions, his inscrutable machinations. What Elder Schwartz couldn't recall, however, was where exactly he had heard these stories. They had come from multiple sources, certainly, and Elder Schwartz could conjure up vague recollections of hushed voices, confidential tones, furtive glances. But, try as he might, he couldn't pinpoint a single specific location, a single recognizable speaker. It would seem that the stories had simply accumulated in his consciousness during the time he had spent in Vila Barbosa, reflexively absorbed into his system like the neighborhood's polluted air.

If Elder Schwartz found it difficult to recall where exactly he had heard the stories of the Argentine, he had an even harder time articulating to himself how the stories made him feel. Where he had experienced—and continued to experience—strong feelings of dread while working in Vila Barbosa, he experienced even stronger feelings when he thought of the Argentine, feelings both more dreadful and more obscure. Months earlier, the thought of being transferred to Vila Barbosa had left him dry-mouthed and sweaty with fear. The prospect of meeting the Argentine, however, was too massive a thing for either his brain or his body to comprehend. It left him feeling oddly weightless, a bit lightheaded.

As Elder Toronto grew more and more desperate to find the Argentine, Elder Schwartz grew more and more resigned. Unlike his companion, he knew that they would find the legendary figure sooner or later, knew that their search for Marco Aurélio had probably been leading them in this direction all along. They would meet the Argentine, pulled in by the man's planetary gravity, and then—and then, what? Again, that woozy dread.

The sun, sinking toward the horizon, cast a rust-colored light over the hazy neighborhood. The two missionaries sat down at the edge of a crumbling sidewalk. Elder Toronto pulled the map of the neighborhood from his bag and spread it out on his knees.

"Should we call it a day?" said Elder Schwartz.

Elder Toronto smoothed out a section of the map, peering closely at the tiny, printed words.

"No," he said, "we'll keep looking."

With his index finger, he traced a path on the map, looked up at the street sign a few yards away, and then back down at the map.

"What are you planning to do when we find the Argentine?" said Elder Schwartz.

"We'll talk to him," said Elder Toronto, "ask him some questions."

"And he'll just answer them?" said Elder Schwartz.

"Whether or not he answers our questions," said Elder Toronto, "I think we'll learn something valuable from speaking with him."

"I don't know," said Elder Schwartz.

"Look," said Elder Toronto, setting aside the map. "I'm so close to figuring this out. Last night, everything felt like a total dead end, like there weren't any cracks I could wedge my fingers into, you know? But today we're making progress. Think of everything we've found out between yesterday evening and today. Seriously— think about it. We've talked to Sílvia, we've talked to Cabral—we have a completely different picture of Marco Aurélio now than we did twenty-four hours ago. There's so much more to work with, and I can solve this, Elder Schwartz. Yesterday evening I worried I wouldn't be able to, but I can. I don't know the answer yet, but I'm getting closer."

Elder Schwartz kicked at a pebble and watched it skip across the dirt road.

"But what are we even trying to accomplish here?" said Elder Schwartz. "Marco Aurélio is probably already dead anyway."

"So what if he were?" said Elder Toronto. "What would that change?"

"Well," said Elder Schwartz. "If he's dead, then what are we looking for?"

Elder Toronto squinted at him, as if the question were incomprehensible.

"Look," said Elder Toronto. "It's like a samurai—samurai have all sorts of duties and obligations to other people, and the whole point of being a samurai is that they won't rest until they fulfill those duties."

"What kinds of duties?" said Elder Schwartz.

"You want to know what kinds of duties?" said Elder Toronto. "Think about it this way, Elder Schwartz. If a samurai's friend disappeared, do you think the samurai would just throw up his hands and say, *oh well, what can you do, I'm kind of sleepy anyway, let's just forget about it?* No, he wouldn't. Because a samurai honors the obligations of friendship."

"But we're not samurais," said Elder Schwartz.

"Samurai," said Elder Toronto.

"What?" said Elder Schwartz.

"Samurai," said Elder Toronto. "The plural of samurai is samurai."

"I don't care," said Elder Schwartz.

"Clearly," said Elder Toronto. "Now quiet down and let me think."

Elder Schwartz was about to respond to this when they were interrupted by a familiar voice.

"Elders," said the voice. "How good to see you."

The two of them looked up and saw Sister Beatrice walking down the sidewalk toward them, loaded down with grocery bags. The missionaries jumped up to help her with her load, but she shook her head and set the bags down. The elders shook her hand.

"It's nice to see you, Sister," said Elder Toronto. "How are you this evening?"

She smiled. She said she was just on her way back from the store. She was making a special meal for Abelardo tomorrow because tomorrow was the anniversary of their marriage. The elders congratulated her and asked how Brother Abelardo was doing today.

"He's been a little down for the past few days," Beatrice said. "His gout is acting up and he's feeling pretty discouraged about it. If you two were to stop by, I'm sure it would cheer him up a bit."

"Abelardo," said Elder Toronto. "Of course."

"He'd be so pleased to see you," she said.

Elder Toronto said they'd be happy to stop by—there were a couple of questions they'd like to ask him. Beatrice smiled and said that this must be a serendipitous meeting then. Elder Toronto nodded in agreement. The two elders picked up the bags of groceries that Beatrice had set down on the sidewalk and the three of them started walking.

THE ARGENTINE

They say that as the above-ground deputies and the subterranean minions gathered in the dimly lit interior of the Argentine's general store, both groups regarded one another with no small degree of mistrust. By this point in the neighborhood's history, those six above-ground deputies had grown old and grizzled, each one now commanding dozens of deputies of their own. Their knees creaked and popped as they sat down on their overturned grocery crates.

For their part, the subterranean minions—their skin ghostly and smooth from being deprived of sunlight for so many years—opted to remain standing, and lurked in the shadowy corners of the store. As was their custom, the minions spoke to one another in whispers, causing the above-ground deputies to glance back at them with growing unease.

Tensions rising, the door behind the counter opened and the Argentine stepped out. In the time since that last decisive meeting with the deputies, the Argentine had aged considerably. His skin had wrinkled, his hair had grayed, his posture had stooped, but, as he revealed with a pained grimace, his square teeth remained as white as ever. He stepped out in front of the counter and greeted the men and women in attendance. Then he cleared his throat and began to speak.

"I've made a mistake," he said, his voice grown scratchy with time, "Without realizing it, I've spent the past several decades constructing an elaborate prison for myself. Just this morning, I recognized what I've done. Vila Barbosa has become a physical extension of my own mind."

He paused, allowing this to sink in. The mouths of the deputies pursed in consternation, the heads of the minions tilted to the side, perplexed. None of them spoke. The Argentine continued. He said he realized that this affliction was a unique one, that it must be difficult for them to understand. He explained it like this: that it felt like he was asleep, aware that he was dreaming and he wanted badly to wake up. Because everything around him was an extension of his own imagination, he could comprehend it all. He could discern the motives behind even the most eccentric actions, anticipate the punch line of every joke, avert any disaster. Nothing could surprise him, nothing could challenge him. He paused again.

Breaking the silence, the tattooed deputy said, "So you'd like us to help you come up with a solution?"

The Argentine smiled sadly. He said that he had already anticipated the ideas that they would come up with, and they were all completely inadequate. Both the deputies and the minions shifted uncomfortably.

"The reason I've called you here," said the Argentine, "is because I've already come up with a solution, and I need you to spread a message to the people of the neighborhood. I'm holding a contest of sorts, open to anyone who would like to enter."

This sent a murmur of surprise through the deputies, a flurry of whispers through the minions. The Argentine silenced them all with a dangerous tilt of his head. Duly chastened, they turned and faced forward in their seats and offered up their rapt attention. After allowing the silent anticipation to build, the Argentine unfolded the details of his sinister challenge. When he finished his explanation, the terrible possibilities now abundantly clear, a shudder ran through the room.

"Now go," said the Argentine, and the group dispersed into the night.

CHAPTER 20

In spite of Beatrice's best efforts, the little nook of a house where she and Abelardo lived had the atmosphere of a tomb, the light bulbs somehow never bright enough to fill all the dark corners, the walls perpetually grimy despite diligent scrubbing, the air always laced with the smells of mildew, illness, and decay. Beatrice and the two missionaries entered the house to find Abelardo seated at the kitchen table with a guest, the two of them hunched over a chessboard. The guest sat with his back to the door, with Abelardo sitting across from him wrapped in a thick, crocheted blanket.

While Abelardo usually suffered through his ailments with a certain amount of gusto, giving the impression that on some level he relished his battles with the myriad sicknesses that ravaged, but failed to destroy, his body, tonight Abelardo looked exactly like the dying old man that he was. His skin, a cadaverous gray, resembled cheap newsprint in the dim light. His head trembled perceptibly and his lips twitched with movements that didn't quite form words. A white glob of spit had collected at the corner of his mouth. He looked up from his game and nodded weakly at Beatrice and the missionaries.

Following Abelardo's gaze, the guest turned in his chair. When he saw who had entered, he stood, revealing himself to be a similarly ancient, but much more robust, old man. He was neatly dressed in the uniform favored by the old men of the city—sandals, chinos, and a short-sleeved button-down shirt undone nearly to his navel. The top of his head was completely bald and the remaining hair on the sides was trimmed close to his scalp, giving an impression of tidiness and control. In contrast, his eyelids, lips, and chin sagged dramatically, conveying the sense that over the course of his life, gravity had affected the guest's face more severely than it had the rest of his body.

"Good evening," said the guest, his voice marked with a faint accent.

The missionaries returned his greeting and immediately set to work putting away the groceries. For her part, Beatrice remained in the doorway, her posture stiff and formal, her hands folded in front of her.

"Luis," she said, "what a nice surprise. If I had known that you and Abelardo were meeting tonight, I would have baked something for the two of you."

"Please," said Luis, "I would hate to have inconvenienced you. And besides, I came here strictly for the company—I wanted to talk about the old days in Vila Barbosa, and Abelardo is just about the only other one left who remembers them."

He smiled and Abelardo nodded gravely, his eyes staring vacantly at the chipped and faded chess set before him.

"We always enjoy your visits," said Beatrice. She gestured at the elders, still unloading the grocery bags. "Luis, have you met the missionaries?"

"Not these two, no. I haven't had the pleasure."

Abelardo shuddered beneath his thick blanket.

"This is Elder Toronto," said Beatrice.

Elder Toronto set down the tin of olive oil he had pulled from the grocery bag and shook hands with Luis.

"And this is Elder Schwartz."

Somehow, Elder Schwartz had knocked the lid off the container of honey that Beatrice had bought, and his fingers were covered with the sticky, viscous result. He held his hands up in mute apology and Luis nodded in understanding.

"It's nice to meet you," said Elder Toronto, returning to his task of putting away the groceries.

"Likewise," said Luis.

Elder Schwartz, having rinsed his hands clean under the kitchen faucet, dried them on the towel and rejoined Elder Toronto in unloading the grocery bags. Luis watched the two elders for a moment, while Beatrice and Abelardo watched him watching.

After a moment, Luis said, "I understand you've been looking for me today."

"Excuse me?" said Elder Toronto, setting down a bag of cevada on one of Beatrice's makeshift shelves.

"I said, I understand you've been looking for me."

"No, I heard," said Elder Toronto, "it's just—"

He looked carefully at the old man.

"Oh," said Elder Toronto.

A slight smile crossed Luis's face.

"I hear you've been asking after the Argentine," he said, "and that's what people call me. I've lived in this country, this neighborhood, for longer than most people in Vila Barbosa have been alive," he shrugged his shoulders and pursed his droopy lips, "but still I'm a foreigner to them."

The man had both missionaries' full attention.

Luis said, "I'm assuming this is about your friend Marco Aurélio?"

Goosebumps prickled Elder Schwartz's arms.

"That's right," said Elder Toronto.

"I met him a couple of weeks ago," said Luis, "and we spoke at length. Abelardo tells me he's gone missing since them."

"Yes, he has."

"Well," said Luis, "I'd be happy to talk to you about it, although I'm not sure if I'll be of much help."

"Yes," said Elder Toronto. "Please."

Beatrice said, "You're welcome to stay for dinner—you and the elders could talk it over here."

Luis shook his head.

"Thank you, but I'm afraid I've tired out your husband," he said.

Abelardo didn't disagree. Instead, the frail old man pulled the crocheted afghan tighter against his thin body.

"Some other time then," said Beatrice.

"Yes, of course," said Luis. "You're always so hospitable."

Elder Toronto stepped forward.

"We're still available to meet with you tonight, though," he said.

Luis shook his head. "No," he said. "Not tonight. I need my sleep."

"First thing in the morning, then?" said Elder Toronto.

Another faint smile flickered across the old man's face.

"Do you know the street Alto das Almas?" said Luis.

Elder Toronto said that he did.

"I live at the top of that street. Come by around seven tomorrow and we'll talk over breakfast."

"No," said Abelardo, speaking for the first time since the missionaries had arrived, his voice a wavering croak. "I don't think they'll be able to make it, Luis."

Elder Toronto looked from Abelardo to Luis.

"We'll be there," he said.

Luis said he would look forward to it, and the muscles of his face hoisted the edges of his drooping mouth into a smile.

"Abelardo, we'll finish our game another time," he said, gesturing at the chessboard.

Abelardo didn't respond and Beatrice wished Luis a good evening as he stepped out from the dim, musty house into the clear night. He shut the door and the room was silent. Abelardo leaned his trembling head back against the wall and sighed.

CHAPTER 21

When the elders got home to their downstairs apartment that evening, nobody was waiting in the darkness with a gun. Nobody threatened their lives. Nobody demanded to know what they knew about Marco Aurélio. They turned on the lights and found each room to be decidedly empty. The sensible reaction to this state of affairs, Elder Schwartz believed, was to go straight to bed and sleep for as long as circumstances allowed. He was on his way to the bedroom to do just that, when Elder Toronto stopped him.

"Hang on."

He stood, hands on his hips, in front of the extensive grid of index cards he had created and taped to the wall the night before. Finding the card he was searching for, the one labeled "Junior Cabral," Elder Toronto pulled the pen from his shirt pocket and added several lines of text to the front of the card.

"What do you need?" said Elder Schwartz.

"What?" said Elder Toronto, still writing intently.

"You told me to hang on. What do you need?"

"Right," said Elder Toronto. "I could use your help. For starters, could you hand me one of these blank cards from your desk?"

"I'm really tired," said Elder Schwartz. "I think it would be better if I just went to bed."

"Don't be silly," said Elder Toronto. He finished what he was writing on the Junior Cabral card and turned around. "Come on. Hand me a blank card, would you? You're closer to the desk anyway."

He held his hand out expectantly. Elder Schwartz picked up a blank card, crossed the room, and slapped it into Elder Toronto's hand.

"Thank you," said Elder Toronto.

He taped the card to the wall and wrote "Luis (the Argentine?)" across the top of it.

"Now, what do we know about this guy?"

"Nothing," said Elder Schwartz. "We know nothing about him."

"Come on—you're being lazy," said Elder Toronto. "We know a few things. He was at Beatrice and Abelardo's house. What does that tell us?"

"That he's a friend of Beatrice and Abelardo."

"I would say acquaintance—'friend' assumes too much—but that's good work."

Elder Toronto wrote "Acquaintance of Abelardo and Beatrice" on the card.

"What else?"

"We know he lives on Alto das Almas," said Elder Schwartz, "and we know he talked to Marco Aurélio just before he disappeared."

"He told us both of those things, but we have no way of verifying them yet. I'm inclined to believe the first statement; I'm not sure about the second one."

He wrote them both on the card anyway.

"Hand me those highlighters, would you?" he said, pointing at the cup of pens on Elder Schwartz's desk. Elder Schwartz crossed the room, retrieved the highlighters, and handed them to Elder Toronto.

"Thanks," said Elder Toronto. "Now give me just a minute."

He hovered over the cards, highlighters uncapped, marking the occasional line of text in pink or yellow. He paused over each card, deliberating silently before marking a line here, a line there. The process dragged on. Elder Schwartz tried to leave a few times, but each time he did, Elder Toronto stopped him, saying that he'd just be another minute or two, that he could really use Elder Schwartz's input once he finished.

At one point, Elder Schwartz asked what they were going to do when President Madvig arrived the next morning.

"I can't think about that right now," said Elder Toronto.

"No, seriously," said Elder Schwartz. "What if he gets here while we're meeting with Luis?"

"He won't," said Elder Toronto, still hovering over his cards. "When he does an area visit, he usually gets there around the end of companion study. He won't be here until ten."

"Fine," said Elder Schwartz, "but what do we do once he's here? Put everything on hold?"

Elder Toronto made a mark on one of the cards.

"No," he said. "We'll need to bluff him. We'll say there's so much to show him in our area that we need to split up. So you'll take President Madvig to visit some fake investigators, and I'll take whichever of the assistants he brings to visit Junior Cabral."

"And they'll just be totally okay with that?"

"We'll see which assistant he brings," said Elder Toronto. "It'll be easier if it's Elder Silvestre, but even Elder Saramago I can handle."

"But how?" said Elder Schwartz.

"Too many questions," said Elder Toronto. "Let me concentrate," and he returned his full attention to the cards.

Finally, many minutes later, Elder Toronto capped the highlighters and took a step back from the wall. The entire process of evaluating each card had taken a full hour.

"What do you think?" said Elder Toronto.

"I don't know what I'm looking at," said Elder Schwartz.

Elder Toronto stepped up to the wall and pulled his pen from his shirt pocket to use as a pointer.

"I've highlighted in yellow everything we know to be true—the verifiable facts."

He moved his pen to a line of pink.

"In pink, I've highlighted what is probably true, but that we can't know for sure. Everything that's left blank is information that's probably not true or is completely unverifiable."

"Okay," said Elder Schwartz.

"So," said Elder Toronto, moving his pen, "take, for example, the card I made for Sílvia. We know for sure that she works in that lanchonete, and we know that when we went there with Marco Aurélio, he said something that upset her. We don't know what he said, but we know he said it. Those are the things we know for sure, so that's in yellow. Here's what I think is probably true about Sílvia—you see that's highlighted in pink. She was probably romantically involved with Marco Aurélio, and she was probably a con artist. What I don't think is true is that both of them lived in Vila Barbosa for so many years and never ran into each other until that day when you were transferred here. A lot of people live in Vila Barbosa, so it's possible, but I just don't buy it. I suspect they were in contact before that day. Anyway, I've done the same thing with all the other cards as well."

Elder Schwartz looked over the cards and saw a lot of unhighlighted text, with an occasional line of pink and an even more occasional line of yellow.

Elder Toronto put his pen back in his shirt pocket.

"I realize there's not much up there that we know for sure," he said, "but part of the problem is that the bulk of our information comes from three sources—Grillo, Sílvia, and Junior Cabral. The man we thought was Grillo wasn't Grillo. He's probably, in fact, the man who killed Grillo, so everything he told us is suspect at best. All we know for sure is that a guy named Grillo lived next door to Marco Aurélio, and that Grillo and his wife were murdered. We don't even know for sure that Grillo was Marco Aurélio's brother. I think it's possible, maybe even probable, but we don't know. Next we have Sílvia and Cabral. Both of them were or are con artists, which once again renders the information we have from them very suspect."

"I think Cabral did it," said Elder Schwartz.

"Did what?" said Elder Toronto.

"All this. I think he's the one we should be going after."

"He's definitely a major player," said Elder Toronto, "but we've got one disappearance and three murders to account for. I think it's unlikely that he'd kill Galvão, the man he himself hired to find Marco Aurélio, so that means he couldn't be responsible for everything."

"But we don't absolutely know for sure that he's the one who hired Galvão."

"True," said Elder Toronto, "but I still don't think Cabral is behind everything."

"Who do you think did it, then?" said Elder Schwartz. "The Argentine—this guy Luis?"

"First of all, I'm not sure Luis is actually *the* Argentine. Second of all, Cabral seemed pretty intent on shifting our focus to the Argentine. As we already discussed, I'm not sure what to make of that."

"Okay, fine," said Elder Schwartz. "So we figure that one person is responsible for kidnapping Marco Aurélio, or whatever it is that happened to him, and a second person is responsible for hiring Galvão to investigate the disappearance. Then we can figure that the first person is also responsible for the murders, right? Because they didn't want whoever hired Galvão to find Marco Aurélio? We just have to decide for sure which of the two people is Cabral and which is the Argentine. Right?"

"Maybe," said Elder Toronto.

"What do you mean, maybe?" said Elder Schwartz. "What do you think is going on instead?"

"I have a few different theories."

He looked at the cards on the wall.

"Are you going to tell them to me?" said Elder Schwartz.

"Not yet," said Elder Toronto. "I need to think through them some more. And I want to get your impressions on a couple of things without biasing you with my ideas. We also need to figure out how to approach this meeting with Luis tomorrow morning."

"I think it's time for you to just tell me what you're thinking."

"Like I said," said Elder Toronto, "I think it would be better if I didn't bias—"

"No," said Elder Schwartz, "I'd like to know what you think is going on."

"Look," said Elder Toronto, "If you're going to be difficult about this, you might as well just go to bed."

"Great," said Elder Schwartz, and went to bed.

CHAPTER 22

As he fell asleep, memories of Marco Aurélio's baptism two months earlier bobbed to the surface of Elder Schwartz's mind:

A hot day—a steaming pressure cooker of a day. The members of the Vila Barbosa ward, seated in warm metal folding chairs, immobilized by the heat. Even the children of Claudemir and Fátima overheated into red-faced stillness.

They had trekked via bus from Vila Barbosa to Parque Laranjeira, where the Mormon congregation had a building of their own, and, more important, a baptismal font. The heat-exhausted members of the Vila Barbosa ward room filed into the building's vast Relief Society room, whose front wall contained wide double doors, now propped open to reveal the font—a sunken, tiled pool about the size of a walk-in closet. The members of the Vila Barbosa ward sat down in the metal folding chairs that were already set up for their use.

Marco Aurélio and Elder Schwartz, both dressed in ill-fitting white jumpsuits, sat in the front row of folding chairs.

"You've never done this before, have you?" whispered Marco Aurélio.

Elder Schwartz shook his head.

"Seems straightforward enough, though," said Marco Aurélio.

"Yeah," said Elder Schwartz.

Marco Aurélio nodded. He folded his arms, his fingers worrying at the bunched fabric of the jumpsuit.

"Pretty straightforward," he repeated.

The service began with Abelardo giving an opening prayer, which quickly metamorphosed from a simple invocation to a rambling jeremiad, lasting one minute, then two, then three. In all likelihood, it would have kept going indefinitely if Beatrice hadn't leaned forward and whispered loudly to her husband that that was probably enough. Abelardo paused at his wife's advice, and then closed the prayer and sat down. The rest of the group opened their eyes, except for Bishop Claudemir who had fallen asleep, his head still bowed as if in contemplation. Beatrice led them in singing a hymn, their voices weaker than usual in the overwhelming heat. Then Fátima, in her gravelly voice, gave a brief talk reminding the tiny congregation of the key principles of baptism—that baptism meant a rebirth and a washing away of our sins, that it meant we promised to obey God's commandments and He promised to bless us with His Spirit. She closed her talk by saying how glad she was that Marco Aurélio had chosen to take this very important step.

As she returned to her seat, Marco Aurélio stood up.

"Listen," he said, "I know this isn't on the program and I'm not sure if it's allowed or not, but I'd like to say something before I do this. It means a lot to me how kind you've all been—the elders and the rest of you—and I want you to know that this baptism isn't something I'm taking lightly. I'm honored to join this company of saints." He turned to Elder Schwartz. "I'm ready when you are."

While Elder Schwartz and Marco Aurélio stepped out of the room, Claudemir and Abelardo stationed themselves at the edge of the font to act as witnesses. In the hallway, Elder Schwartz opened the narrow door that revealed the tiled stairs leading down into the water.

"Go ahead," said Elder Schwartz, and Marco Aurélio stepped down into the font. Elder Schwartz followed, the water bracingly cold in contrast to the oppressive heat of the day. He descended the stairs until he was in up to his waist, cold water creeping up the fabric of his jumpsuit.

"Ready?" said Elder Schwartz.

Marco Aurélio nodded. Elder Schwartz raised his right arm and said that he baptized Marco Aurélio in the name of the Father and the Son and the Holy Ghost. Then, with his hand behind Marco Aurélio's back, he lowered him into the chilly water. Elder

Schwartz watched him go all the way under, tiny bubbles escaping from his nose, his dark hair wreathing around his head. He pulled him back up above the surface. Marco Aurélio coughed and sputtered and wiped the water away from his eyes.

"Okay," he said, and the two of them left the cool water for the stifling air above.

CHAPTER 23

Luis sat on the curb in front of the little general store, his arms resting on his knees. A frayed straw fedora shaded his eyes from the morning sun. When he saw the missionaries approaching his store, his sagging face lifted into a polite smile. He stood up.

"Elders," he said, "good morning."

He shook their hands and invited them inside his store. The space was small—not much bigger than a newsstand—but appeared both amply and tidily stocked. The wooden shelves lining the walls, their surfaces smooth with a dozen layers of paint, held the kind of basic food and home goods that were ubiquitous throughout the neighborhood's households—rice, beans, farofa, soap, sugar, coffee, goiabada, canned palmito, string, olive oil.

"This way," said Luis, opening a door behind the front counter. They stepped through the doorway into a tiny kitchen, its table—which took up most of the space in the room—set for breakfast with fresh rolls, warm milk, coffee, and a bowl of fresh fruit. Luis removed his hat and hung it on a hook next to the door. The corners of the kitchen were piled high with books.

"Please," he said, gesturing at his table, "have a seat."

Elder Toronto and Elder Schwartz sat down. Luis picked up the small pitcher of warm milk.

"Milk?" he said, and both elders said yes. He filled their cups and told them there was chocolate powder if they wanted it. He filled his own glass with coffee.

"I hope you don't mind," said Luis. "I know you're not allowed."

"Go right ahead," said Elder Toronto.

Luis added two spoonfuls of sugar to his cup and stirred it in.

"You know a little about the church, then," said Elder Toronto.

"I've met several of your colleagues over the years," said Luis.

He took a sip of his coffee and added another spoonful of sugar.

"The older I get, the more of a sweet tooth I have," he said, stirring the coffee.

"So have you ever received the missionary lessons?" said Elder Toronto.

"Oh yes," said Luis. "Many times."

He pushed the bread and the bowl of fruit across the table toward the missionaries.

"Don't be shy about the food," he said. "If you don't eat it, I'll probably end up feeding it to the dogs. I eat so little these days."

The elders obliged him, each taking a roll and a piece of fruit—a slightly green banana for Elder Schwartz and a red persimmon for Elder Toronto. They pushed the rolls and the bowl of fruit back across the table to Luis, but he shook his head.

"Just coffee for me this morning."

Elder Schwartz peeled his banana and took a bite. Elder Toronto mixed a spoonful of chocolate powder into his milk. He licked the spoon and set it on the table.

"This breakfast is very nice, but I'd like to get to the point," said Elder Toronto. "What can you tell us about Marco Aurélio?"

Luis took a sip of coffee.

"I'm afraid you'll be disappointed," he said. "I can't tell you much."

"Well, anything you can tell us will be extremely helpful," said Elder Toronto.

Luis picked up a roll and tore it in half. Lips pursed in concentration, he spread a thin layer of margarine on one half and took a bite as the two missionaries watched expectantly. He set the roll down on his breakfast saucer and brushed the crumbs from his fingers.

"Early last week," he said, "I took a meeting here in the store with your friend Marco Aurélio. He had, shall we say, a business proposition for me. I found him to be articulate and professional. His proposition intrigued me, so I told him to go ahead with his plans. Then we shook hands, and that was that."

"And what was his proposition?" said Elder Toronto.

"I'm sorry," said Luis, "but Marco Aurélio made the presentation in confidence. It would be unprofessional of me to tell you."

Elder Toronto raised an eyebrow, waiting for more.

"I'm afraid I've disappointed you," said Luis. "I wish I could be more helpful."

Elder Toronto leaned forward.

"I think you can tell us more than that," he said. "I think you're holding out on us."

Luis took a sip of his coffee.

"I really didn't want to get your hopes up," he said. "I've told you all I can."

"All you can or all you will?" said Elder Toronto.

Luis smiled.

"I forget sometimes how young you elders are," he said. "Just boys, really."

"You need to tell us what the two of you talked about," said Elder Toronto, undeterred. "Junior Cabral seemed to think that Marco Aurélio was in some kind of trouble."

"Junior Cabral," said Luis with a shake of his head. "He's as clever as he is cruel, you know." He took a bite of his roll and chewed it thoughtfully, eyes downcast in contemplation. He swallowed and looked back up at the elders. "Although not quite so clever, perhaps, as your friend Marco Aurélio?" His wrinkled mouth turned up in a faint smile.

"Don't turn this into a joke," said Elder Toronto.

"Who said I was joking?" said Luis.

His red-rimmed gaze fixed on the old man, Elder Toronto rolled the persimmon, which he had eaten none of, in impatient circles on the tabletop.

Elder Schwartz, for his part, had woken up that morning hopeful that this whole mess might soon be drawing to a close. It was quickly becoming clear, however, that their visit with Luis would resolve nothing. He folded his arms and sighed.

"Tell me," said the old man after a minute. "Why do you think I would know anything more about your friend's disappearance?"

Elder Toronto rolled the persimmon under his hand.

"Because I've heard the stories people tell about you," he said.

"So have I," said Luis. "They amuse me."

"Do they?" said Elder Toronto.

Luis took a sip of his coffee.

"You like those stories, don't you?" he said to Elder Toronto, smiling. "And why not? It's the kind of thing you're looking for right now, isn't it? What you think you want is a tidy narrative."

"What if I do?" said Elder Toronto.

"You're a smart boy," said Luis. "You should know that a story like that isn't going to satisfy you. It might satisfy someone like your friend here," he nodded at Elder Schwartz, "but not you. Not in the long run. Take a moment and think about how you've felt during the past few days."

"We're getting off track," said Elder Toronto, fingers tightening around the persimmon.

"I'll confess now," continued Luis, "that I've been following your little investigation very closely. And as I said, I'd like you to think about how you've felt during the past few days."

Elder Toronto tossed the now-bruised persimmon from hand to hand, his face a blank.

"You've felt good, haven't you?" continued Luis. "Energized. Engaged in the world around you. Untroubled by thoughts of what awaits you after your mission. You may have even felt flashes of joy." Luis smiled. "It's the thrill of the chase."

Elder Toronto set the persimmon back on the table.

"Am I wrong?" said Luis.

Elder Toronto looked down at his hands.

"In the swirl of these invigorating emotions, you might believe that what you're yearning for is a solution to this mystery, but I can tell you from sad experience that for people like you and me, these so-called solutions can only disappoint. What you're truly longing for right now, my friend, is more mystery—a continuation of this thrill that comes from an active mind being challenged."

"No," said Elder Toronto. "What I want is a solution that explains Marco Aurélio's disappearance, and I want it to be true. I'm just trying to help my friend. This isn't about me."

Luis nodded gravely, his gaze coming to rest on the bowl of fruit in the middle of the table. After a moment, he looked up at Elder Toronto.

"They say I've built a labyrinth beneath this neighborhood," he said. "It's preposterous, of course, but there's a kernel of truth somewhere in there. Mazes fascinate me. It's an interest I inherited from my maternal grandfather. He designed them for wealthy aristocrats in the old country. He would make up the plans and then oversee their construction on the grounds of the estates. Usually they were built of shrubs or even just flagstones laid out on the lawn. Occasionally his patrons requested something more substantial—wooden fencing or brick walls—but that was very rare.

"The mazes were always well designed, but never too difficult to navigate, as per his patrons' requests. The mazes he built for me, his young grandson, however, were a different story; drawn on the backs of rejected plans, they filled the great expanse of the draft paper, minutely designed and astonishingly intricate. I spent hours attempting to solve each puzzle, wandering through the passageways with my finger, or, if I was feeling bold, a pencil. Finishing quickly meant disappointment for both me and my grandfather. I relished my time spent inside the mazes searching for a route through the complex arrangements of walls and doors. My grandfather, for his part, prided himself on the intricacy of his designs, his ability to keep me occupied and wandering. He talked, on occasion, of a never-ending maze that would somehow go on forever, with paths that never re-crossed themselves, and walls that offered up infinite possibilities to the intrepid solver. I often tried to imagine what that might look like. After the aristocracy fell, my grandfather's occupation vanished, and he drank himself to death in a matter of years. He's long dead now, but my affinity for mazes has continued.

"I envy this situation of yours, this investigation into your friend's disappearance. What you have is an incredibly complex labyrinth of possibilities. Yes, you must continue to collect evidence—the puzzle remains incomplete—but you must also meticulously evaluate your evidence, because in this mystery, nothing is straightforward. Three of the major players, for instance, are con artists by trade. As you have probably already recognized, behind each statement they've made and each action they've taken, shadowy passageways branch off in every direction. What ball of twine will you use to navigate them? What minotaur lies in wait? Even this conversation you're having with me—I look into your eyes and I can tell that you haven't decided whether I am a senile, old crackpot or a criminal mastermind, and as you explore either—"

"This isn't some game," Elder Toronto interrupted. "I want you to tell me what happened to Marco Aurélio."

At this, Luis's wrinkled face sagged. His posture drooped and even the light in the room seemed to dim slightly. Luis looked nearly as tired as Abelardo had the night before.

"Elder Toronto," said Luis, sounding as old as he looked. "If you ever get to be as old as I am, you might find that there's something infinite in a mystery like this, something divine."

Elder Toronto shook his head. He threw the persimmon that he held in his hand onto the tabletop. Rolling away, it fell off the table's edge and hit the floor with a soft thud.

"Let's get out of here," he said to Elder Schwartz.

The two missionaries stood up to go.

"Before you leave—" said Luis. "You may not give much weight to anything I've told you, but I do have one request."

"What?" said Elder Toronto.

"That you be more cautious," said Luis. "The people you're dealing with—regardless of their possible roles—are far more cunning and far more ruthless than you seem to imagine."

Without acknowledging the old man's request, Elder Toronto turned and stormed out of the little store, Elder Schwartz following close behind him.

THE ARGENTINE

They say that in the years following its announcement, a handful of brave souls took up the Argentine's challenge. None of them passed the test. As each of them failed, one after the other, the Argentine's patience grew thin. He had each unsuccessful challenger kidnapped, tortured, killed. Not surprisingly, this cut back on the already feeble allure of the challenge. Fewer and fewer made the attempt.

The rules of the challenge were simple, which wasn't to say they were easy.

"I want you to spread the word throughout the neighborhood," the Argentine had explained on that night in his general store, his deputies' grizzled faces eagerly upturned, his minions' pale heads cocked to listen. "I want you to tell them I've become a prisoner of my own mind, and the only way to free me is to successfully deceive me. You tell them that anyone who can fool me, stump me, trick me, or surprise me, I will reward with everything that I own and control. If, on the other hand, they fail, they forfeit their life."

After so many years and so many failures, however, those who took up the challenge employed increasingly unlikely tactics. They presented him with elaborate lies, labyrinthine hoaxes, intricate scams. Some contestants, as the Argentine referred to them, tried to stump the Argentine with obscure bits of trivia, an approach that only annoyed the Argentine, as in the case of the runny-nosed bookseller who asked him how many stones were in the Great Wall of China.

"370 million," said the Argentine.

The bookseller sniffled at this.

"Are you sure?" he said.

"Are you saying I'm wrong?" said the Argentine.

"I would say that number seems quite low," said the bookseller.

"Then tell me the correct number," said the Argentine.

"Ah," said the bookseller with a sniffle, "in fact, I don't know the exact number myself."

"And why not?"

The bookseller pulled a tissue from his pocket and wiped at his nose.

"But don't you see," he said to the Argentine. "The only way to find that out would be to dismantle the wall. That's why I asked you."

"Idiot," said the Argentine, and had the man executed.

Other approaches proved no more successful. A lovely young woman in an aubergine dress began by telling the Argentine the story of a young prince who traveled to a far-off land, only to discover the inhabitants of this distant kingdom—each and every one of them—turned to glass. Astonished at what he found, the young prince wandered among these gleaming, transparent lords and ladies, knights and fools, blacksmiths and cowhands, each of them immobilized by this strange enchantment. Baffled by what he found, the young prince wandered the countryside, looking for someone who could explain this strange situation. One day, as the young prince passed a little pond in the forest, a voice called out to him. Approaching the edge of the water, the prince saw a large fish—green and scaly, not made of glass—poking its head above the surface. You there, called out the fish, and the prince crouched down at the edge of the pond. He asked the fish how it had learned to speak. The fish explained that it, too, had once been an ambitious young prince. He had arrived in the land many years earlier.

The young woman in the aubergine dress paused.

"*What did the fish have to say?*" *said the Argentine.*

The young woman said, "For that, sir, you'll have to wait until tomorrow night."

"No," said the Argentine, "I know this trick," and he had the woman executed.

One day an old magician tried his luck.

"Inácio the Magnificent," announced one of the two brawny armed guards, deputies of a deputy, before escorting in a scarecrow-like figure in a top hat and tails. His costume, threadbare and shiny, had seen better days, as had Inácio himself, his thin hair and drooping moustache a uniform, unnatural black against his wrinkled skin.

Approaching the front of the store where the Argentine sat in a sturdy wooden chair, Inácio waved his arms with a creaky flourish and, in a voice stripped bare by decades of performance, said, "Inácio the Magnificent, at your service."

He bowed, and the Argentine applauded politely.

"Your excellency," continued Inácio, "Today I will perform a feat most astounding. Using the immense powers of reflex taught to me by an ancient Eastern sage, I will, from a gun fired at my head, catch a bullet in my teeth."

He produced an ancient-looking revolver from his jacket. The two guards stepped forward, hands on their own weapons.

"It's fine," said the Argentine, and the guards stepped back.

As the act gained momentum with Inácio's explanation of the great risks involved, the magician began to move, not like a younger man, but like a man who had trained his body over decades to captivate an audience. With a grace only slightly creaky with age, he removed a cartridge from the cylinder and presented it with a bow to the Argentine.

"If you will," said Inácio, "please mark the bullet so that you may identify it later."

Inácio turned his back to the Argentine, who removed a penknife from the pocket of his pants and carved an obscure symbol into the tip of the bullet.

"All right," said the Argentine.

Turning with another bow, Inácio the Magnificent took the cartridge and returned it to the cylinder. He turned to the two guards.

"I will now select a volunteer to fire the weapon," he said.

"Stop," said the Argentine.

Inácio the Magnificent turned back around.

"The cartridge I marked," said the Argentine. "You've hidden it in your mouth."

At this, Inácio's face brightened, even his drooping moustache perking up.

"No," said Inácio with a smile, "no, I haven't. It's not in my mouth."

He opened his mouth wide, lifting his tongue. Empty.

"See, you're wrong!" he said, grinning now, practically jumping up and down in excitement. "See, look! It's still right here in my hand!"

He lifted his hand to the Argentine, revealing that the bullet, now free of its case, was, in fact, still in his hand.

"You were wrong!" he repeated. "You were wrong!"

The Argentine smiled sadly at this. With a wave of his hand, he signaled to the two brawny deputies, who crossed the room to restrain Inácio the Magnificent, each of them gripping one of his tuxedoed arms.

"Wait," said Inácio, his elation evaporating. "What's this?"

"I'm sorry," said the Argentine. "It was a good try."

"Stop," said Inácio, as the guards dragged him across the room. "I fooled you. You thought the cartridge was in my mouth."

"No," said the Argentine, "I fooled you. I tricked you into telling me that the bullet was in your hand."

For his insolence and his failure to deceive, the shabby magician was burned alive in a stack of old tires.

And still, improbably, the contestants came, one after another, each failing to deceive the increasingly despondent Argentine.

• • •

Some say that the Argentine anticipated all of this, that he understood from the beginning that his challenge was an exercise in futility. What he had created could not be undone, and the challenge only served as an outlet for his frustration, a means of punishing the residents of Vila Barbosa.

Others say that he still holds out hope—dim though it may be—for a contestant clever enough to deceive him.

Until that day, however, the Argentine remains trapped in his own imagination, a prisoner of his own power. By day, he roams the subterranean system of tunnels, halfheartedly recording acts of cruelty that he's already conceived of. By night, he lies awake in his bed, terrified by his own omniscience.

CHAPTER 24

Whenever—many years later—Mike Schwartz thought back to that day, he could remember only vaguely their walk home from Luis's little store. All he could summon from his murky recollections were brief snatches of conversation here and there. He could remember Elder Toronto insisting that the man they had just met was a lonely old crank, that they needed to go back to their apartment and take a second look at some of the information on the note cards.

"That whole meeting was a wash, then?" said Elder Schwartz.

"No," said Elder Toronto. "We still have enough information to take to Cabral. We fulfilled our end of the deal, and now he'll have to tell us what he knows."

"But how are we going to visit Cabral?" said Elder Schwartz. "President Madvig is going to show up at our place any time now."

"I told you last night," said Elder Toronto. "You distract President Madvig here in Vila Barbosa and I'll take care of the rest."

"I need something more concrete than that."

"Fine," said Elder Toronto. "We'll hash something out when we get back to our place. Just let me think for a minute."

"You know," said Elder Schwartz, "President Madvig could already be there."

"I doubt it," said Elder Toronto, and started walking a little faster.

Even all these years later, though, Mike remembered with an alarming degree of clarity what happened when they arrived at their apartment.

They should have seen it coming.

The two missionaries stepped into their dark front room and before they could turn on the light, someone closed the door behind them. Elder Schwartz was knocked to the ground with a blow to the back, and Elder Toronto yelled at him to run. Elder Schwartz scrambled to stand up, but a booted foot kicked him in the leg. As the foot wound up for another kick, Elder Schwartz recognized the man attached to it as the bald police officer who had come to investigate the murder of Ulisses Galvão. On the other side of the room, his partner, the officer with the moustache, held Elder Toronto's arms behind his back while the third attacker, the man who had claimed to be Grillo, his muscular body even more imposing than either of the two policemen's, hammered at Elder Toronto's torso with his meaty fists.

The bald policeman kicked Elder Schwartz again, this time in the gut, and the air went out of him. He curled into a ball, not breathing. Just as his diaphragm began to resume functioning and Elder Schwartz could breathe again, the bald policeman stomped on his shoulder with an audible crack, and then kicked him in the face. Everything went dark in one eye. Moving methodically, the bald policeman picked him up by the throat, throttled him until he almost lost consciousness, and then threw him to the ground. Elder Schwartz curled up into himself, whimpering.

The bald policeman turned his back to Elder Schwartz and joined his two fellow assailants. The broad backs of the three men formed a musclebound veil that obscured from view what, exactly, they were doing to Elder Toronto. Still, watching from between his fingers, Elder Schwartz caught flashes of the violence. Fake Grillo pounding Elder Toronto's face—a swelling, bloody mess of its former self—again and again and again. A kick to Elder Toronto's knee that sent it bending back in the wrong direction. Something skittering across the floor—a bloody tooth. And then another.

The three men stepped away and Elder Toronto collapsed to the ground. When he started to push himself up with his wobbling arms, the officer with a moustache picked up one of the desks and threw it down against his struggling body. Elder Toronto didn't try getting up again and lay there wheezing dangerously.

The men crossed the room and Elder Schwartz curled up into an even tighter ball. The officer with no hair gave him one last brutal kick to the back of the head. Before he blacked out completely, the last thing Elder Schwartz saw through his one still-functioning eye was the three massive men walking out of the apartment, leaving the flimsy metal door partly open behind them.

PART TWO

CHAPTER 1

It was one of those Arizona summer mornings when the heat arrives like a biblical plague. With noon still a long way off, backyard thermometers already registered triple digits. Swimming pools, bathwater warm, provided no relief. Morning news programs advised the weak and the elderly to stay indoors. Air conditioner repairmen waited by their phones in tense anticipation. Dusty, brown lizards hid in the shade. The streets of Sandpiper Flats, the subdivision where Mike Schwartz lived with his wife and children, were deserted.

Inside the Schwartzes' beige stucco home, the four-ton-capacity air conditioner strained to keep the temperature down.

"I'm telling you," said Jason Jenson, sprawled out in an armchair in the Schwartzes' living room, "this juice supplement is where the action is."

Only nine A.M. and already the sun had rendered the closed window blinds practically transparent. Light streamed in, unbidden.

"Juice supplement?" said Mike Schwartz.

"Not now," said Connie Jenson, waving a sleepy hand at Jason. "It's too early in the morning."

"He's interested," said Jason. "You're interested, right?"

"Yeah," said Mike.

He propped himself up with one of the pillows from the couch.

"Should one of us go check on the kids?" said Alison Schwartz.

"They're fine," said Connie.

A steady stream of thumps, giggles, and squeals emanated from the bedroom on the other side of the wall. The kids had built a fort in Jodie's room, which, amazingly, had kept the whole lot of them—seven kids, all told—entertained for half an hour and counting.

In contrast to their children's current exuberance, the two couples lay sprawled around the dim living room, still in their pajamas, moving as little as possible. This way, said Alison, they'd generate less heat.

Jason, though, was sitting up straight in his recliner now, starting to come alive. He and Connie were visiting from Utah, staying with the Schwartzes for a couple of days before wending their way to Disneyland. Connie and Alison were sisters, which made Mike and Jason what, exactly? From his pile of pillows on the floor, Mike wondered what the term would be. Connie was Mike's sister-in-law, but Jason, as her husband, was one more step removed by marriage. So he wouldn't be Mike's brother-in-law. Or would he? This ambiguity briefly troubled Mike, but the unease dissipated as Jason, nobly situated in the recliner, began to speak.

Although a few years younger than Mike, Jason exuded a snappy competence that made him seem, if not older than Mike, then at least more capable. Drawing power from the savvy aura that surrounded him, Jason began holding forth on the new juice supplement he was involved with—both drinking and selling. He said that someone in their ward introduced him to it. After drinking it for a week, Jason felt better than he ever had in his life. He went back to the guy in the ward and told him he wanted to get involved. And so the guy got him all set up, and now Jason was selling the stuff himself.

"So it's one of those pyramid schemes," said Alison, who had little patience for Jason.

"No," said Jason. "No, no, no, no, no, no, no. No, Alison. It's not a pyramid scheme. This is legitimate. It's a networked personal business opportunity, and we're selling something that people need."

He said that the founder of the company—a good guy, a member of the church—had served his mission over in Asia somewhere, Jason couldn't remember where exactly. But while he was over there, he worked in this rural area where—he discovered—everyone lived to be very old. Nineties at least. And they were all really proud of this, and they'd tell people that it was because of this berry that they ate.

"It's a berry that doesn't exist in the West," said Jason. "Or at least it didn't until now. There's not even a name for it in English."

He explained that after the company's founder got back from his mission, he remembered this berry and started to investigate. He went back to this region of Asia and got some samples of the fruit and brought it back to be analyzed. And when he discovered all the amazing properties it had, he knew he couldn't keep something so great to himself. So he founded the company and developed the juice supplement. And now he just needed people to sell it, so that the juice could help as many people as possible.

"He's just a really good guy," said Jason. "He's using the power of nature to create greater wellness opportunities for everyone."

"And how is this supplement supposed to work?" said Alison.

Connie rested her hand on her sister's arm.

"I was skeptical at first, too," she said. "But then I tried some, and let me tell you. I feel amazing. See, how it works is—actually, Jason, you explain it. You're better at it. Tell them about the Negatoxins."

"I'll get to that," said Jason. "So, they analyzed this berry, and what they found is that the reason it's so amazing is because of this chemical or molecule it contains. The name the company uses for it is Positrol. And Positrol is so amazing because when you consume it, it eradicates all of the Negatoxins in your body. Obviously, Negatoxin isn't the official scientific term for it—that's just the word the company came up with. The thing is, if you use too much scientific jargon, you run the risk of coming across as an elitist with the people you're selling to. But I'm getting ahead of myself—you'll learn all that in the home-business training.

"What I'm saying is that over in Asia, the people who eat this berry live to be ninety, even a hundred years old on a regular basis. That's their average age, and I'm not even kidding, and now, that same berry is available worldwide through this supplement."

"This juice stuff works, then?" said Mike.

"Sure," said Jason. "The main thing, though, is that this company is amazing. Their business model is really, really smart. And I'll tell you what the best part is if you decide to get involved. Do you get paid for helping people find this juice? Yes. A whole lot, if you play your cards right. But is that the best part? No. The best part is that you're giving people the gift of wellness. This stuff, Mike? This stuff saves lives."

"So it's been working out well for you," said Mike.

"I'm telling you, Mike," said Jason, "if Connie and I keep on track like this, I can quit my other job by the end of the year. I'm not even kidding. That's how well we're doing with this juice supplement. Ten-hour work week, here we come. And that's great, because you know what that means, Mike? More family time. Because that's what this is all about."

"Interesting," said Alison.

Jason shook his head with a good-natured smile.

"Alison, I can see you're not totally convinced yet, but when we head out for California tomorrow, I'm going to leave a case of the juice with you guys, and I'd like you to try some. I'd really love it if you two just took some time to think it over."

Jason's face glowed in the sunlight permeating the closed blinds, and Mike found himself nodding, saying yes, that all sounded wonderful.

CHAPTER 2

To make it through the day, they'd all need to get out of the house. Too many warm bodies in a confined space. The water parks would be packed; more likely than not, they'd spend most of their time waiting in line under the vengeful sun. The shopping malls stayed cool, but were unlikely to occupy the kids' attention for long. They decided a movie would be the best option, it didn't matter which one. Something the kids would like. The theater would be air-conditioned, that's what mattered. But first they needed to eat.

Earlier in the week, Mike had bought frozen pizzas for the occasion, but everyone agreed that turning on the oven would be a terrible idea. So Mike and Alison offered to drive over to the grocery store and pick up stuff for sandwiches. It would be easier than bringing everyone along.

As he and Alison crossed the sweltering parking lot toward the store's main entrance, the asphalt soft beneath their feet, Mike looked up with his one good eye to see the blue sky filling with long, wispy cirrus clouds. A wind had picked up, hot and dry, and an empty paper bag blew across his feet.

With a cheerful whoosh, the automatic doors welcomed them into the cool interior of the grocery store. Mike found a cart, the metal chilly against his skin, and they began patrolling for supplies: rolls from the bakery; lettuce, tomatoes, cucumbers, and bean sprouts from the produce section. In the refrigerated dairy aisle, Mike broached the subject of the juice supplements Jason and Connie were selling—it sounded like an interesting venture, he said.

"I think it works for Jason and Connie," said Alison. "Cheddar or mozzarella?"

She picked up a package of each, weighing them in her hands.

"Mozzarella's the safe choice," said Mike.

Alison dropped the brick of mozzarella into the cart.

"Seriously, though," said Mike. "It sounds like a good opportunity."

"Are you being serious about this?" said Alison, wheeling the cart toward the deli meats.

"I don't know," said Mike. "Even if Jason's exaggerating a little—"

"You would hate selling things," said Alison.

"Maybe," said Mike.

They stopped the cart in front of a wide array of deli meat.

"Jason loves that kind of thing," said Alison. "He loves it. You know that."

"Yeah," said Mike. "True."

"Plus, it's snake oil, Mike."

"But still," he said. "A ten-hour work week—think about that."

Alison leaned in to examine a package of sliced ham.

"I mean, if you're really serious about this, we could look into it."

"Well," said Mike.

He left it there, unsure what he wanted.

"What meats should we get?" said Alison. "We should get a few different kinds."

"Turkey for sure," said Mike. "And ham."

Alison picked out one of each and put them in the cart.

"What else?" said Alison. "Beef?"

"What about another turkey?" said Mike. "I think everyone likes turkey."

"Some variety would be nice, though," said Alison.

They stood there side-by-side, basking in the cooler's refrigerated drafts, contemplating the various meat options before them.

"Schwartz?" said a gravelly voice from Mike's blind side, and Mike turned his head.

The man who addressed him wore a somber blue polo shirt and a slightly rumpled pair of slacks, neither of which fit him especially well, the pants cinched to bunching around his narrow waist, the shirt draped tent-like over his slender torso. His hair, just beginning to gray at the temples, was neatly combed in apparent compensation for the chaotic face below it, a rugged terrain of scar tissue and drooping skin. A series of pink scars crisscrossed the man's throat. He had a scuffed leather bag slung over his shoulder and leaned heavily on a simple, wooden cane.

"Mike Schwartz?" repeated the man in his gravelly voice.

"Yeah," said Mike. "Do I know you?"

"Sorry," said the man, his hodgepodge of a face twisting into a smile. "I forget sometimes that people might not recognize me. They had to do a lot of work on my face."

Mike shook his head, the man's identity still not registering.

"It's me," said the man. "John Toronto."

It took Mike several seconds to respond.

CHAPTER 3

Outside, the sky, so blindingly clear that morning, was now filled with dark clouds.

Inside the burger place, the two men ate for several minutes without speaking, the only sounds in their booth being the occasional crunch of a French fry or the rattle of ice in their paper cups. Both men focused their full attention on the apparently crucial task of eating their hamburgers: taking a bite and then staring at the burger as they chewed, mapping out with their eyes where the next bite would come from. Every so often, one of them might look out one of the restaurant's plate-glass windows at the effects of the increasingly violent windstorm outside; garbage rolling down the sidewalk like tumbleweed, an elderly couple leaning dramatically into the gusts as they crossed the street, a magazine blowing out of the hands of a woman who was waiting for a bus. However, neither man made eye contact with the other, confining their gaze to their food and to the world outside.

At the grocery store, after introductions and a bit of small talk, Alison had offered to head back to the house alone to give Mike and John a chance to catch up—she could come pick Mike up a little later. Toronto had jumped on the offer, suggesting that he and Mike grab a bite to eat at the fast-food place across the street, and when they were done, he could give Mike a ride home himself. So it had been settled, and here they were.

When the burgers were gone, Toronto broke the silence with his gravelly voice, asking Mike how he had been and what he was up to. Mike ran through the vital statistics—married eleven years, three kids, a job in the city planner's office. Toronto said that sounded terrific. He said that in his line of work, he saw so many dysfunctional marriages, so many people who cheated on their spouses, or maybe just couldn't stand them, that it was nice to see a couple who obviously loved each other like Mike and Alison did. Mike thanked him.

"Are you a marriage counselor, then?"

"No," said Toronto, scratching at his scar-ridden cheek, "I'm kind of an independent contractor. Nothing too glamorous."

Mike nodded like he knew what Toronto meant.

A few yards away, a teenaged employee with surprisingly good skin pushed a mop in a rolling yellow bucket across the floor, humming softly, his eyes lingering on a nearby table of high school girls, who were now engaged in a heated discussion. As the boy passed the booth where the two men sat, the yellow bucket nearly snagged the dangling strap of Toronto's leather bag. Toronto lifted the strap onto the bench and hugged the bag a little closer.

Mike had watched Toronto dote on this bag throughout their meal—he treated it like it was a well-behaved dog or a small child, resting his hand on it lovingly, stroking it reassuringly, and holding it as close as possible. Mike wouldn't have been surprised to see Toronto drop a morsel of food into its obedient mouth. Mike wondered what the bag contained.

On the outside, it was nothing special, something between a satchel and an attaché case. The brown leather, scuffed along the bottom, was cracking in places. A buckle was missing and a deep scratch ran along the bag's front. One of the handles was wrapped in electrical tape and the strap, several shades lighter than the rest of the leather, looked like it came from another bag. Whatever was inside, there was a lot of it—the bag bulged with its hidden contents.

"So you're in town on business?" said Mike.

"I'm actually just passing through."

Mike nodded.

Toronto said, "I don't mean to be rude, but I'm curious—is that a glass eye?"

Mike turned the eye in question away from Toronto.

"It's not glass," he said, "but it is prosthetic."

Toronto said he wouldn't have noticed if he hadn't been looking for signs of lasting damage. He picked up his cup and took a drink.

"Apparently I was in a coma for a while," said Toronto, his fingers gently patting the bag sitting next to him, "and then just in really bad shape. I don't know, I really don't remember. When I was finally stable enough to move, they shipped me back to the States and I spent months in the hospital. I was in physical therapy for a long time. I still have to walk with a cane."

"I'm sorry," said Mike. "It wasn't as bad as that for me. Some internal bleeding, and a broken collarbone. And my eye."

"Still," said Toronto.

Mike shrugged.

"Things have worked out okay for me," Mike said.

Toronto nodded. The nearby group of high school girls laughed at some private joke. Toronto hugged his bag closer. Mike looked outside at the darkening afternoon sky.

"Could you excuse me for a minute?" said Toronto, standing up from the booth, picking up his cane, and limping back to the restrooms.

His leather bag remained behind, alone on the bench.

The teenaged employee had struck up a conversation with the nearby table of girls and now leaned on his mop, chatting amiably. Outside, the wind continued to blow, the sky clouded and prematurely dark. Crossing the floor of the restaurant, a tired-looking manager in an ill-fitting uniform and a headset approached the young employee with the mop and told him he either needed to be mopping out here, or back behind the counter filling orders. Conversing with customers wasn't included in either option. The boy nodded and the manager walked away. The boy rolled his eyes for the benefit of the girls and began to mop a few feet away from them in silence.

In his booth, Mike stared at the leather bag that Toronto had left behind. What was in there? He glanced up at the restroom doors, then at the table of girls engaged in conversation, then at the young employee mopping halfheartedly with his back to Mike. Nobody was watching. He looked back at the restroom one more time and then stood up, leaning over the table and lifting the bag over to his side of the booth.

Instead of finding, as he had expected, a chaotic space roiling with papers, Mike was surprised to see that the inside of the bag was organized into a neat assortment of pockets, dividers, and compartments. He saw a bundle of yellowing note cards in one pocket and pulled it out of the bag. He recognized the cards as the ones Toronto had made in their apartment in Vila Barbosa all that time ago. In the ensuing years, further information had been added in different colors of ink, but always in the same recognizable handwriting, information like "birth name: Sílvia Maria da Graça Meirelles Sousa" or "never actually served time" or "did have brother named Grillo" or "has tattoo of bleeding hummingbird on shoulder; usually keeps it hidden."

Mike put the note cards back and pulled out a thick stack of photographs from a different compartment. They were separated into categories by tabbed dividers as follows:

Pictures of Places. Flipping through this section, Mike saw the apartment where the elders had lived, Marco Aurélio's house, Sílvia's lanchonete, the high-rise building where Cabral's office was located, the cheery little house where Claudemir and Fátima lived, and several buildings, parks, and homes that Mike didn't recognize.

Pictures of People (most of these images grainy, likely captured through a telephoto lens). Although this section contained pictures of many people Mike had never seen before, he did recognize several. Fake Grillo, for instance, sitting at a table outside a bar with a woman who pointed angrily toward his chest, her mouth open in accusation. Junior Cabral stepping out of an armored car. The policeman with no hair frisking a kid who stood, arms and legs spread, facing a cinderblock wall. Sister Beatrice pulling her wheeled grocery basket through a street market. Wanderley the cab driver sitting on a curb smoking a cigarette. The blurred face of a woman who could be Sílvia looking out the window of a bus.

Pictures of Their Personal Belongings. Mike didn't know what to make of this section. He saw a wooden string of rosary beads peeking out from the pocket of a skirt; a diver's knife sitting on a dresser; a small shelf of comic books; a battered cavaquinho resting against a painted cement wall; a makeup brush in someone's hand; an open dictionary on a threadbare couch.

There were more categories and more pictures, but Mike returned the stack to its compartment.

He pulled a manila folder from the bag and found photocopies of various official documents inside, all of them written in Portuguese: birth certificates, marriage licenses, writs of divorce, criminal records, deeds, wills, affidavits, death certificates. He recognized very few of the names on the documents.

Another folder held a collection of maps, some of them hand-drawn, some of them torn at one edge, obviously removed from a larger atlas. The maps ranged in scale from streets to neighborhoods to cities, and in focus from utility lines to average annual income to historic landmarks. A picnicker's map, yellowing at the edges, depicted Vila Barbosa before it was settled—a topographical view of its steep, grassy hills; of its cool, green eucalyptus groves; of its many winding streams. A crime map of the neighborhood featured dozens, maybe hundreds of multicolored flags, each one with a simple icon representing a different type of crime—a fractured car for a vehicle break-in, a cartoon ski mask for a robbery, a knife for an armed assault. The top of another map, this one hand-drawn in a blue, smudgy ink, proclaimed itself a key to the thirty-seven secret entrances to the Argentine's system of tunnels. A simple black-and-white map so large that Mike couldn't fully unfold it tracked the electrical lines that ran throughout Vila Barbosa. A minuscule map the size of a business card charted an elevated train system—never actually built—that connected the various points of the neighborhood.

Next to the folder of maps, Mike found a yellow legal pad, its dog-eared pages covered in handwritten, retrospective algorithms, a multitude of possibilities arranged into arrow-connected boxes, for example:

> Did Marco Aurélio ever ask Abelardo about his connection to Luis?
> if yes=>Did Abelardo tell him anything about their shared history?
> if yes=>
> if no=>
> if no=>Was Marco Aurélio unaware of the connection?
> if yes=>
> if no=>

Another legal pad contained timeline after timeline, each one charting known events in the lives of Marco Aurélio and those connected to him. One timeline compared and contrasted events from the stories people told about the Argentine with known events in the life of Luis, owner of the little general store. Another timeline charted significant events in the development and decline of the Mormon congregation in Vila Barbosa. Still another timeline, stretching for pages, noted down to the minute everything that happened to the missionaries between Ulisses Galvão's appearance at church on Sunday and their meeting with Luis just days later.

Behind the timelines, he found a manila folder marked "Audio Surveillance Transcripts." He flipped through the pages and pages of meticulously recorded conversations, most of them in Portuguese. Mike's skills in the language were rusty—beyond rusty—and so only the very occasional fragment of meaning popped out at him: *. . . what kind of idiot do you think . . . not just the police . . . if she's scared . . . how many times . . . that third cupboard . . . something I pride myself on . . . can't stop thinking . . . Aurélio never . . . share of the money . . . regardless of how messy it was . . . not like she's your wife . . . it's what I keep telling you . . . those two Mormons . . . not a gun . . . without . . . bound to find him . . .*

Next to this, was a folder full of unlabeled statistical graphs, charting sets of data that Mike couldn't decipher. There were box plots, line graphs, histograms, pie charts, pictographs, scatterplots, and bar graphs.

Another folder contained dozens of police-style sketches. At first glance, they seemed to be photocopies, each one an identical depiction of Marco Aurélio's face. As he examined the sketches more carefully, though, Mike could see minor variations in each version—the ears a bit higher in this one, the jaw slightly firmer in that one, the cheekbones just sharper in another. Furthermore, no single depiction got it quite right. In fact, if Mike had been shown any one of these sketches in isolation, he may not have even guessed that it was supposed to be of Marco Aurélio. Strangely, though, all of the depictions put together somehow captured something that eluded any single sketch.

In a zippered compartment was a pouch filled with several small objects. Mike emptied its contents onto the table—a worn padlock key; a pair of women's sunglasses with one lens missing; a dented policeman's badge; a thin, gold wedding band; a brittle, creased bit of leather. Mike returned the objects to their pouch, and put the pouch back in the bag. There was so much more in the bag that he could look through—more unexplored pockets, compartments, and folders—but Mike saw the door of the men's room begin to swing open. He closed the bag and returned it to its spot on the seat across from him.

Toronto stepped out of the bathroom, adjusting his ill-fitting pants. With the aid of his cane, he limped back to the booth and sat down. He held the leather bag close to his body and smiled apologetically. Mike smiled in return and folded his hands, which had begun to shake. The contents of the bag had left him unexpectedly enraged, his ears ringing with the physical reverberations of the anger, his muscles clenching, the vision in his one good eye blurring at the edges.

"I have to ask you before we go," said Toronto.

The girls from the nearby table stood up with their trays in hand and Toronto waited until they had passed before continuing.

"I have to ask you," he said, "if you've thought much about what might have happened to Marco Aurélio."

"No," said Mike, working to keep his voice level.

"Really?" said Toronto. "The mystery of it never intrigues you?"

Mike clenched his fingers together.

"No," said Mike. "There's no mystery. The Argentine had him killed."

"Interesting," said Toronto. He hoisted the leather bag into his lap. "Tell me why you think he would do that."

"Why? Because Marco Aurélio tried to con him. It didn't work, and the Argentine had him killed."

"And what leads you to believe that Marco Aurélio's con didn't work?"

Mike felt like he was twenty years old, a missionary again. He gritted his teeth.

He said, "Nothing leads me to it, it's just what I think happened."

"But what evidence do you have to support that theory?" said Toronto, unbuckling the latch of his bag.

"I don't have evidence," said Mike. "It's just—" He took a deep breath, composing himself. "Fine. Let's say that's not what happened. Do you have a better theory?"

"I'm glad you asked that," said Toronto with an eager smile. "Now, I can't quite account for all the details yet." He opened the leather bag. "What I mean is, I think Marco Aurélio accomplished something truly astounding, and so obviously I can't fully—"

"No," said Mike, so forcefully that Toronto's eyes opened wide in surprise.

"No," Mike repeated. "I see where you're going with this and it's pathetic. Just stupid. Stupid"—the words sputtered out of him—"It's stupid to think about. Is that why—did you track me down, or what is this? Because this wasn't an accident. You didn't just accidentally run into me today, let's be honest here." He laughed, a short, barking laugh. "And, I mean, going along with your stupid plan back then," he shook his head. "No. Even for a couple of kids, I can't believe how stupid—you're supposed to be smart or something, but I really don't see what's come of that. Because you're a mess, you know? If you're still trying to figure it out after all this time—it's pointless and it's sad, because there's nothing to talk about. Nothing."

As Mike ground to a momentary halt, he could see that Toronto's mangled face had twisted itself into an expression of— what? Betrayal? Embarrassment? Regret? Mike couldn't tell. He pressed on.

"And now you're going to try and convince me that Marco Aurélio pulled off some mystical, incomprehensible con that we somehow played a part in, and what? He's still alive and well somewhere, enjoying the spoils of his impossible scheme? That's not—that's just not—I mean, that's a great explanation for you, isn't it? Right up your alley, because all it does is create more mystery. You don't actually—" Mike waved his hands, groping for words. "See, I'm not going to claim that I've given the question that much thought because honestly, it's not worth the effort. But you're no more interested in solving anything than I am. And do you want to know why I know that? Because the solution here is obvious. Whatever happened, it was ugly and mundane and completely inconsequential. Marco Aurélio was a petty crook. He was just some loser who got in over his head with the wrong people and they killed him—that's all. So don't try to turn this into something it's not. This is just—" He shook his head. "This is just ridiculous."

Mike paused and took a breath.

"I won't do this," he said, composing himself. "Okay?"

The expression on Toronto's face, which Mike still couldn't decipher, intensified briefly and then resolved itself into something more neutral. He closed the leather bag, latching it shut again.

He said, "I should get you back home."

• • •

Toronto pulled his rental car up to the curb in front of the Schwartzes' beige stucco house. Mike opened the door and got out. The wind had not subsided, and dark, meaty clouds loomed overhead.

"Listen," said Mike, calmer now, leaning into the blue compact car, his hand on the open door, "you're welcome to come in if you'd like."

"Thanks," said Toronto, "but I should hit the road."

"Well," said Mike, and paused. He knew he should say something, but he wasn't sure what. As he tried to think of what it could be, he saw Toronto's ragged face assume the same inscrutable expression that it had at the restaurant just a few minutes earlier. This time, though, Mike recognized it as a look of pity. The anger that had diminished on the drive over returned in its full magnitude and Mike slammed the car door shut. He stepped up onto the curb.

A fat raindrop hit the sidewalk, and then another. Thunder in the distance. Mike braced himself against the wind.

Inside the car, Toronto leaned across the front seat, looking up at Mike through the passenger window, that same expression of condescending pity on his scarred face. He lifted a hand in farewell. Without acknowledging the gesture, Mike turned and walked up the driveway. The drops were falling steadily now, dark spots on the pale concrete, the deluge close at hand. He heard Toronto put the car into gear and pull away from the curb. At his front steps, Mike paused and turned back around. Stepping backward onto his porch, he took cover from the now-heavy rainfall. Through his good eye, he watched Toronto drive away until his small, blue car turned a corner and disappeared.